Summer Fever

'I am a bastard to women. I am no good. I make them suffer and therefore I have to suffer.'

Amber gets off the hammock and stands, her face and strong shoulders bathed in gold by the sudden intrusion of sun.

'Kneel!' she demands, and though the haughtiness in her voice seems authentic, I notice something curious. As the sun shines in her eyes I see that they are filled with tears. She drops to her knees in front of him and takes his penis in her hand. For a minute or so she caresses him gently, her fingers working from the root to the tip of his cock. He has a look of almost pained rapture on his face.

'I deserve everything I get,' he says in a husky voice.

Amber takes this as a cue to change tactic. Sliding her hand under his balls she squeezes as tight as she can. I see him wince.

'More. I need to suffer. Please.'

She squeezes again. Then she twists his poor flesh as if wringing out a cloth. He doesn't cry out or buckle or try to extricate himself from her touch although he is shuddering and his face is contorted.

'Have you suffered enough?' This time I can hear quite clearly the distress underlying the authoritarian harshness.

'I can never suffer enough for what I have done.'

He sounds almost haunted.

'Punish me now, please.'

Summer Fever

ANNA RICCI

BLACK
lace

Black Lace novels contain sexual fantasies.
In real life, make sure you practise safe sex.

First published in 2001 by
Black Lace
Thames Wharf Studios,
Rainville Road, London W6 9HA

Typeset by SetSystems Ltd, Saffron Walden, Essex
Printed and bound by Mackays of Chatham PLC

ISBN 0 352 33625 0

Chapter One

'Wow, wow, wow ... oh, unbelieeeevable.'
The girl's song rises from the radio in sweet excitement as I open my legs in the passenger seat of Steve's car. Each time he changes gear he slides his hand under my skirt; sometimes high, sometimes low. I move as close as I can to him, getting wet at the thought of his next touch; wanting him to put his hand inside my knickers, to feel the moisture. He would be pleased. Steve is a bit older than me. He used to be my art teacher. Now he's my teacher in love. I want to learn how to gratify and delight him; how to master and control my desires. Steve tells me I'm a quick learner but most of the time I'm sure I don't live up to his expectations.

The scent of cut hedgerow rushes past, followed by the smell of the sea; the fresh-air fishy tang that used to remind me of beach holidays as a child. Now it makes me think of something entirely different – the scent of lovemaking; hot bodies on cool sheets, clinging to each other in the sand while the gulls cry overhead. Steve removes my knickers with one hand; quickly and expertly. I close my eyes and drink in the fragrance; intoxicatingly strong in the open-topped car. I feel languid and full of anticipation for the long hot weeks ahead. It's a great time to be alive, to be seventeen with the vast summer sky above and my whole life in front of me. We're taking the long coast road to a summer of love and crashing seas, of beach parties, of entire nights lying in each other's arms. I want to make love on the sand at dawn.

The next time I feel Steve's hand steal up my thigh I clamp my legs together to keep it there, trying to squirm down to his knuckles, needing his touch for a moment longer. I flash my eyes at him, moisten my lips, wanting him to feel my excitement, my gratitude. But there is a hardening in his pale eyes and his head moves slowly from side to side. His fingers, almost as if punishing me, withdraw quickly; hard as the pincers of a crab. He gives me a light nip; it's playful but hurts, and I know it will leave a mark.

'You must be patient, Lara,' he says. He smiles, but his dark hair flopping onto his brow shadows his gaze and makes him look stern and mysterious. I know he is annoyed. Steve doesn't like me to take the initiative.

So I pull down my skirt, bring my knees together and turn away to look at the scenery; the long grasses, thrashing together at the roadside, deep and vigorous as we pass. Then, as the car rises on a bend and we look down, they are merely a surface, rippling like the fibres on a carpet. Way off towards the horizon lies the slit of silver ocean, still and distant with shiny promise. And I daydream – I fantasise as I often do when Steve isn't with me. Only now, more and more, I do it when I'm with him too.

In my fantasy I always wear a dress of silver silk. It is elegant and old-fashioned with a low neckline that pushes up my breasts. The bodice is cut close to my body so that when I move, and especially when I get excited, the silk caresses me like the touch of a hand. Steve is standing in the doorway to a room in an old house, his arms reaching out to me. When I walk towards him I look like a lady. But when he carries me to the bed I am a whore – the lower panels of my dress parting to reveal the thinnest gossamer stockings held up by tiny exquisite beaded suspenders. I laugh and squirm in his arms wanting to kiss him, to devour him; hoping my struggle will snap the flimsy supports beneath my dress so my writhing thighs and moisture will be apparent to him. In my daydreams Steve never tells me to be patient.

The room we enter is small in area, but tall and circular, part of a turret; a room fragrant with cold and witchcraft. As he carries me to bed, through the special indoor gloom of summer, the incense of dry flowers begins to fill the air. The bed is large and deep; lush in careless folds and ridges of pink satin. I am shivering so he frames me with the thick smooth sheets and places his body beside me like a shield. Then he begins to undo each button on my dress, from the swell of my breasts down to the top of my pants. My underwear is brief and thin, almost as thin as tissue. In my bra are two holes where my nipples peep out like rosebuds. My panties contain a slit down the middle which will tear, very easily, one way or the other. For a moment Steve stares at it, letting his hand rest just above. I wonder how much of my moisture is visible. I lift my hips a little, wanting him to touch me. But he remains completely still, his light eyes soft, his strong regular features almost boyish with wonder.

Taking time to look at me, into my eyes; to touch me, my skin, every inch of it as he exposes it; taking in my growing feverishness, my expectation, he gradually peels away my silver shell, and edges me towards the beginnings of slow wonderful orgasm. By the time he takes my nipples in his mouth one after the other, dampening the thin gauze of my bra with his kisses, my legs are bent and open, my hands clutching at and pushing his partly clothed body down towards me. When I am almost out of my mind with longing, the tips of his fingers steal into the opening of my pants, to where my juices gather like honey glaze inside the gauze and trickle out. He only needs to touch me lightly around the clit for me to be on fire; thrusting my hips, my sex lips up towards his hand.

3

'Please,' I whisper. 'Please, now, go inside me.'

Steve smiles down in sympathy. 'I want to make it as good as it can be for you,' he says gently, allowing me to place my hand on the top of his belt, then move it down to the bulge of his cock.

I start to move my fingers, fondling his erection, desperate to free it; to make our pleasure complete. But he stops my hand with his own. With a deft movement he undoes the belt himself, then slides quickly down my body, denying me the immediate delight of his hard, ready cock. He kisses me, small butterfly kisses on the inside of my thighs, over my abdomen and down, down over my pants, over my lips, until I writhe with delight and expectation. Then I feel his tongue probing the opening in my pants, pushing it that way and this, lapping at the juice that now seeps constantly. When his mouth is over my clit, teasing it, and I hold his head hard, tiny delicious contractions start inside me. There are ripples of pleasure around all my openings. I am almost out of control and will shortly force his mouth even harder on to me. Nothing in the world will matter but the pressure needed to give me the orgasm that is desperate to explode inside of me. But am I failing him, giving him no pleasure at all? In a tortuous mix of bliss and confusion I force myself to lift his face away from me. He isn't surprised or angry. In my fantasies Steve always understands when I am ready, knows when I can't wait for him any longer. His eyes glisten with happiness and pride that he has brought me to this state of arousal. His fingers are warm but not damp as he strokes tears of frustration from my eyelids.

'Now, Lara, you need me now, don't you?'

And only then, as he swiftly pulls off his remaining clothes, does he let me caress his cock, run my fingers along its velvety shaft, circle my thumb over its warm oily tip. His eyes close briefly, very tight, and he sighs before opening them again – the only signs that his excitement is as intense as mine.

'Show me where you want me, angel,' he says softly.

In my dream he lets me nuzzle the head of his cock between my legs, just inside the tear in my pants, waiting for me to give the signal that I need him right inside me. So expert is Steve in the build-up of intensity in his lovemaking that this always happens almost immediately. I dig my fingertips into his back, my nails into his buttocks; his cock comes inside me, slowly at first, but soon strongly and hugely; filling me up. He moves his body almost imperceptibly when I begin to cry out, to beg for release till I almost sob with pleasure and frustration. Then, suddenly, it happens. Steve changes from the slow tantalising lover to a man possessed by demonic desire, pounding into me so hard I think I'm going to break apart. Both of us are wrapped up in the urgency of our need for deliverance; harmoniously intent on the pounding of his cock, of his body, merging with mine. I am dissolving, breaking up towards his hardness. My hips rise to meet his thrust. More and more and more until I will burst open in growing ecstasy. God, oh God, oh God . . .

'Lara, angel. Come back to me, wherever you are.'

My eyes jolt open and the thrashing grasses at the roadside have gone. We are just above, riding at full speed past the banking, dipping sands that seem to smooth for miles towards the sea.

For a moment I've forgotten where I am, who I'm with. I stare at Steve as if he's a stranger, taking in the long, strong thighs in the driving seat; the bronzed knuckles on the steering wheel; his other hand playing thoughtfully with my hair; his cool inquisitive eyes.

'Sorry, I was in a dream. I'm back now.' I laugh, but I feel strangely cold, even afraid. The truth is, that in the few months I've had with Steve, our relationship is nothing like the wonderful uplifting pictures in my head.

Most of the time I'm apprehensive when he wants to make love, often tense and rigid. I rarely become wet in response to his urgent caresses and demanding hungry kisses. He tells me my tightness is sweet, that his cock feels good squeezed into my narrowness, that it makes him want to come quickly. Often he does. Often it is all over in minutes. I try to make the right sounds. I tell him I love him, over and over. Sometimes I cry. In my naivety I hope he'll think it is in orgasm. Steve is my first lover and I can't come for him. But I like being as close as that; his body inside mine. Sex is as close as you can get. Afterwards he holds me on his chest and calls me his angel, his child. I know I must be a disappointment, but this summer I'm determined to learn how to please him. Now I smile at him, let my fingers stray to the tiny seed buttons on my blouse. I undo a couple, pretending I'm hot, but my hands tremble. I want to excite Steve but I don't want him to think I'm a tramp. He has strong views on the behaviour of young girls, often complaining about them parading themselves in short school skirts, wearing mascara and lipstick with their uniforms. What first attracted him to me, he says, was my naked face and my innocence, my eagerness to please. I am not to be brazen, not to flaunt myself in front of other men. Unless, of course, he wants me to. Then, I must paint my face; wear the sheer provocative clothes he buys me; sit in the pub with no underwear on. But only when he wants me to. But it's alright. He smiles back at me and the car is slowing down. I want him to stop driving, to hold me against him, kiss my mouth, my neck; slowly undo all my buttons, to my waist; take time to kiss my breasts. There will be no urgency, no pressure. Maybe nothing more will happen. It can just be a foretaste of the night to come.

The car draws into the side of the road, bouncing a little as Steve drives over the shallow grass verge. He turns to me, placing two fingers on the exposed flesh at the top of my breasts, then roughly slides his other hand up my thigh to my knickers. He presses his thumb inside my lips, over the cotton, finding my clit. He massages it briefly, but then withdraws.

'You'll have to excuse me, little Lara,' he says. 'I need to take a leak.'

He opens the car door then looks back at me, his eyes sparkling.

'You can join me if you like.'

My face reddens. I don't know what I'm supposed to do. I don't know what he wants.

'I'll just stay here,' I murmur and sink behind my hair.

I watch him walk away to unzip himself and pee against a bush some way up the road.

He takes a packet of cigarettes from his shirt pocket and turns so I can't see his face. He stands smoking and looking down towards the sea.

'What am I supposed to do?' I say the words aloud, plaintively, to the soft wind.

'Just be your sweet, beautiful self ... I should say,' a voice comes lazily from the back seat of the car.

I turn around so quickly I make myself dizzy. I had forgotten our passenger.

Jake's eyes, faintly glazed by dope, smile gently into mine. His eyes are brown; soft and deep. So different from the pale, distracted blue of his brother's.

'Arrogant bastard.'

The slowness of his voice and the warmth of his gaze, although possibly caused by the reefer now carelessly discarded over the side of the car, have a relaxing, almost hypnotic effect on me. When he leans forward and his hand comes up to massage my shoulder I don't push him away.

'I scared you, Larissa, I'm sorry.'

His eyes search my face.

'Steve's not arrogant you know,' I whisper, trying not to look into those eyes.

I watch his shoulders come towards me and away; towards me again as his fingers ease my tense muscles. At a quick glance Jake and Steve look alike – the same dark good looks; slender but strong build. But close to you can see that Jake's features are mellower and his shoulders broader.

* * *

7

Two weeks ago Jake had carried me into a bedroom when I felt faint at a party. The room was spinning and I looked around desperately for Steve. I began to sink down a wall when I felt someone's hand catch my upper body, and an arm slide under my legs. Jake picked me up and turned my face to his chest. My surrender into the swirling blackness, my head on his shoulder, was blissful. I felt completely safe. When I opened my eyes he was lying beside me, propped up on one elbow, stroking my brow and watching me. Neither of us said a word.

It was late evening. The yellow blind at the window was half down and the light in the room was golden. All he did was stroke my brow and brush the hair from my face, yet the longer it continued, the closer he seemed to me, the more intense the small pinpricks of pleasure all over my body became. Then the door swung open and Steve was standing, once more the school teacher, furious, judgmental.

'What the fuck's going on here?'

Jake and I separated quickly, and immediately I felt guilty and unsettled. Jake explained the situation and left with his eyes smiling at me. Steve pulled up the blind harshly so that cold light entered the room; he opened the window so that cold air rushed in, too. Then he went to get me some water. When he returned I was sitting on the edge of the bed crying. Only then did he seem concerned. But I couldn't explain that it wasn't because I felt unwell but because I wanted him to stroke my brow, again and again and simply lie close to me as Jake had done.

'Steve's not arrogant,' I repeat now, aware of the uncertainty in my voice. Jake's hands have stopped on my shoulders. 'He's nicer to me than any other guy I've known.'

'Oh, yes, and how many would that be, Larissa?'

His voice is muffled as he pulls his T-shirt over his head. I can't help staring at his chest; its light olive colour, the taughtness of his muscles and the faint line of

8

dark hair in between. When his head re-emerges and the T-shirt is cast aside, he catches me gazing at his torso, his belt and the area around the zip of his jeans.

'I wouldn't do that if I were you. You'll give me a hard on and my big brother will take umbrage in a truly spectacular manner.'

I turn away from him, my face blazing, but I don't object when I feel his hands move gently through my hair, stroking my skull and stealing down the back of my neck. He continues to knead, then release, his fingertips against the tightness of my upper body.

'You exaggerate everything, Jake,' I say weakly, trying to stop myself leaning back into his touch; telling myself I have no choice. He's too strong and is somehow drawing me towards him.

Suddenly I hear the driver's door open. I sit upright so quickly that I smell the fragrance of my hair as it swings forward; the shampoo scent with the sun in it.

'She's so tense, Stevo, really knotted up and no fucking wonder,' Jake says cheerfully.

When I glance at Steve I can feel guilt in my expression; heat in my face. But he leans over and brushes my mouth with his own. Then he turns sharply to Jake, who's now stretched out on the back seat, a fresh joint in his hand.

'Next time leave her alone. You don't know how pathetic you look sometimes.'

Jake laughs. He laughs while Steve revs up the engine and speeds off into the late morning sun. Steve drives so fast my hair streams out behind me. From time to time I imagine it touching Jake, blinding him momentarily before his fingers part it and his mouth, not his hands, caress my neck and shoulders before stealing round to the front of my body. I wriggle on the seat tilting my head back on the rest. I stretch my legs as far as I can. In my short skirt they look good, already quite tanned from a few hot weeks. My thighs are damp with sweat and the feeling is not unpleasant. Steve looks straight ahead, concentrating on the road and turning up the radio.

9

Need to be your lover, baby
Need to be the guy
To hold you hard in the soft moonlight
Love you till you cry

The breeze moulds my cotton top to my breasts. It's a present from Steve; shell pink, brief and flimsy. He likes me to wear it without a bra. I look down at my nipples; hard and dark against the straining material. I have small breasts but large nipples: 'a precious mouthful' Steve always says. But he never takes them in his mouth long enough, never kisses them as softly as I'd like. As we speed through the ocean-scented air my nipples harden more. I want them to be touched. I feel shivery and strange. Steve is consumed by his wild joyless driving and no longer puts his hand on my thighs, yet it feels as if I am being touched. I begin to ache faintly between my legs; pressing my lips together, longing for some added pressure; wishing I could put my finger there, the way I do when I am alone.

I feel a tap on my shoulder; I hold my breath, not sure if I've imagined it. It comes again. I turn to see Jake smiling at me and holding up a half-smoked joint. He puts it to my lips and I close my eyes and inhale deeply, holding the hot harsh-sweet smoke in my mouth as long as I can. Then I swallow and, when I open my eyes again, Jake is leaning towards me, very close, his eyes shining and his face vibrant. The song on the radio has worked itself into a mellow guitar refrain with a soft underlying bass sound. As we smile into each other's eyes it feels as if he is transmitting this guitar beat to me; it travels through my body, making my skin tingle and my heart race. Most intensely, though, inside his gaze and the pulsating music, I can feel my clit throb. I press down on the seat, feeling tiny blissful contractions start up all over my lower body. I bite my lip and try not to squirm. Something in the way his eyes shine convinces me he knows.

I feel as if we are floating, alone together; detached

from the car; nothing but the vast blue sky around us. I'm becoming more and more aroused as I look at him, more inclined towards abandonment. I have to force myself to turn away, mouthing 'Thank you' just before I do.

Steve is now driving as though possessed and I wonder if he has noticed the interaction between Jake and I. Normally the speed we are travelling at would scare me but with the dope, the music and the desire pumping through my veins, it only makes me more excited.

From the back seat Jake is singing along with the music.

> *To hold you hard in the soft moonlight*
> *Love you till you cry*

His voice is not deep and rough as I would have expected, but higher and more melodic, seeming to instil each word with new meaning.

When he sings 'hold you hard' I feel my whole body shiver. 'Hold you hard', 'love you hard'; it all becomes intermingled. I imagine his cock, brick-hard in his jeans. I imagine undoing his zip; caressing him; seeing the look on his face. He's singing for me, I'm sure of it. I cross my legs, clenching all the muscles in my lower body in an attempt to satisfy my intense arousal. He must know what he's doing to me, I think, half in ecstasy, half in despair. I can't help but move my hips a little and then I discover with delight the rough cord handle of my handbag. I lift myself on the pretext of securing my skirt against the wind, simultaneously positioning the cord so that I can easily settle my crotch on it. Brief feelings of shame and embarrassment come and go as I clench the muscles in my buttocks and abdomen, then release them and bear down on the ridged cord. My clit pushes out against the flimsy gauze of my pants and I rub myself again and again on the harsh fibre.

I am lost in my pleasure, intent on rubbing myself harder and longer, catching my breath as the small deft surges of bliss come more frequently. It takes me some

11

time to realise that the car is slowing considerably and our surroundings have changed. We are in the middle of a thick mass of tall trees on the long driveway leading up to Old Beach House. Steve has switched the radio off and all I can hear is the wind in the trees and now and then a spatter of birdsong. I am damp with sweat and flushed; the throbbing between my legs is still there but dulling now because I know that soon we must stop. I close my eyes, numb with frustration and disappointment. Then I realise that the reason Steve is driving so slowly is because of the surface of the driveway. It is stonier and more uneven as we progress. As the car jolts its way forward the cord between my legs begins to rub and push against me with much more force than I was able to muster myself. Waves of redness begin to fill my head and my womb constricts sharply as the heaviness in my abdomen increases unbearably. I am going to come. I can't help it but I must try to let it happen silently and motionlessly. I move forward in my seat sitting on my hands, frantically fighting the urge to move in abandonment and make my situation obvious. 'I want to. I want to.' The words go unsaid, but scorch through my brain. Sweat trickles between my breasts and my pants are soaked with excitement. Then the car bounces over a small pothole and the cord between my legs sears a jagged blissful course through my lips.

'Oh Jesus, Jesus,' I whimper, unable to stop myself.

'Lara, what's wrong, angel?'

Steve finally turns to look at me and I stare back, dry mouthed and jolted into reality, unable to believe he has done it again. One more unfulfilled orgasm. Tears fill my eyes as the car comes to an abrupt stop.

'I'm alright,' I whisper and tidy my hair with trembling hands, letting the wetness cool on me and the now dull throbbing subside completely.

Jake leaps up from the back seat and climbs over the closed door. Only then, as he walks away from me, his broad shoulders gleaming in the sun, do I notice my surroundings. We have drawn up in the rather neglected

12

courtyard of a large, old, building with pillars around the door. Strange tropical plants sprout from behind pock-marked statues; tall slender strips of greenery waft together like groups of people whispering. In the stronger gusts of wind, patches of them bend precariously deep, bowing to us in the warm breeze. Laughter and music can be heard creeping into the air from the rear of the house: guitars and singing; a tinkling sound like a mandolin. Then a girl appears from behind a wild blowing palm at the side of the house. She wears a silver dress, similar to the one I picture in my fantasies. But hers is of a lighter, easier material, and she wears it in a relaxed manner. She doesn't look as if she'd want to pretend to be a whore. She walks slowly as if in a dream. She is older and taller than me, with a light but assured step. Jake goes immediately towards her and lifts her off her feet, swinging her around as her pale hands cross over and clutch his tanned shoulders. Her hair is a glorious dark cloud around them both. Damp, small and miserable in the car, I hate her.

Steve is redoing the buttons of my blouse to re-establish a chaste neckline.

'You're all damp and trembling. What is it Lara? Tell me.'

He puts his arms around me and for a short while I cry weakly against his shirt.

His shoulder feels warm in the sun. I think how nice he smells, how good it will be to sleep on him all night for the next few weeks.

'I scared you. That's what it is. Driving too fast. That's it, isn't it? You should have told me. You should always tell me when I upset you.'

I smile to reassure him but my gaze is drawn beyond him to the pillared darkness of the door of the house; so dark on such a blue-bright day. Jake and the girl with the cloud of hair, arms entwined, disappear into the shadowed entrance without a backward glance.

'I only want to make you happy,' Steve says.

* * *

13

All that long afternoon the sun moves over the dancing leaves and the tall trees on the periphery of the garden sway in unison. Steve and I drink and sing and joke around with five or six other couples on the wide expanse of close-cut lawn. I drink wine from the bottle too fast and dance barefoot in the grass. The more I drink, the more confident I become. I stop looking towards the house to see if Jake and the girl are going to reappear. I stop needing to be so close to Steve and begin to enjoy the looks from other men as I sit on the grass with my skirt riding up too high. Then someone dances too close to me, sliding his hands down my buttocks and moving me nearer and nearer the thick bushes at the back of the garden. He holds me so hard to him I can feel the urgency of his erection as if we were naked. Reckless with drink I let him burrow his cock up my skirt and want him to carry on until I become hazily aware of the discomfort in my abdomen as he presses against my full bladder. When I push him away with some inept excuse he becomes annoyed, calling me a prick tease. Steve strolls over, looking almost embarrassed. 'She's not used to the booze,' he explains and the guy shrugs in a conciliatory fashion and walks off. I feel cheated, although I don't really know why, then I tell Steve I am desperate to pee. He looks firstly exasperated then sympathetic and hastily takes me behind some tall lush-leaved trees. My balance is so precarious, as I squat in the dark summer shadow, that Steve has to stand behind me, holding me up. In my drunkenness it strikes me as hilarious that I should be in this predicament with my rather stern but gorgeous ex-teacher and I begin to laugh uncontrollably. Hot liquid spurts from me as I cling on to Steve's leg and try not to wet my skirt. When I've finished Steve bends down to wipe between the legs with the large fleshy leaves of a scented bush. My mirth is infectious and he laughs as he strokes the last of the moisture from me, one arm around the small of my back to help me keep balance.

'Bet you never thought you'd be doing this a year ago.'

I giggle. 'When you were teaching me the joys of perspective.'

'God, Lara, I sometimes wonder what I'm doing with you, I really do.'

He smiles up at me. He, too, is fairly drunk but still very much the grown-up, the one in charge. I know his words are spurred by affection, but suddenly I feel anxious and afraid. I watch as he drops the leaves onto the glistening pool I have made, which is already sinking into the hot, pitted earth. I notice I have peed a little on the edges of his shoes. The fickle effects of the alcohol leave me cold and ashamed. I can no longer look at Steve. But he cups my chin in his hand and forces me to face him.

'I keep forgetting how young you are,' he says. 'The little girl I used to teach pottery to. You're right, a lot has changed in a year and I'm not sorry. But I should take better care of you, Lara.'

He says the last words in a voice thick with self-chastisement, far more than is necessary.

We stand holding each other for a long time, me shivering a bit and Steve stroking warmth down my back and whispering over and over again, 'It's my fault, Lara. I need to look after you, teach you better. It's all my fault.'

I still feel soiled and drained, but as he kisses my forehead, reiterating his feelings of guilt and blame I sense that the control has shifted from him to me.

Timidly at first, but then gaining courage I place the palm of my hand lightly on the front of his jeans. Then I press harder cupping my hand gently around his balls. His cock, semi-erect to start with, swells and strains against the rough tight denim. I stroke him again and again watching his face lift from my hair, his eyes blink in surprise; he opens his mouth to speak but then doesn't. He pushes my shoulders back as if wanting to reject me, but seems helpless to stop his penis coming towards my hand. I watch with fascination as his pleasure turns to near pain. I keep touching him and stopping, touching

15

him again, even when he groans and begs me not to. I dig my nails around the contours of his straining dick pushing my fingers behind his balls into the tight area between his legs. I know he is struggling for control.

'Not here. Christ, Lara, not out here in the open.'

I know that I won't unzip him and let his cock go free; hard, moist and aflame in the summer air. The feeling of power I have over him is exciting me too, giving me small needling surges of pleasure between my legs. I know I won't relieve him with my hand or, better, my mouth. But neither will I stop. Suddenly the prospect of making him come inside his jeans fills me with almost overwhelming excitement. Instinctively I know that after the ecstasy has ebbed away he will be annoyed with himself and more so with me. But still I don't stop. Now I am rubbing my cupped hand roughly, almost brutally, as quickly as I can along the straining shaft. With delight I watch a tiny patch of leaked semen darkening his jeans. Just a few seconds more . . . then, to my astonishment he suddenly pushes my hand away and, breathlessly, furiously, he comes down to kneel in front of me and with a deft movement has lifted my short skirt and pulled my pants savagely down to my ankles.

'See how you like it then,' he says bitterly and begins to lick and probe with his tongue every fold and hollow and every secret place between my legs. But he does it in a harsh animal fashion and I am reminded of a dog that used to roam near my house when I was small, how it would run up and jab me with its snout, in a similar manner. As he grips my buttocks and thrusts me towards his face I feel the depth of the humiliation I have forced on him by making him no longer in charge.

'Hold me to you,' he says in a cold muffled voice, his head covered by my pink skirt so that he looks odd and foolish. I feel embarrassed, cradling his head lightly but looking around me, glad that the trees and the dense bushes are there. To the right of us stands the turreted end of the wing of the house, stark and looking deserted among the surrounding green. Halfway up is a balcony and a shuttered window. One of the shutters is half-open. Suddenly I become convinced that Jake is in there with the dark-haired girl. For a second I stare upwards, fearful that they will come to the window and see us. But then I think, why would they? Lying naked and entwined, pulsating in their own wetness, why would they rise from each other to look at a silly drunk girl, her bare legs shivering in the sun. A girl trying to feel something as the man she believes she loves bites and nuzzles and probes between her legs. A girl feeling only amazement that any man should want to bury himself in her unresponsive unwashed cunt, bitter with the taste of stale pee and the salty sticky aftermath of solitary unfulfilled fantasies.

A sudden rogue wind blasts through the lulling breeze, unbalancing Steve enough for him to fall away from me, and my fingers fall away from him. Although taken by surprise he smiles up at me wanting to see some sign of need from me, the agony of unfulfilled desire on my face. But as he looks at me I am looking upwards to where a dark green shutter now bangs intermittently. In the lulls of silence between slamming wood I am sure I can hear a woman's voice, at first sobbing as if she is enduring the unbearable. But then it changes. It changes into a sound that resembles music, a long undulating wail that rises and shakes and cries out towards heaven in joy.

'Let's finish this later,' Steve says quietly and rises, stroking my face absently as if he knows, and wants to banish, the wonder in my mind.

The sun is low in the sky and the crooked leaves in the trees are dark with unbroken glossiness. Only an occasional drunken voice creeps over a silence now too sacred for guitars. Spent by alcohol and revelry we all doze in long chairs, sometimes kissing and touching. But we are inside ourselves, essentially lonely. It isn't until the trees glow red and the sun behind them sinks completely to the unseen ocean that Jake and the girl serenely come back to us, hand in hand.

* * *

Twenty summers have passed since then and now I travel that long coast road again. Today I am alone in my car apart from sketch books, pencils and colour swabs; the tools of my trade. My dress is new and flimsy in red and marigold dyes, splashes of optimistic summer hues, but it is not short. It does not reveal. The nearer I get to the old house the more unsure I become; so at odds, in my bright dress, with the warm but dull day; frightened by my desire to revisit the past, and the implications of my motives for doing so.

I glance at myself in the driver's mirror. Stace told me to wear make-up. 'You're in business now,' she said. 'You have to look the part.' And she watched as I frowned over the mirror, my hand shaking as I smudged shadow onto my eyelids, trying to look eighteen again. Finally, as if I was the child and she the mother, she rubbed it all off and started again. Gently and expertly she made me glow with life and expectation. She laughed at my gratitude. I was thinking, If only you knew what's in my mind when I see my face like this; what I hope for. 'Oh Mum, you know it's what I want to do, what I'm training for.' I watched her tall, slender body walk out of the room, walk towards some new experience or heady encounter and I thought, I used to be like you. My days used to be filled with hope and excitement. Hope was taken for granted, never to come to an end. Now, the face in the mirror looks drained beneath the glistening eyelids and the warm moist mouth. I stop the car and sit a moment, staring at the colourless beach below and listening to the wind in the grass. This is not a blue-bright day, like the one long ago and others that stand out like jewels; the summers of my past. Today the sun hides and I see only emptiness when I look at the sea. But I can't go back; I have an appointment to keep. But not yet.

I get out of the car, wrapping myself in Stace's long cardigan. I smell her scent from it, the spicy sweetness around the collar and I am comforted, thinking of how she looks, perfumed and dressed to go out, her lipstick bold and her head high. I can't imagine Stace unsure of how to get her man.

I walk down to the beach through the long grass. I take off my shoes and dig my toes into the sand between the tight roots, stopping a while to look towards the blank shoreline, almost expecting to see the reel of all those years ago unfold before my eyes. The young girl, with her skirt already half off, lifted wildly up so that her feet point towards the sky. When she and her lover sink to the sand her head bumps slightly and he falls a little too heavily against her open thigh.

'Oh, that hurts a bit,' a half-nervous, half-excited giggle in the voice. The memory is vivid and wonderful, yet sad too. The voice is so clear in my head that I slump, overwhelmed, to sit in the thick grass and I hear it again. But it is not in my mind, it is near me, just as tremulous, just as young – somewhere in the sea of rustling green – very near.

'I'm not sure.' Then a small female cry, 'Yes. OK. Oh . . .' Silence. Two gulls sail by overhead, uncannily close together, their wings almost touching. One of them cries as it leads the other higher into the sky.

Holding my breath, I softly part the reeds at my side. I see nothing at first but more thick strands of green. But I can hear them. Voices, probably silenced by passion when I first came, are now clear, oblivious to my presence.

'You'll like it, you will, come on sweetheart. I'll do it for you, too. Come on, you know what I can do for you.' My heart racing, I move slowly into the green, sliding on my thigh, moving my dress up so that it doesn't tear. My fingers move gently on the feathery tips of grass. Lower down, their shafts graze my flesh. I stop abruptly when an intermingling of faint female moans and loudening male cries make me realise how close I must be. I lie flat and, closing my eyes for a second, part the grass.

When I open my eyes again the lovers are beneath me,

19

quite far below in a hollow of sand where the grasses have dispersed.

He is young and dark, slender but taut, as Steve once was. He is kneeling, but his thighs are thrust forward and he holds her to him, the girl with straight hair the colour of sand. He holds her to his cock and looks up to the sky in ecstasy as her pale hair veils out in the wind, her head bobbing quicker, quicker.

Suddenly he pushes her harder onto him, clasping her head. Her hand, previously resting on his thigh, arches as her nails dig into his flesh. He throws his head right back and groans, then releases her quickly, falling back, gasping on the sand. She collapses over him, her face turned to the side, her mouth beside his cock still open, her small body heaving, her arm across his chest as if seeking an embrace. He strokes her hair almost absent-mindedly. Across his pelvis, strands of its goldness stretch, plastered down with his seed. Eventually he moves his body up, bends down to kiss her face. She lifts her mouth to meet his. Laughing, he takes the sticky hair from her mouth, wraps his arms around her.

'I want to make you happy, angel, you know that, don't you?'

She murmurs something against his chest. Looks up, smiles. For several seconds they rest there holding each other. Then he moves her away, gently but briskly, finds his rumpled jeans, puts them on, glances around.

'Damn it. Where's my jacket?'

She is looking around her as he turns and walks up the hollow, in my direction. I crouch further down. Immediately below me, where the grass starts, is a line of her clothes – dress, bra, sandals, all thrown at an angle to each other. His jacket is there too, so heavy and dark compared to her things. He picks it up and takes out a small metal flask. Turning to face the road he drinks contentedly. Behind him in the curve of the sand the girl sits quite erect, cross-legged, patting down her bare arms and legs as if clothed, as if brushing something from herself. She looks at his naked back for several seconds as if expecting something, then turns away and looks down at her feet, spots a scrap of something scarlet near her toes. Glancing up at his still averted back she picks up her tiny pants, spits into them then wipes her mouth. He comes back to her and she rises to meet him, half runs, a small golden-haired nymphet.

He presses his hands hard into her buttocks as she pushes herself against him.

'I love you,' she cries out and she sounds joyful. 'I love you,' she says, snuggling against his hardening cock.

I rise from my hiding place, trampling the grass in my haste to get away, tearing at some of the tall stalks, stumbling on others.

Back in the car I part my skirt to rub at the small criss-cross marks on my legs. I look at my calves, my thighs, only faintly tanned by the still early summer. They are still firm, but rounder than they were all those years ago. I remember my slender legs snaked easily around Steve's back. I remember pushing, rubbing my clit against him, wanting to come, wanting so much, for him. And those words, 'I want to make you happy, angel.' That's what he called me too.

I draw back the roof of my car. A pale sun is smeared behind the thinning clouds. I find a station on the radio that plays rock music. I'm tired of driving this long road with only silence and the pictures in my head for company.

> *The day I came to see you,*
> *I wore a dress of fire.*
> *I died inside our sea of flames,*
> *We burnt out all desire.*

The music of my youth.

> *I sit and sing by moonlight and read the gypsy's palm.*
> *You never give a backward glance as you leave the*
> *   stranger's land.*

I comb my hair in the mirror. It's shorter now. I can no longer hide behind it, but it's fashionably layered and still thick. Once my hair was the colour of pale sand, too. It could be again with the help of a long hot summer sun, or a cosmetic. Imagination. I dab some more of Stace's berry gloss on my mouth. Open my lips, smile wide. My teeth are white and strong. I remember the first time I took Steve in my mouth, trying not to gag, All those times. The teacher and the pupil. The protector. The master. I still believe he wanted to make me happy.

You take her by the hand and leave the stranger's land.

I fling back my almost blonde hair, turn up the music and rev up the engine. A faint sunlight falls on my legs, my neck, my wet lips.

The car screeches from gravel to smooth flat road. A short way along, I pass the young couple leaning on a motorbike. The girl wears a short, though somehow demure-looking, dress on her small, neat body. She has painted her lips and carefully runs her tongue over an ice cream. Her lover watches her benevolently. Further down the road the bike roars past. The girl is at the front, her slender thighs open and commanding, her fair hair streaming from a helmet. His face is buried in it as he clings to her back. I laugh and turn the radio full up.

There is no longer a gate at the start of the long driveway to Old Beach House. The opening is flanked by some roughly cut-back bushes. The trees beyond look higher but not so impressive or luxuriant as I recall. As I drive slowly onwards I see signs of preservation of a few unique features in this wild spacious garden – the small circular grass glades, neat with their fountains still running; the tiny benches and tables, in need of varnish but intact and well-placed; crystalline ponds with oriental flowers, small and threatened-looking in a rampant jungle of tree ferns and lopsided, top-heavy larches and chestnuts. Such a curious mixture of neglect and conservation as if the owner wants to hide himself from the world, but not entirely, as though a quiet desperation for company still exists.

Then the house is in view – the pillars fronting the heavy oak door, a door obstinately closed on this warm June day. The tall windows at the front are now curtain-less and dull looking. There are no cars, no people, no sound apart from my radio.

I switch it off and drive round the side of the house, where the turreted wing stands. I stop the engine and gaze upwards. The balcony is empty, the green shutters closed. For several seconds I remain, as if waiting for someone to appear, the shutter to open. It doesn't. I try to compose myself, remember I'm here in a professional capacity. I find some mineral water in the glove compartment, gulp some down, then dampen my face and the back of my wrists. I take a perfume from my bag, the same one I wore all those years ago, 'Burlesque', the sweet but musky scent of Eastern markets. I am about to spray some on my neck and down my breasts when I catch sight of my face in the mirror. I see the fear in my eyes, so strangely framed in shimmering dust, but there's excitement there too. You are a mature woman, I tell myself. You have done well. Go and show him how you've changed. I put the perfume back in my bag and take my briefcase from the passenger seat. I leave the car and walk briskly to the front of the house to mask my nervousness. I watch, as though in slow motion, as my finger reaches towards the doorbell. I wonder absently if I should have worn nail polish. The sharpness of the ring I hear from within the house takes me by surprise and immediately I want to turn, to run, even as the blood seems to drain from me. I gaze fixedly at the door, unable to believe I have actually come here with the half-formed, crazy ideas I have in my head. But no-one is coming. It takes me several moments to take this in. I ring once more, then glance at my watch; check the hour, the day. Afternoon of the third of June. No mistake. I am seized by fury. So typical. The gentle eyes and the soft voice,

23

but no real concern for other people. Props of the actor; the artist as a human being.

Now, sure that I'm alone, and with cooling adrenaline, I decide to take a look around. Then I'll leave my card and phone later from some cosy civilised hotel room.

On the far side of the house is a tunnel of intertwined greenery leading to the rear garden. It is just as it was, poignantly fragrant in the light afternoon warmth. I remember one afternoon, another party, it had just started to rain and I was first inside to take shelter. My dress was thin and I felt chilled. There was a flower, a tiny white one, growing from the wall of the tunnel. I had turned to pick it. Then a hand came around my waist, caressing my abdomen, the fingertips stretching downwards so that I arched up to meet them. I knew, even in the gloom, that it was not Steve's hand. It was too broad. But I pressed myself against him, let my buttocks strain against his erection. He moved closer, so did I. We rubbed against each other very gently, very slowly, but enough for me to feel the flame start to lick inside me, flickering between my legs. Then I heard approaching voices and knew there wasn't long. I placed my hand over his, frantically guiding it down. I pushed the tip of his index finger so hard against the top of my lips that my hand trembled afterwards. Then he stroked me, once, softly, almost imperceptibly, as if all he wanted was to touch the gauze of my skirt, feel the warm moisture seeping through the flimsy layers of material. Then he let me go abruptly and turned me around to face him, so I could say, 'You!' in an outraged voice and look at him with loathing and he could feign amusement. Then the others caught up and Steve nudged my breast with his elbow as he searched for his lighter. The sensation in my still erect nipple made me catch my breath.

Out in the daylight again I am surprised how little this part of the garden has changed. Varieties of luxuriant, scantily flowered bushes grow high and wild with spaces in between and underneath – green and scented niches for lovemaking. The tree ferns, tall swirling clumps of

24

them, waiting to tease and graze excited flesh in the high breeze, flatten to a mattress of fragrant lushness when it is calm. The emerald lawn – hard and flat, a sponge for secrets and juices of the body. The tall pale grasses where Steve and I lay till it was pink with the evening sun, him asleep with my head on his chest, me touching his cock as an insect covers a piece of fruit, unable to be at peace, wanting more.

Then I see something new. There's a summer-house – wooden, but for two stained glass panels at the front with clear glass between them making a door – an odd but intriguing mixture of styles. I approach, the designer in me curious. I walk in the shadow of the big house watching the sun play on the coloured glass, mottling the clear glass with leaf shadow. Suddenly I stop, blink a few times and move rapidly back against the wall. A girl stands behind the glass with red tumbling hair and she is naked. She stands sideways and reaches out a hand. Her tall, strong body is now front on, as if she's looking straight at me. Quickly I crouch down, hiding myself behind a curtain of loose ivy, but I can't resist peeping out as the glass door opens. The girl's long-legged frame comes towards me, her arms clutching the unbuttoned man's shirt somewhere around her waist, exposing a heavy, large-nippled breast and a glimpse of amber pubic hair. She walks almost jauntily on bare feet smiling to herself and pausing to call over her shoulder.

'Was I good for you today, my darling? As you say, alive and deep. Was I deep enough for you?' Her voice is low and Germanic. She ends her words with a mischievous laugh.

Then she walks more quickly, almost playfully, as if she expects to be chased. But after she passes me, frighteningly close, I have no wish to watch him follow, so I shut my eyes and pray he does not spot me. His footsteps crunch by on the gravel and I realise with a lurching sense in my stomach that I recall even this, his ambling even-stepped walk. As he passes he throws his cigarette end into the ivy where I hide. I can't make myself look at him but I catch his scent, the familiar mixture of incense and soap and the fresh sweat of excitement.

I crouch there a few more minutes, dazed and saddened, pondering my next move until it occurs to me that they might notice my car tucked into the side of the house. I stand up, brush down my dress and clutch my briefcase. Then I walk as calmly as I can, back past the stained-glass summer-house, giving it a casual but interested glance in case I am being watched, then I saunter past my car. I fight the desire to get in, race off and phone later to cancel my appointment. Only the thought of Stacey's expression when I arrive back with portfolio, luggage and faded make-up propels me towards the entrance of the house. But some ten feet before the door I stop, gripping the handle of my briefcase like a child at a new school. The door is opening and out into a quickening breeze comes the girl with the auburn hair. Jeans, like a blue velvet skin, adorn her endless legs and her naked breasts are shackled lightly under a tiny jumper. Immediately, she sees me standing at the side, but there is no surprise or curiosity in her eyes. Instead, she gives me a small sly smile, as if she and I are involved in some conspiracy. She strolls a short way down the drive, then wrenches, from under the shadow of the trees, a motorbike. She anchors it beneath her as if mounting a beast. Without a second glance, she roars down the drive with her hair flying.

My heart races as I look back towards the door. He is standing in the shade, watching me. We both take a couple of steps towards each other. I am suddenly unnerved by the gathering breeze which pulls at my dress, lifting the light material around my legs, holding it tight against my chest. Now he stands in the daylight, with his hand to his eyes as if the sun is strong not, as it is, intermittent, flitting in and out of the clouds, or as if I am far off and he can't be sure I am there. I move as if in a trance, watching myself walk. His old jeans are splashed with paint and bleach stains, his thighs lightly muscular; easy, welcoming. The pale shirt he had earlier given to the girl is open over a still-strong chest and a tanned torso. His hair is shorter now but still thick and wavy and attractively flecked with grey. The extra years suit his features. He has small lines around his dark eyes; fine ones around his mouth. The bold sensuality of his youthful face has been tempered by something I didn't expect – a trace of reserve, regret, even compassion.

Now we stand only six feet apart. His hand, with shirt entrapped, is thrust in his pocket in a posture I remember. But the look in his eyes is alien to me. They travel over my face as he seems to search somewhere inside his head. I grow cold all over. I can't believe he doesn't know who I am. With this terrible possibility comes the consciousness of the over-fluttering of my skirt, how old my face must look, how unrecognisable my body. The sun coming and going through the clouds, lighting up then darkening the space between us, makes me dizzy. I will have to say something.

But before I do there is an abrupt change in his expression. As if he has just got the punch line of a joke, he smiles broadly then laughs; comes towards me with his hand still in the pocket of his jeans.

'Larissa,' he says. 'Well, my God, it is, isn't it?' Then he repeats it, softly, 'Larissa.'

I feel a flush spread on my face as he looks me up and down, his eyes casual, running over my breasts, my thighs, my legs, making me hot and cold, charged with energy, then suddenly weak and powerless.

To regain my composure I take my gaze from him and smartly snap open my briefcase. I pull out my business catalogue with the embossed pastel cover that I am so proud of and offer it to him.

'Elmac Design,' I tell him briskly and continue foolishly, 'That's me. I'm here to look at your house.'

He looks straight into my eyes, a frown playing on his brow. He reaches for the catalogue and somehow, whether through nerves from one or both of us, or a gust of the mischievous wind now determined to add its own chaos to the afternoon, the folder is dropped. It opens on the ground between us, fanning out a carelessly anchored batch of colour samples to the wind. We stoop at the same time and our hands collide, pinning down a square of peach satin.

'Mmmm, nice feel,' he murmurs, his dark eyes so near mine glowing, while his mouth, though soft, is straight and serious. I leave my hand under his, not attempting to struggle free. I hold his gaze defiantly though the wind tears my skirt from my thighs, dishevels my hair and makes my eyes water. I feel the wetness on my lashes as I look into those warm eyes. I have waited twenty years for Jake Fitzgerald.

Chapter Two

'*I*'ll show you around then.'
  He regards me casually as we stand in the vestibule. His hand is on the glass door to the hall. My eyes are not adjusted to the inside light and I blink, but can make out nothing beyond the glass. Then I remember that by afternoon the sun is long gone from this part of the house. The garden and the kitchen at the rear will now carry all the light.

  'I've been here before,' I remind him as we stand inside the large rectangular hall.

  The once ornate tiles on the floor are dingy and worn and the high walls, buff-coloured and bare but for one or two odd groups of framed photographs, small as stamps on an envelope. There is something quite different about the way the hall looks but I can't remember what. Jake leads the way briskly towards the wide staircase, ignoring the ground floor rooms at the front which I don't even remember seeing the first time I came. As I stand at the foot of the stairs, looking behind, trying to work out what has changed so much, Jake calls down to me.

  'I thought you were here on business. You seem to be doing a lot of reminiscing.' Even with the distance between us I can still hear the smirk in his voice.

'I'm just trying to get a feel for the space, an impression,' I say briskly.

I climb the stairs rapidly, aware of the sound of my new high-heeled sandals on the bare wood, as if the very sound of them will betray my ambivalent reasons for coming back. There used to be something on the floor – carpet, tapestry matting, something. Jake is standing on the wide landing watching me, but as I approach he turns away to open with difficulty two rather oddly placed glass doors. They open inwards, creaking into life, disgorging some dust and loose plaster from their fittings.

I follow Jake onto a small balcony, gripping the ornate iron railing. He puts his hand over mine and I look into his eyes, startled.

'Don't worry,' he says, 'it's all quite safe. I've had it checked. I wouldn't lead you into danger, now would I, Larissa?'

I look down at the expanse of rear garden. The smaller ferns beneath the high ones bounce and curve in a small swirling sea. The leaves of the tall trees at the periphery of the garden are yellow-green and full of youth. Just standing near Jake again, seeing his bare arms, his strong hands, makes me buoyant and full of expectation. I fight hard to keep my thoughts on a mundane level.

'We'll have to get these windows fixed.' My voice is neither businesslike nor that of a friend to another. It sounds timid and flat.

'What?' Jake moves his elbows back from the railing, finds some cigarettes in his torn shirt pocket, lights one. He doesn't look at me at all.

Through the dancing green branches, the sun glints intermittently on the glass door of the summer-house. I think of the naked girl with the red hair. I wonder if he is thinking of her too.

'Perhaps after the frames are done, the fittings and such like, it might be an idea ... I saw the stained glass on your summer-house. We could repeat the colour.' I know I am speaking too quickly.

'Who's we?' He turns to me with a grin.

Close to, his skin has a tanned dusty appearance, like a workman after a hard day. There is a trace of sweat in the air, mingled with warm cotton and a faint tang of spice. I wonder if it comes from Jake or the girl. I notice a smudge of paint on his chin. I resist the urge to touch it.

'You're the designer, Larissa,' he continues in a slow jaded manner. 'Tell me what you think and, within reason, we'll do it. You'll recall that I'm an easy kind of guy.'

'I never found you easy.' The words are out before I can stop them. I smile to make the statement seem lighter.

He laughs briefly, shrugging it off.

I lean back against the railing, facing him, trying to keep my breathing even. The breeze lifts my hair. I hope I look appealing. My pelvis is tilted towards him; thin cotton strains across my chest. My nipples are hard and I want him to see.

He continues to smoke, glancing around the garden, then, as if forced to appraise me, he looks back, slowly taking in my neck, where my fingers now rest, rigid against my skin to stop them trembling; my mouth, which I try to make soft and casual; and, finally, my eyes, which I know will show him the truth.

'Lara Macintyre,' he says quietly. 'The little girl my brother screwed. The first-year student with the shiny hair and the new clothes – the clothes that *he* bought for her.'

Something in his tone angers me. Yet I am embarrassed too. It is true that I had been different from the others at art college. I kept myself for Steve, studying religiously and waiting around even after he had left teaching and gone some distance away to do his degree in architecture. I waited around because he always came back and he was kind. I feel a sudden sadness at the realisation that it had all been so wrong, even in the beginning. To mask this from Jake I look up brightly.

31

'Everyone fancied you like crazy in our year, you know.'

'Yes,' he says mildly, 'I do know. I shagged most of them eventually.'

Furiously, I turn away from him and stare down at the garden. The intense green of it is suddenly wild and frightening in the wind. But not me Jake, I think.

He is standing right by me now, so close I can feel the warmth of his body. I feel oddly comforted. He throws his cigarette, half-smoked, out into the restless air and greenery. It travels for a while, curving, a dot of fire, then lands dead in the gravel.

'I always looked out for you didn't I, Lara?' he asks quietly, as if reading my thoughts.

I turn and smile weakly at him, remembering the times he, not Steve, collected me at the station when I'd visited my parents for the weekend. The times when Steve was too involved in exams to travel, and Jake took me to the pub with his friends. How he'd come and sit beside me if I was being harassed, how he'd walk me back to my neat sterile little flat but never come in. And yet, when we touched there was always something there or perhaps I'd just imagined it. Just another fantasy.

I look out over the eccentric contours and wild textures of the well-remembered landscape. It is as if the ghosts of the past, recumbent in couples in all its lush niches, raucous, exuberant, then stilled by passion, are finally being borne away on today's breeze. I look at the clouds racing across the sky and back at the garden. How deserted, how devoid of joy it seems. How quickly summers pass when you're older.

'Look, maybe it would be better if someone else does the work,' I say in a resigned voice. 'After all, you weren't prepared for me. You know what they say about friends and business.'

Suddenly he grabs my wrist, urgently, as if I'm leaving immediately. I stare at him and my breath comes faster. I feel exhilarated but frightened too. His grip is harsh but I don't want him to let me go.

'Larissa,' he says.

'Don't call me that. It's not my real name.' My voice shakes and I am ashamed.

His hold relaxes and his hand slides over my wrist. 'Larissa,' he says so softly it is almost inaudible. 'The nymphet martyr.'

His hand cups mine, then moves again back over my wrist, back and forth, down again, a gentle soothing motion as if I have been injured and he is trying to heal me. And I feel it again, the quickening in my blood, the urge to go nearer and nearer to him. He is standing so close I can feel his breath on my lips.

'I always wondered why you called me that,' I whisper, glancing into his eyes.

'Larissa is Greek, the martyr, but a nymph also,' he says solemnly. 'I used to watch you with Steve, trying so hard to please. You were so unhappy.'

'I think I prefer to be simply a nymphet,' I tell him, feigning amusement.

I gaze down at our hands through the veil of my hair and I know I am not going to leave.

It takes Jake a further hour to hastily show me the rooms on the upper floor, none of which I recognise. They are all so empty and mournful. At the front of the house the pale, afternoon sun casts a deep green shadow through the trees, covering everything. The rooms at the rear are, by almost hideous contrast, white with sunlight but open and lonely. All are in varying stages of neglect. A few have no floor coverings and bare walls, but here and there I am surprised by items of odd furniture or a sculpture; a collection of luxuriant overgrown plants; ancient-looking vases and bowls in corners and sometimes in the centre of rooms. In one room, next to where I remember the bathroom to be, a four-poster bed, swathed in silk and lace, stands on bare boards. It is positioned next to the brazen light of an uncurtained window.

Jake reads something in my expression and says briskly, 'I'm an artist. I need props for my models.'

'Yes, of course.'

I think of the red-haired girl in the summer-house.

An archway marks the start of the corridor leading to the west wing and the turreted room. I think back to that afternoon twenty years ago when I gazed up at the shadowed balcony and the banging shutters, my skirt raised and Steve with his head between my legs; how I heard the cries of a woman in a way I'd never heard before, unable to tell if they were of pleasure, pain or grief. I never discussed it with Steve and, as I see Jake following my gaze into the gloom of the archway then swiftly averting his eyes to look at another door immediately in front of us, I know I'll never mention it to him either.

'You'll remember this, Lara,' he says cheerfully and opens the door, bidding me to enter first.

The room is small and square and a tree in late blossom taps at the window. It is the tree I remember first, the rhythm of it like a large flowered hand on the glass as I knelt on all fours on the rough beige matting. Steve was entering me from behind. I wore a wine-coloured corset and nothing else. He had bought it for me and it was expensive but it felt harsh and tight. All evening, as I sat with Steve and his friends on the same corded boxy sofa that I look at now, drinking and talking, I felt the corset grow tighter, my breath shorter. Steve kept looking at me with fondness and whispering, 'Wait till later, little Lara,' but when the time came I was so dry with apprehension I had to go to the bathroom to smear some face cream between my legs. Even then I couldn't respond. I stare now at the same rush flooring; at the spot where I bit my lip and waited for him to finish so that he could turn me round and hold me, the spot where semen spurted from him after I moved, unable to even fake pleasure. My eyes mist over as I gaze around the rest of the room, the tawny walls, the pale shaded lamps and in a corner, I'm sure, even the same stereo system that was there then.

The room looks as if it is never used now. It is almost as if the perfumes we wore then, the incense we burned, the dope we smoked, remains, impregnated in the air. If feels as if the voices and the music are still there. All we need to do is listen hard enough. Slightly dizzy, I turn to Jake, half expecting to see the twenty-year-old with the teasing eyes and the olive skin, the man who could so easily have become a model as an artist.

'Nothing's changed,' I whisper.

'The way we were, Larissa,' he laughs.

'Sometimes it doesn't seem that funny.'

'I know,' he says and in the shadow I can't read his expression. We both look towards the window where the pink flowers now brush the glass in an almost friendly manner, waving. I think how beautiful they look, how I never saw them as beautiful all those years ago.

'You're not thinking of that bodice thing he made you wear?' Jake says suddenly.

I look at him in astonishment trying to recall his presence that evening. Then I wonder how he could have known what I was wearing anyway.

'I saw it in his room,' Jake continues. 'In a box all decked out in tissue paper.'

His voice sounds flat. 'It was one of the few times he let me and my drunken buddies sit with his swanky friends. And you were so scared. I heard you, you know, throwing up in the bathroom when I went to get a beer.'

'God, Jake, that was probably the dope,' I say, managing to laugh.

Suddenly drained, I go to sit on the boxy sofa. He comes to join me. Unexpectedly I catch a faint scent of blossom, as if the tree is transmitting its essence to us. Fortuitous and wholesome. With only Jake and I there, the room seems welcoming, a haven in the rambling forgotten house of eclectic objects and crystal-clear memories.

'I told him when I saw it, whatever it was, that it would frighten the life out of you, that he must be crazy.

You know what he said, Lara? He told me he knew you were out of your depth sometimes but it turned him on. He liked the way you dug your nails in, clinging to him like some frightened animal. He said you liked it too.'

He laughs shortly, shakes his head.

I can't think of a single thing to say. I feel shocked yet buoyant at the same time, as if something has been cut loose in me. For some reason I am very glad he has told me.

I squeeze his hand.

This time it is me who wants to leave the room first, while Jake lingers by the door, gazing around with a strange absent look. Just as he reaches for the door handle there is a loud rushing sound and the tree swipes one of its laden branches hard against the glass. Startled, we both look towards it. The mass of flowers retreating, shaken, from the window look thicker, softer and more intensely pink than I ever remember seeing them.

Jake slips his arm around my shoulders.

'This place freaks you out, Lara. It used to then and it still does.'

'Maybe it's more the people than the place,' I say quietly.

In the dusty sunlight of the hall he looks weary, the lines around his eyes showing the years. I have a moment's urge to touch them, smooth them away. But instead I glance at my watch.

'Look, I'm feeling a bit drained and I need to find somewhere to stay. I'll come back tomorrow, OK?'

He looks at me as if he's trying to work something out, takes another cigarette from his pocket, taps his chin with it, still searching my face.

'Could I just use your bathroom?'

He lights the cigarette, says nothing.

'Jake, your bathroom? I think I'm a bit too old to stop the car and pee behind a bush.'

'Yes, yes of course, I'm sorry. I was just thinking . . . anyway, it's over there. You'll remember.'

He indicates the door with a sweep of his arm. Once

more there is warmth in his eyes as I walk down the hall.

I do remember the bathroom, but not like this. Compared to the run-down eccentricity in the rest of the house it is luxurious, ornate even. The old tub is still there in the centre, but renovated, pristine white, with large gleaming taps. The floor and the walls are of blue and green marble, a large frozen whirlpool. Two floor-to-ceiling mirrors adorn the window wall. The French windows, unfrosted, are open. There is a tiny balcony. Branches sway on either side of it, whispering and clashing gently.

I sit on the lavatory, peeing gloriously, breathlessly looking around – another bath, sunken, takes up the far corner, the light settings like candles high on the walls. There are numerous jars of soaps and spices on the floor and on marble shelves. Two glossy chairs, sculpted like hollowed gravestones, are piled high with fluffy towels. I stand in front of the mirror, fluffing up my hair, pinching colour into my cheeks, listening to the wind in the trees.

I recall white tiles, everywhere, clinical like a hospital, black and red lino on the floor; I bled on it once. Steve was pounding into me, here, standing with the door locked to get away from Jake and his friends. It was the start of my period and I hoped it wouldn't show, but after he finished it trickled down my leg, one small line of blood then more, till both my thighs were streaked with it and it formed little scarlet pools between my ankles, large petals on the black. I was so ashamed. Steve was shocked and concerned. I remember he sponged me with warm water and cotton wool. I remember the sensation as he bathed gently between my legs as if I had been hurt. The hot wet dab again and again around my clitoris. I wanted to tell him that I liked it and wanted it to go on, but, of course, I didn't.

I take a final look in the mirror, lifting my skirt to see how my new heels flatter the shape of my legs. I lift the hem higher, drawing in my breath as if, despite the locked door, I might be discovered. I admire the sheen, the expensive look of my new satin knickers; white, still my preferred colour. I smile at this, thinking how some things never change. Then I touch myself – once, then twice with my middle finger, hard and lingering over the sleek tightness of my pants. Immediately, I begin to feel aroused, seeing in my mind Jake leaning against the balcony with his shirt half open, feeling his hand on mine, his arm warm around my shoulders. Guiltily I let my dress fall, smooth it down and walk to the door. I can feel the moisture gather inside me. Outside in the now sunless hall I don't see Jake. Then I notice him coming towards me from the darkness of the west wing.

'Ah, there you are,' he says, as if I am the one who has been somewhere unexpected.

'I can see that you've made up your mind.'

He takes a strand of hair from my neck, lifts it back over my shoulder. His hand stays there a moment, a moment in which I feel a quiver in my breast that goes through my body, my abdomen, and remains, a warm heaviness between my legs.

'I'm sorry? Made up my mind about what?' I lower my lashes. Still, I feel his eyes on me as if he can see through the flimsy brash cotton of my dress, to where my legs grow weak and the crotch of my fine new knickers feels warm and damp.

'Well, you'll be staying, of course,' he says lifting my chin, looking into my eyes. He smiles fleetingly, a hard dry smile. 'It would be best for you. Of course, you know I have the room.'

I feel as if I'm being accused of something.

'It's up to you, Jake,' I say as evenly as I can.

He laughs, gives me a broad, amused smile.

'I think we'd better get your luggage.'

It is early evening. The clouds and the quick unpredictable breeze have gone. The sun is clear and peaceful in the pale sky. I am helping Jake prepare a meal in his large old-fashioned kitchen. But for a few modern appliances this room, too, appears to have changed little since I last saw it. The light worktops once strewn with beer cans, ashtrays and half-full coffee mugs are now empty but for neatly arranged utensils and a few bits of pottery. Searching in the cupboards for herbs and garnishes I find the shelves well-stocked and spotless.

'Dare I say I detect a woman's touch about this place?' I remark as I splash dressing on the salad.

Jake, who is rhythmically chopping vegetables by the sink, stops abruptly. There is silence. I swallow hard, wishing for the buzz of sound from the old days, the laughter and music.

As if reading my thoughts, he turns around and indicates a bench by the window holding a portable music system.

'Help yourself, Larissa,' he says. 'Choose something.'

He turns away again.

'I'll open some wine.'

Several untitled tapes lie near the player. I put one on at random. For a while there's no sound and I hover nervously with my finger poised over the fast forward button. Then the air is filled with the sound of a church organ. I stare at the player in horror, wanting to turn it off. The last time I heard this slow beautiful music is the last time Jake and I met, fifteen years ago at his parent's funeral.

'Hand maidens, Lara.' Jake's voice comes right into my ear.

'Jesus Christ!' My whole body jolts with fright and I whirl around.

'The answer to your earlier question.'

I have knocked his arm and the glass of wine he carries spills much of its contents down my leg, over my sandled foot and dies on the floor in a small trickle. My face flames and tears come to my eyes. The organ song rises poignantly to the ancient kitchen rafters, as if imbued with new significance, as if intent in going higher. Like a film unwinding I remember the funeral in flashes – the weather; a wet blustery day in summer, about this time, how our too-thin clothes added to the misery. Jake's face, I suddenly remember Jake's face. Now I need the music to stop. I begin to shake. I want to run away.

He stands in front of me all these years later smiling, with his hands tracing a path from my chin to my temples, his index finger on my cheekbones as if on the contours of a sculpture. I can't believe I'm here again, in this bizarre old house, with its whispering gardens and this man who uses his words and his eyes and his carefully aimed gestures to throw me off balance. I feel a tear escape my eye and wet his finger.

Then he kisses me. While my cheeks burn and the water in my eyes stops me seeing his expression, he comes forward and brushes his lips against mine; once, twice, three times, his mouth comes briefly and sweetly to mine as my lips begin to open.

Then he stands back and for seconds our eyes lock in perfect understanding, as if we probe into each other's minds, searching back over the years for the reasons we did things wrongly, for the occasions when things could have been different. I feel my lower body move towards him; the warm liquid feeling and tingling between my legs. My sex strains towards his cock. I am sure he will be hard. I must feel the edge of his erection, just the pressure of it against his jeans, just a touch, enough to brush myself against. Now it is me who goes to kiss him. My eyes are clear now and he looks at me with a strange expression. I see the fear and the solemnity there but still, when my mouth comes to his, he responds almost savagely, his lips covering mine, his tongue probing, his mouth hard against my own as his hand is in my hair, pushing my head to him. I feel his other hand flat and strong spread across the small of my back, pressing my abdomen against his cock. My breasts are forced against his chest, the discomfort melting into a hot urgent pleasure. My legs are opening, my hips move. I am straddling his hard cock. My lower body goes to him in waves and waves as his tongue probes my mouth. Half-faint in the intensity and duration of our kiss, I am writhing against him unable to stop myself.

But suddenly we are apart again. As quickly as he held me to him, Jake is now pushing me away. He holds my shoulders at arms length and looks at me. We are both breathless but he controls his breathing far quicker than I do.

He says in a perfectly calm way. 'It's so good to see you.'

I might be a friend or a sister he has met at the station. I flick back my hair and gaze at him. I feel languid and warm, my abdomen is heavy with need and my lips are swollen with desire. Liquid is seeping into my pants.

'What's going on here?' I finally manage to whisper.

Then I watch in amazement as he sinks to his knees, and begins to undo the ankle strap on my sandal. I watch the tiny grey flecks in his beautiful hair, feel his breath on my skin.

'What are you doing?'

'I'm going to make you better, Larissa,' he says as he undoes the other strap.

His head is near enough to kiss me between the legs. I begin to ache again. I am very wet. I wonder if he can smell my arousal. When he bids me take my foot from the shoe with a tug at my ankle, I do it straight away. I step out of the other one and he begins to rub the drying wine from my legs and feet. Long, gentle strokes down my ankles, across my instep; massaging the heat and tiredness from my toes.

'Such beautiful feet,' he murmurs, 'I always thought you had the most perfect feet.'

I am getting wetter. I long for him to reach up to feel how damp my knickers are, to put his hand inside, to feel the moisture leaking down my inner thigh. I long for him. Instinctively I reach down to touch his hair, barely letting my fingers graze the top of those wonderful dark curls.

But then he is standing again and I take my hand away, not knowing whether or not he has felt my touch.

41

'Let's continue this outside,' he says, in a businesslike way, collecting the bottle and the two glasses.

I follow him bare-foot through the patio doors into a deep lilac evening, filled with cool scents. I'd forgotten he is a couple of inches taller than Steve, a good few more than me. Without my heels I'm suddenly as vulnerable and unworldly as I ever was twenty years ago.

Unnervingly the music hasn't changed although the tape is well through. I can't imagine anyone other than Jake having a tape of the music played at his parent's funeral. I remember how he always did things differently, how he painted landscapes when the preference was for moody still life, how he never portrayed people in an abstract way, although it was the fashion. He always made faces terribly real, more real on canvas than they were in life. A wildness in the eye, a serenity in a gesture – nothing escaped him. So observant, intuitive. So tender.

'Don't worry. It'll be a different tune in a minute.' Jake inclines his head back towards the kitchen. 'Now, you sit there, Lara.'

I sink, tired and bewildered onto the old garden chair he has set several feet from a table. He fills my glass and hands it to me.

'Jake, the music's fine. I didn't say anything.'

'You didn't have to. I could always read your face. Come on, give me one of those beautiful limbs so I can bring it back to life.'

He sits with my feet between his thighs and for a while I watch his strong well-shaped artist's fingers knead and caress my toes, the ball of my foot, then higher towards my ankle. If I stretch my toes just a little I will touch his cock. I imagine doing this, the tip of my foot reaching out, finding him already hard, nudging his erection against his jeans, feeling it swell more. Oh, God. I close my eyes and throw back my head, afraid to show him my longing, how little I can control my need for him, still.

'You remember don't you, Lara – that tune?' His voice is soft as the final bars of the organ melody fade.

'Yes, of course. I remember everything.'

The next tune on the tape is completely different, hard rock, another one from the old days. How like him to put two such dissimilar tracks together.

> *You're a girl from a different world*
> *Can't wait for you any more*
> *Flash your eyes then let me be*
> *Send kisses from your door*

Jake's hands slide up and down my calves massaging my tendons then rubbing the muscles below my knees. I drink too quickly and keep my eyes closed. His upper body drops further over my legs. I am drawn to the scent and the warmth of him as, engrossed and rhythmical, he pummels then strokes the feeling through my muscles, my veins, the surface of my skin. He works like a physiotherapist, but it doesn't feel like that. With every dip of his strong shoulders, his head coming down, I want more and more to open my legs to him, to lift my skirt, wanting his mouth on the place where the juices run. I want him to put his hand up my thigh, feel the wetness leaking from my knickers to the soft skin there. I want him so much.

I take a large gulp of wine, and to stop myself feeling like this, stop myself begging, I visualise, as I haven't done for years, the day of the funeral. Steve and I were near the open grave, much nearer than Jake and his girlfriend, whoever she was; Stace, two years old in Steve's arms, straining to look into the hole in the earth at the rich auburn wood of the coffin. Steve was pale, but emotionless. Jake had tears running down his face. His girlfriend, not knowing what to do, gave up stroking his arm and went to smoke self-consciously under a tree. I cried too, not for the parents – I'd only met them once or twice – but for Jake and myself and how I wanted to hold him. And afterwards in the house, in the big kitchen we all got drunk after the relatives left. Jake took his girlfriend into one of the large cupboards and screwed her noisily against the door so we could all hear. That night Steve, the baby and I shared a bed in one of the upstairs rooms, and I woke at dawn to the silent heaving of Steve's averted shoulders as he sobbed into the pillow. I didn't touch him and I hated myself. The three of us left early that morning. We didn't say goodbye to Jake and I never saw him again.

'And now, Lara, I must give you sustenance.' Jake's voice sounds dramatic as I come out of my dream.

He stands and bends over me, placing my feet back on the ground.

'Where were you there?' he asks.

'Years away.'

He scrapes his chair forward to sit close to me, leaning on his elbow and smiling. The tape has finished. The sky is as dark as it's going to get on this blue summer night. Somewhere, a bird cries, not in the garden, but far off, towards the sea. Emboldened by drink, I look at Jake, daring him to touch me, to acknowledge what's in my mind.

But he breaks eye contact swiftly and rises. He seems far less drunk than I am.

'Food and more wine, that's what we need,' he says, 'then you can tell me all about it.'

'All about what?'

I'm sure I don't imagine his rapid glance from my breasts, right down my body to my thighs, where my dress rides up.

'All these years I haven't seen you, I want to know what you've been doing, how you've changed,' he says disappearing into the kitchen. Not as much as you'd imagine, I think as I drain the last of my glass.

I am drinking too much. Our situation is confusing but invigorating at the same time. Jake and I are flirting in a superficial manner, his earlier desire for me dissipated with the coming of the stars and the blackening of the sleepy foliage. He asks me if he's lost his touch, meaning his talent with massage.

I open my eyes wide and say, 'You, Jake, you could never loose your talent for anything.'

He keeps rising to change the music and when he returns, sometimes sits close and sometimes not. I am convinced he is teasing me deliberately but he masks it with a brotherly, hospitable manner. He fills my glass repeatedly and regards me with half-amused, half-intrigued eyes. From time to time he rubs the chill from my arms and even pops morsels of food into my mouth.

'Try this, Lara, a delicacy from one of my hand maidens.'

He smiles broadly, knowing I am desperate to ask more, but, like the Jake of old, revels in the torment of my curiosity. When I shiver he immediately removes his shirt and puts it on me as if I am a child. His fingers rest near my neck too long, then he watches me as I try not to gaze at his shoulders in his old, tight, paint-spattered T-shirt.

Our conversation consists mainly of his questions, delivered in a slightly superior, world-weary manner and my replies, gushing and defensive.

'How's old Stevie?' he asks, using the pet name I have for his brother, although I know he always hated it.

'In America now. We're not together, haven't been for ages. In fact, never for any real length of time after Stacey was born. We make contact; phone calls and things.' I stop. I am talking too much.

'So he never married you, then?'

I blink, astonished, and shake my head. 'Didn't you two keep in touch at all?'

I refuse yet another variety of delicious-looking savoury from Jake's outstretched fingers.

He swallows it himself then leans forwards to take both my hands, holding them quite hard on the top of my thighs so that I feel the pressure. I wriggle back in my chair, unable to stop myself staring at the hard muscles in his chest, remembering the feel of them on me from behind, my face on them, in all sorts of contrived,

45

silly situations, although I never felt them the way I wanted to.

'We didn't have much time for each other, Steve and I,' he continues. 'He was always desperate to move abroad, do big things with his life. Then after the folks were killed, someone had to hang around and keep an eye on this place. He wanted to travel, I stayed.'

He strokes the back of my hand thoughtfully.

'But you didn't come back here to live until quite recently,' I say.

He laughs outright and my face blazes in the cool air as I realise I've given myself away. Then, unexpectedly, he reaches over, raises my hand to his mouth and kisses it extravagantly.

'So you *were* keeping tabs on me, Larissa. I suspected as much,' he says in a quiet, mocking voice. Then he adds softly, 'Actually, I'm flattered.'

'People still talk about you,' I say hurriedly. 'The old crowd. You're quite famous, you know. Then there was an article about the house in one of the papers. The renovations, all about your plans for the summer schools . . .'

My hand begins to sweat in his and I resist the urge to pull it away.

Suddenly the laughter leaves his eyes. I stare apprehensively at the cold dark brown in them. It is as if someone has switched out a light.

'So you just decided to do some background work, arrange a tender.'

He says the word as if it's offensive and my stomach lurches. He pauses. I hear for the first time insects buzzing in the bushes. The sound becomes louder. I can feel it under my skin. The sternness in Jake's eyes reminds me uncannily of Steve.

'You decided to get . . . involved. How like a woman,' he says at last.

He grips my fingers and they hurt. My blood chills.

He takes his hands from mine and almost viciously pours himself another drink, splashing wine on the table.

I hear his breathing and my own. He drinks rapidly, watching me with supercilious eyes.

A new sterility, harshness, creeps into the evening. The outline of the trees behind him is suddenly ragged and ugly; the light spilling out from the kitchen no longer magical, but flat and barren.

> *I knew that there would be a danger*
> *It's just the way that women are*
> *Now I see you once again*
> *Please take me to your Shangri-la*

Suddenly I have an image of Jake at a party dancing with some girl, his hand hard on her buttocks, his arm around her waist. He is winking at me over her shoulder. I am wearing a new white dress that Steve has bought me and no make-up because he wants me to look virginal. That is how it was – me trying too hard and still doing the wrong thing. Never doing what I wanted.

I feel grubby, drunk and exasperated. Suddenly I have had enough of Jake's arrogance and sarcasm, of my own defensiveness.

'Look, I'm bloody good at my job. Why do you think your agent accepted me?'

He makes no reply, but drinks deeply from his glass, gazing somewhere over my head to the trees and the sky. His own anger has evaporated and the strange sadness is once more in his eyes.

I pick up my own glass and drain it swiftly.

Now I am more tired and confused than angry. I need to take a shower and I don't even know where I'll be sleeping – my hold-all remains like a forgotten pet at the foot of the stairs.

Abruptly, having no clear idea of where I am going or what I am going to do, but knowing I need to escape, I stand up. Then Jake rises, a little unsteadily; wine splashes from his glass, down the front of my dress, making me shudder with the chill. I feel the wetness on my breasts, my abdomen, even the top of my knickers.

He doesn't apologise but holds my shoulder, moving his thumb slightly, so that the shirt slides a little. He rubs the wetness of my dress into my skin. My nipples harden.

I feel slightly afraid, yet filled with sickening anticipation. We are standing inches apart. I could press myself to him in an instant, feel him harden against my soaking transparent dress, my damp knickers. I could kiss him, I could . . .

'Why didn't you just get in touch directly?' he says in a soft injured way. Write a letter, something? Agents, Lara.' He laughs bitterly. 'Did you really think I would turn *you* down?'

There is a terrible tightness in my throat. We stare at each other and the word hangs between us. Yes. I did think you would turn me down.

A low aircraft appears from nowhere, scouring the pale sky, its drone loudening then fading, killing all the soft sounds in the trees. Our moment passes. Jake grabs the bottle from the table then reaches for my hand, his mood suddenly exuberant.

'Let's go. Take the air on this glorious night.'

We walk barefoot on the short grass across to the mass of longer strands. On the soles of my feet there is coolness then warmth; softness then harsh scratching. I sway a bit, sometimes stumbling so that Jake clutches me around the waist, holds me against him. I love it when he does this: his grip tightening each time I threaten to lose balance; the palm of his hand spread on the side of my hip; our thighs coming together; the firmness of his body. I feel reckless and jubilant in the heady air. A three-quarter moon perfectly held between two topmost branches of a larch captivates me. Flowered bushes beckon me to rest in their green and pink cushioning, but each time I lurch towards them Jake pulls me back and for a while I walk quite steadily in his grasp.

'My God, Larissa, I hope I'm not going to have to carry you. Twenty years ago I might have been accused of getting you inebriated for my own purposes.'

I laugh and grab the bottle from him, wanting to

appear carefree, throwing caution to the wind, but all the time thinking: Why can't it be twenty years ago, why can't we relive the past?

It's cooler and darker where we walk now. The trees are tall and blocking the sky. All the black-green textures of the garden seem to close in around us as if we are in our own fragrant, secret place. My heart beats faster. I am sure Jake is taking me somewhere to seduce me.

Exuberant in this notion, I stop and turn to him, putting my hand on his chest and, feigning greater drunkenness, fall against him draping my arm around his neck.

'Where are we going?' I murmur into his shoulder and feel, as I knew I would, the swell of his cock on my stomach, making me desperate to rub myself further into his body, caress him there, feel his balls, feel him want to take me.

'We're here,' he says into the top of my hair. His voice sounds sober, oddly final.

I want it to be 1979 again as he leads me into the summer-house. I smell cedar wood and oil paint and a warm mustiness left over by the sun. But, although he holds my hand, there is now a careful distance between us. Jake lights a small oil lamp on a table to our right. And immediately, like phantoms from the shadow, dozens of paintings, large and small, appear in the amber radiance. I catch my breath but say nothing. Jake sits, his arm stretched along the back of a bench by the table. I know he wants me to sit beside him but the pace of events is suddenly too slow for me.

Clutching the bottle possessively against my chest, I sink onto a low-slung hammock near the wall, some six feet from the table. Jake and I watch each other but I am no longer intimidated by his silence. I gulp from the bottle, letting wine trickle from my mouth onto his shirt, down my already damp dress. The edge of my flimsy bra is visible, as is the top of my white knickers. My bare feet and pearly polished toenails are grubby now, but my legs are long and exposed and he is looking at them. I badly want him to touch me. I set the bottle on the floor and fall back too quickly on the thick silky hoop of material, setting it in motion and making my head swim. Fearful I might be sick, I decide to start a conversation.

'Why are they all in here, your paintings? That's what's so different about the house. None of your work is up on the walls.'

'The house needs to change,' he says abruptly. 'I thought that was why you were here. Nothing stays the same.' His voice trails off.

I feel rebuked and ashamed, and have to remind myself I have come here to do a job. I need to show how capable and strong I have become.

The hammock swings gently, in a comforting way. I watch the paintings rise and fall in the lamplight – naked women and boys, women's faces painted ostentatiously or touchingly bare, some smiling, some sad.

Through tired eyes, I'm dimly aware of Jake leaning forward in his chair. He must be going to touch me. I feel my legs fall open.

'You'd better not fall asleep, Lara. I'd struggle getting you back to the house – these days anyway.' His voice comes dimly through the air.

The hammock is slowing to a stop when I feel his caress like a graze, first on my lower legs, then on the soft skin of my thighs, followed by a slight heaviness on my damp dress and knickers. I open my legs wider, imagine him entering me slowly, not removing any of my clothes, simply prising back the gusset of my pants, then filling my wetness with his cock.

'Oh, yes,' I murmur, sliding my hand down over my abdomen, my crotch, trying to meet his. Instead I encounter a soft covering, a blanket of sorts, on the back of my hand.

I look up startled. Jake is kneeling over me, trying to cover my feet and my inelegantly parted legs with a swathe of the copious material.

Humiliated, I push myself up and the yellow wood walls lurch once more. Now the eyes of the painted women, taunting and superior, stare at me. Jake puts his hand out to still the hammock. My face rests against his arm. His skin smells of wood shavings and summer grass.

'I want you to fuck me. Now.'

The sound of my words with their enormity of irrevocable truth overwhelms me.

'I want you,' I repeat, and my voice sounds hoarse.

For a moment there is nothing to be heard but the gentle putting sound of the lamp on the table then Jake says, 'You've had too much to drink, Lara.' As if this is unfortunate and in a different situation he would want me too.

'Besides it's impossible to shag on that thing. It has been tried.'

It is this attempt at lightheartedness, at diffusing the situation that distresses me most. All I can think of is the auburn-haired girl in the afternoon, naked then taking his shirt – the one I am wearing now.

I force myself upright trying to tear off the offending garment. I am aware how childish and illogical I must seem, but I am consumed by the burning shame of rejection and my deeper passion, my desperate need for Jake as strong, but oddly as precarious too, as the flame from the table lamp. The hammock swings dangerously. Jake puts both arms on either side to steady it. Once more we are inches apart.

'That girl this afternoon. I saw you here with her. All this talk of hand maidens.' I stop, breathless and humiliated. I think how ugly I must seem to him.

'You've fucked *her*, haven't you? Christ, Jake, there was a time you'd shag just about anyone.'

He shakes his head, looking at me with resignation rather than the anger I expect. A softness comes into his eyes. He is about to say something kind and I can't bear it.

'You wanted me this afternoon,' I protest in a feeble, shameful voice. 'And this evening. It was obvious.'

'Put your arms around my neck,' he says and I think

51

for a moment I am being reprieved. But then he straightens his back and stands up, his arms sliding beneath my legs.

'I can walk.'

'I don't think so.'

The flame from the lamp flickers then extinguishes abruptly with the swish of my body through the air. There is a dreadful finality about the darkness, as if the walls are closing in, as if there will never be light or open air or any kind of joy again.

Jake carries me outside and I am amazed at the blackness here too, the way it is washed across the sky and clinging damply to the long grass and bushes. I can't believe that this could be the scene of our earlier optimism and flirtatiousness.

He seems to bear my weight easily despite his earlier doubts but now that I know he doesn't desire me I want nothing more than to disappear. I hide my head against his chest, feigning sleep, but he seems to want to talk.

'I remember carrying you like this once at a party. You passed out or something.'

His easy, jocular manner depresses me further.

'I don't remember.'

'Don't you? Steve caught us in a bedroom. He thought I was trying to screw you.'

He laughs. Tears escape from me. I hope he doesn't feel them.

'You were always such a bloody fool, Lara,' he says quietly. 'Getting pissed and trying to be the sophisticate for Steve. He had no idea how to treat you, how nervous he always made you.'

Then, in an almost conciliatory manner he continues, 'There'll be a lot of people around over the next few weeks. I know you want some action and you're a lovely woman. You won't have to look far.'

I wonder if he is being cruel on purpose. Using all my strength, I push against his chest and writhe out of his arms, almost falling to the ground but he grabs for my wrists just in time and pulls me to my feet. Struggling and sobbing in his grip I can't help but notice the bulge of his erection in his jeans.

'I only shag models,' he says in a strained, almost frightened, way and I lift my gaze from his cock to meet his eyes.

'I'm not pretty enough, then,' I hear myself say petulantly.

He grasps my wrists too hard and they hurt. I wonder if he is punishing me for giving him an erection.

'Artists' models are not necessarily good-looking, you should know that by now,' he says shortly, then in a different tone, 'Look, I don't want to get involved with you, Lara.'

'I'm here to work!' I scream at him now, amazed at the fury in my voice. 'I asked for a shag, Jake, that's all, in memory of the old days. That's *all* I wanted.'

He lets go of my wrists and stares at me, speechless. For several seconds I glare back at him, unable to stop the tears running down my cheeks, wondering how such a promising evening could spiral into such craziness.

As if from a captor, I turn away and start to run towards the light from the kitchen. It looks eery and far off. The faintly moonlit lawn is not level under my feet, and pitches more the faster I try to move. I hear Jake's voice calling my name, echoing through the trees. I am lurching towards a place of no escape and I know I'm not going to make it. I slip, inevitably, and the close-shorn lawn hits me cold and hard on the side of my face.

I open my legs in the bed of silk, wide, already aroused. The man above me smiles. I know he is going to take his time. He moves down to my feet, kisses my ankles, runs his fingers lightly over the inside of my calves. My thighs tremble and my pelvis moves upward, begging for his attention.

'Please,' I whimper.

'You must be patient.'

'Stevie, please.'

But he is not Steve. He looks similar but there is compassion not distance in his eyes.

'Lara, look around you. Use the setting, capture the atmosphere. We are only part of the picture. Use it to sublimate your mood. Use it all.'

Startled, I look away from him. A shutter to the balcony bangs closed. But the other one remains open and the three-quarters moon stares in like a ravaged eye. In its light I see that the walls are high and curved and the area of the circular room is small. An owl hoots once, close by. Then I watch while the other shutter, slowly and ominously, creaks closed. Now it is absolutely dark and I sense my lover is no longer with me. I am naked in a sumptuous bed in the narrow tower of the turreted west wing and I am alone.

Chapter Three

'Now ... please, now.'

I twist and writhe under a hot sun. I am in shackles, but they are made of cloth. My movements cause the tightly drawn material to rub and push between my legs. But I feel there is someone else near, unseen, above and around me, and it is his presence that compels me towards orgasm. I thrust my hips towards the warm sky and towards feelings of deliverance.

Then a desert breeze blows over my face and opens my eyes. But there is no blue sky, only the shadowed height of a curved ceiling. I sit up quickly and the room spins. My head falls back, throbbing, onto a mountain of pillows. I look down and see the tangle of sheets around my naked thighs. Sweat glistens between my breasts and my nipples are hard. I feel as if I have recently been touched. I pull the coiled sheeting from between my legs and touch myself. My fingers come away wet. I propel my legs over the side of the bed and look wildly around for the one who has aroused me. But the tiny, opulent room is shaded and silent, empty but for a streak of sun and the faint scent of roses. My hold-all and briefcase lie on the floor with my dress draped over them, my shoes neatly lined up in front. From the muzzy recesses of my mind I try to dredge some clue as to how I got here the previous night. Did I undress myself? Did Jake stay? I ache all over, my mouth is dry, I feel tired, used up. Yet inside it all, I feel a strange exhilaration. I touch myself again, feel the stickiness remaining. I smell the tangy musk from my fingers. I can't believe Jake and I might have shared this exquisite bed and I can't remember any of it.

On a small bedside table stands a bowl of fruit. There is also a jug of water with ice cubes fairly intact, suggesting his recent presence. Propped against the jug is a note.

Larissa,
  Treat the place as your own. I think of you as my guest whatever the circumstances. I will be around this afternoon if you need me.
  Yours, Jake

I pour myself a large glass of water. My hand trembles, and my mouth too, as I drink. I gaze again at the large sloping script.

'Whatever the circumstances.' Is he annoyed at my behaviour or is it that he screwed me after all and now regrets it? 'If you need me.' God, do I need you, Jake. 'Yours.' Yours, yours – it drums inside my head, a taunting refrain as I wander around my narrow surroundings, which feel more and more like a prison as the paranoia of my hangover increases. In a small rectangular recess off the main circle of the room stands a dark-wood wardrobe. Years of burnt incense and dope seep into the air when I open one of its rich drawers. The narrow door next to the wardrobe is locked, probably just a cupboard. I go into the small adjacent shower room and catch sight of my face in a mirror and laugh. Patchy remains of yesterday's make-up glaze my skin. I scrub my teeth with the touchingly feminine pink brush Jake has provided. He might be a difficult bastard but he certainly is a thoughtful host. I wash the final shimmer from my face and make a promise to the subtly pretty woman in the mirror to leave behind the wistful teenager inside and get her priorities right.

With precariously renewed spirit I throw on my favourite, old denim dress and look out my sketchbook. Out on the balcony I munch on some fruit and notice a small opening in the balustrade where it curves towards the adjoining wall. There is a narrow flight of steps leading down to the side garden. I am grateful for their existence. Despite my resolutions I don't feel I can face running into Jake until my hangover and embarrassment have lifted a little.

Walking to the far end of the rear garden, beyond the tall trees I am shocked to find what remains of the old orchard. Now it is merely a small island of trees clinging possessively to the seeds of its early fruit. Around the island is evidence of a fire, not recent. Scorched tree stumps hopelessly pierce the barren earth. I walk quickly on, unwilling to accept this mournful location as the place I lay on Steve's bare chest, crying with happiness and fear the day I found out I was pregnant with Stacey. It was September and the shadow of huge fruit fell over us. Its dizzying fragrance and a brash fickle heat making us promise to love each other forever.

Soon the ground is lush again with low green shrubbery and splashes of wild flowers. This land adjoining Old Beach House used to be my favourite retreat when I first came here, an ideal place to sketch and dream and kid myself that one day I would be Steve's perfect lover. I saw Jake here sometimes, but never by himself. There was always some girl to lie with him in the tiny flowers and laugh at his jokes. He never knew I was here. I would always run off to the sea pool some twenty yards on and hide behind the rocks until he and the girl disappeared or I could sneak away.

The pool is just as it was – tremulous opal under the clear mid-morning sky and lulling gently around the edges, stirred by the force of the underground tunnel to the sea which feeds it. I sit at the edge of the sandy scrub with my feet dangling in the water of the pool's one shallow ledge. Now, with the sun on my face lifting my spirits, I decide that my suspicions of not being alone in bed were nothing more than alcohol-fuelled imaginings.

I open the front of my dress and let the sun fall on my breasts.

Then I sit on the grass, leaning against the rocks, trying out some ideas for the house on my sketchpad. I worry about the bleakness that has set into the building over the years; the strange way that bits of it survive valiantly but quite independently of each other; the easy comfort of the kitchen; the opulence of the bathroom; the eerily preserved seventies room; the strange and frightening magic in the room where I'm sleeping. After a while, I put down my pencil. My head is still too muzzy to concentrate.

I lift my dress over my head. I am wearing nothing underneath. I smile at this, thinking I would not have done this twenty years ago. Five or six feet of the stone ledge falls away to deepening water. I ease myself into the blue depth, gasping at the sudden change in temperature. Then I swim the thirty feet or so to the other side of the pool before diving deep to where the water is an inky green and shadowed by the sides of the pool and the mysterious hollows and dark places that I can't make out. I twist and turn and dip while my breath lasts, enjoying the freedom of my hair flowing from my scalp, in front of my face; the water against my skin, free to invade me, caress me, hold me. I feel suddenly liberated, vigorous. It occurs to me that I still enjoy, need even, my times of solitude. There's something to be said for being without a man. I surface again and float in the water trying to make myself as still as possible. I think of the time Steve and I swam out here to this deepest part and he told me that just below us was the mouth of the tunnel to the sea and if you got too near you could be sucked inside, out to sea. I said I wasn't scared to swim down with him, although he must have known I was. About six or seven feet down, a sudden warm current moved against my body sending me fleeing upwards. It took

Steve several seconds back on the surface to calm me sufficiently for us both to swim back to the edge. 'I was lying to you Lara. It was just a joke,' he kept saying, and he smiled. Then he removed my swimsuit while I was still shaking. He fucked me with no preamble, quickly, forcefully. Now I can smile at the memory as I lie motionless, quite serene in the trusted bulk of water.

Then a large splash and a violent upswell near me jolt me out of my equilibrium.

I roll over in the pool with my heart thudding as the head and torso of a young man break the surface. For several seconds we tread water near each other, staring, breathless.

'Thank Christ,' he says at last, 'I thought you were fucking dead.'

He looks at me with large hazel eyes, heavily lashed. Something in the seriousness of his expression makes me laugh. His accent is odd; lightly tainted with Cockney, sweet.

'As you can see, I'm not . . . quite.'

It seems natural for us to swim together to the edge of the pool. We sit on the ledge which is now only marginally covered due to the ebbing tide. He sits cross-legged; tanned and muscular in his white shorts. Yet compact too. His hair is silky black, short, sticking up at the front like a small boy's.

'Greg Lansdowne,' he says and stretches out his hand to shake mine enthusiastically. 'I do the summer school. Classes, models, rooms. Arrangements, that's my thing.'

The robustness of his handshake and the effect it has on my upper body cause me to remember my nakedness but I don't believe Greg has noticed. He leans back on his elbows and gazes at me earnestly. I am conscious of my unmade-up face and the fact that I must be ten, if not fifteen years older than he is.

'I do a bit myself,' he continues, thrusting himself forwards to sit, legs splayed, upper body leaning towards me. I notice a large tear up the inner thigh of his shorts. Just a little more . . .

'Dressing up, transformation. That's my thing. It's important to be other people. Like a bit of acting, you know?'

'Sorry?' I enquire and drag my gaze from his beautifully packaged crotch to his shining little-boy eyes.

'Modelling. You can really let yourself go. Clothes maketh the man and all that. And you, you're a model too?'

'Oh no, I . . .'

'*I* know,' he says suddenly, gleefully. 'You're Lara, aren't you?' He stretches across to slap my knee playfully.

'Yes, but how did you . . .?'

'J F told me you were coming. He was pretty up about it. You're his sister-in-law or something.'

'Actually, I'm not, and I'm sure he *didn't* know . . .'

'Fuck, yes, you really look the part. Have you ever considered . . .?'

'Would you please stop interrupting me.'

He retreats visibly, moving back as if I've slapped him, looking downwards. I wonder if he'll spot the tear in his shorts.

'I'm sorry,' he mumbles, 'I talk too much, I know.'

I laugh. 'God, no. I am. Stace, my daughter, calls it my "somebody's mother tone". It's bloody pompous. I'm just a bit stressed . . . and hungover.'

I lean across him and squeeze his hand. For the first time I see him glance at my breasts. He brightens immediately. Like a puppy allowed back in the house, he moves closer, his eyes glowing with renewed enthusiasm.

'Tell you what, Lara. I've just the thing for that morning-after feeling. I've got it in my bag. Is it OK?' he says, glancing backwards.

'Of course.' I smile and watch while he scrambles to his feet, his lovely young buttocks half-visible through his damp shorts. He is exquisitely proportioned – neither tall nor small. His legs are not overbuilt and his shoulders not too broad. I think of him as some lithe creature of the wood scampering off to do his duty to the ladies of the forest in their castles. What had Jake called me? The nymphet. The sprite and the nymphet. I giggle as I glance down at my body, faintly golden in the noon sun, maybe even reddening slightly around the knees. I don't suppose Greg has anything as sensible as sun-cream in his bag. The ends of my hair, fair and soft, have dried out and waft in front of my face. I run a hand over my breasts, still firm. I suck in my stomach. Then I open my legs slightly in the warm water which is now so shallow as to be almost a glaze, wetting my thighs then letting them dry again. Am I still a nymphet? I laugh again as a small amount of sea laps around my sex lips.

'I see you've started without me,' Greg says, holding up a large bottle of water in one hand, the fingers of the other concealing something else.

'I'm sorry?'

I have the grace to close my legs. He hands me the bottle and I drink deeply from it to relieve my arid mouth and throat. I let it spill from my lips and trickle between my breasts and into my pubes and join with the other water. It feels good to do this in the sun, making me shiver with pleasure at the coolness of the bottled water.

'Happy stuff,' says Greg. 'That's what we're going to do.'

He sits at an angle with his legs bent over mine. The position seems natural, unthreatening, even protective. I look at him trying to gauge what it is in this man with the sensitive mouth, the classically handsome, yet gentle features that invokes such a feeling of ease in me. And I think, honesty. Maybe you haven't learned to lie – yet.

I put the bottle of water down on the ledge. The sea has deserted it completely. The stone is turning from dark to pale yellow. I feel as if we are on an island, the only two people alive.

Greg unfurls his hand and reveals a perfectly rolled joint.

'Happy stuff,' he whispers.

'Oh Greg, I don't know. I haven't smoked for years. Christ, sometimes it used to make me flake out.'

'This won't,' he says softly, 'I promise. I'm an expert.'

'Don't tell me,' I say, moving my lips closer to the upheld joint, near enough to see the small green pools reflected in his eyes, 'it's your thing.'

'Right,' he says and slowly parts my lips before inserting the reefer.

I laugh at the sky. When I turn one way, the sky is coming down to our own little drop of sea. His and mine. All the birds come to our bushes to sing together. The wind is drinking our sweat and our salt-water hair. I roll over on my stone bed and the sky is holding out ballerina skirts of the leaves in the trees.

Sometimes I feel Greg's legs, still bent, still in the same position, touching me insistently, sometimes I feel his skin melting into mine. But he doesn't move. Then I am melting into the stone. If it sucks me back hard enough it will meet with my clit and graze me, then cut me apart in orgasm with its big yellow tongue, mouth, body, whole-earth self. I laugh; always laugh. He laughs too. The reefer passes between us like a small vessel across the blue sea-sky.

I asked Jake to shag me, last night. He didn't.

I don't say the words to Greg. I transmit them. He transmits back – Why?

I don't know.

All the sky and small clouds and the fragrant green stuff and our own little tankard of sea will tell him that.

I don't know.

All the sea creatures that lived and died on this stone are with me now, holding me in perfect understanding. Then suddenly I come down. The sky is back to where it was and the birds have moved on. I look up at Greg and he is looking down at me.

'OK?' he whispers.

'Yes. You were right. It was good stuff.'

'Did you really ask J F to shag you?'

I sit up quickly grazing one of my hands as I try to keep balance.

Greg reaches out to steady me. With the touch of his young hands on my old shoulders I suddenly feel very sober and foolish. I rise abruptly and walk over to the heap that is my dress and pull it over my head.

'Lara, please, don't go. Please.'

It is the sheer panic in his voice that changes my mind.

I walk back to him, and he grins up at me like I've given him the most wonderful gift in the world. Then he stretches up his hand and moves a little. There is a loud ripping sound as the frayed material on his shorts gives up completely. His semi-hard cock slides down onto the yellow rock.

'It's your thing!'

I sink to my knees and we cling together consumed with mirth.

'Fuck,' Greg gasps against my shoulder. 'Trust me!'

I feel his swelling cock against my leg. I look up to the vast sky. An aftermath cloud of dope, craziness and hope floods my senses.

'I'd like to do both,' I hear myself say.

Greg sits on the ledge of the pool with me on his lap. My legs are wrapped around his back and my fingers nurse his growing erection as if it were a small scared animal.

He looks at me with those big eyes. 'You trust me not to let you fall,' he says quietly.

'If you do, it's not the end of the world. We'll fall together, get . . . wet together.'

I kiss the silk of his hair, his smooth forehead, each of his velvet eyelids, his perfect nose, his full lips. I feel slightly stoned again, out of myself as if I am watching someone else. I feel free.

His cock gets stiffer under my touch. I open my thighs wider and nuzzle the root of it with my wet lips.

'Are you in love with Jake?'

'I don't know.'

'You won't fall in love with me, will you?'

There is a strange apprehension in his eyes. I lift myself a little and slowly let his cock fill me up. Then I squeeze him quickly, then relax my muscles again, as hard as I can. I feel very warm, but in control.

He touches my nipples with trembling fingers. The sensation makes me contract myself again. Greg bites his lip and shudders. His eyes are closed.

'I won't fall in love with you, I promise.' I brush my lips over his eyelids. He clasps me firmly to his chest. My nipples tingle and I rub them on his smooth hard skin. I am getting so wet I must be leaking on him.

'You're so very young ... and beautiful. But you make me forget myself. I don't know who I am any more. And ...' I gasp suddenly as he presses me down and simultaneously thrusts himself into me so forcefully it almost hurts. Again and again and again. There's a growing redness in my head. I feel myself smiling.

'... And it's too wonderful to lose ...' Oh Jesus, I'm going to come.

'Too ...' Not yet, make it last.

'Liberating!' I scream as, suddenly, he bucks his hips violently upwards, driving me into a long almost unbearable climax. I collapse onto his shoulder and he continues to plough into me, quicker now, his hands clasping my buttocks like vices.

'I feel just like that,' he says, his voice shuddering with his need for release, 'I don't know who I am ...'

Half conscious in the afterbliss of orgasm, I look at him in vague wonderment.

'... Sometimes it's pure hell ... Oh, Lara, darling.'

The way he says 'darling' through gritted teeth makes him seem much older.

'... Sometimes it's sheer ... literal ... magic!'

He thrusts into me once more and this time comes violently, groaning and holding my head against his chest. And suddenly, unexpectedly, I come again; just a small climax, a swift intense feeling like the opening and closing of a claw inside me. The delightful shock of it makes me dig my nails into his back, then, one or both

64

of us shuddering in ecstasy causes us to lose balance. Down we go, into the cool inky depths of our drop of sea; entwined, then unfurling from each other like sea creatures. We resurface, apart, laughing and come together to kiss, once; joyfully, as if we celebrate a triumph.

Jake stands in the kitchen, preparing food, in the same paint-spattered jeans, his back to us as we come in from the fragrant warmth of noon. At the far end of the worktop sits the red-haired model. She is barefoot and wearing a robe but, with my own juices glazing my thighs, I suddenly know with certainty that she hasn't been fucked but would like to have been. Her foot swings towards Jake and she looks at his averted back with a mixture of sorrow and agitation.

'Ah, Larissa,' he swings around as I come in. 'Food,' he says, holding a plateful of salad towards me. You really must eat . . .'

Then he notices Greg. Our eyes meet. I try to smile.

'Both of you . . . must eat.'

He puts the plate down on the worktop. It lies there like an orphan, away from all of us. He folds his arms; looks at Greg.

'All organised for this afternoon?'

Greg goes to the plate, blind to, or unconcerned by, my embarrassment. He picks up some tomato and cucumber; swallows it quickly.

'Yep. No problem. Students, models, all briefed, arriving in due course,' he says with a wide smile.

'Good.' Jake glances at me, lets his eyes travel absently down my body and rest between my legs. I feel my face flush as Greg comes over and pops some salad into my mouth. I stare at him fixedly trying to swallow. He winks at me. I feel as if I'm in a play and no-one has told me my part.

Suddenly, the red-haired girl gets up, flicks her hair from her broad shoulders and looks between Greg and I.

Her expression starts as near insolence but ends, on her wide slavic features, as a sulk.

'Gregor,' she says quietly, emphasising the 'or' in an almost comic manner, 'this afternoon you must be pretty for me. You understand? This bastard here doesn't make me feel pretty today.'

Then she sighs, turns and leaves the room. She walks like a ballerina but she's much too tall.

'Sure thing, Amber,' Greg calls after her. 'Can do that, yessir.'

Jake gazes at the closed kitchen door.

'Oh well, boss,' Greg says as he walks off with the plate of salad, 'guess you can't win them all.'

'Strange morning,' Jake murmurs, picking some paint from his nails.

'Yes it was, wasn't it?'

When, from nowhere, a burst of laughter escapes me, he quickly masks his curiosity with a bland smile.

It's the music and the loud female protests that make me open the door.

'No, no, you are asshole *and* bastard. I say we have to be like little girls – innocent.'

'Jesus.' Jake's voice is tired and exasperated.

A run of honky-tonk piano notes rush impertinently into the silence. I enter quietly but, I hope, with confidence.

'Feel free to spectate,' Jake had said earlier as he prepared, under my protest, another salad. 'You are a guest and a relative, almost.'

Now I enter the room which contains perhaps a dozen seated strangers, all ages and mixed gender, sketchpads in hands. They are trying not to look nervous but grow more uncomfortable at the tense scene unfolding on the four-poster bed in front of them. On a sumptuous white coverlet, like cake icing, Amber sits in a tiny ballet frock, legs bent and arms stubbornly folded over her knees. Her hair is twisted into a tight knot and her eyes are painted in smoky hues. Despite this, and the fact she is wearing no knickers, her fraught, disconsolate expression does indeed make her look like a little girl. She begins to rock slowly back and forwards on the bed. Sitting beside her is a model with lush, dark pinned-up curls. Her back is naked and averted. In contrast, to Amber she sits almost eerily still.

Jake smiles at me, almost sheepishly, as if it's me and not the students who are losing out because of Amber's performance. He approaches her and puts his hand on her knee. She looks up at him in reproachful silence. He sits between her and the motionless dark-haired model. I wonder if she is meditating. Jake leans across and whispers something to Amber, plants a brief kiss on her neck. Finally she nods and touches his hair in a conciliatory fashion. One long golden leg stretches unselfconsciously across his lap. I quiver with yearning and jealousy.

'Now,' says Jake briskly as he softly rubs the limb that imprisons him like a beautiful exotic snake, 'Amber wants to do sweetness and light today. She wants to be enchanting but she wants to be happy. I'm sure you can manage that, Greg.' He ends on a weary, terse note.

I look around the room but I don't see Greg. The students start to rustle paper and pick up pencils. Jake leaves Amber and comes towards me, smiling. I feel strangely misplaced and uncomfortable and have decided to leave when a blast of tenor sax fills the room and on a string of wild runaway notes the dark-haired model turns dramatically, swinging her well shaped legs athletically over Amber's. Her eyes, too, are heavily made up, but her mouth is bare and glistening and reminds me of one I have seen before. Her compact brown body is naked to the waist and . . . she has no breasts. As the realisation dawns, the model smiles directly at me, tantalisingly, beautifully. Then she moves swiftly into position behind Amber. The froth of a skirt in the middle of the perfect male-female body seems so appropriate. There is a murmur of approval from the students.

'You look a bit pale.' Jake pulls a chair from against the wall and I am glad to sit.

I stay for half an hour. Each sketching session lasts about five minutes. During those periods Amber doesn't move at all but lies on her side, legs together, looking down at a cutting of blossom in her hand which grazes the top of her pushed-up breasts. Greg moves frequently, a leg over Amber's, as the music switches from soulful clarinet to light capricious piano; an arm around the front of her body, placing his hand over hers on the thin branch. Sometimes he smiles almost ghoulishly, unsettlingly male underneath his slick dark eyes. Sometimes in profile, his face turned upwards and his body hidden by Amber's, he is regally, unremittingly female.

At first I marvel at how motionless Amber is, apparently almost asleep in her restful pose, but gradually I become aware of a subtle change in her expression. Now and then, almost imperceptibly, she bites her lip; tightens her eyelids. By the time the session is nearly over her cheeks are flushed beneath her pale powder. Something quickens inside me: an empathy, an instinct. Sweat dampens my body, a hot dull pressure starts up between my legs. I'm aware that, unconsciously, I am pressing my lips together for extra friction. I remember the touch of Greg's young fingers on my breasts that morning and marvel at his cunning.

'OK, sweetheart,' Jake, beside me, says suddenly in a loud voice. I don't immediately realise he is addressing Amber and not me.

I jump, startled, and he notices, gazes straight at my hot face.

'Do you still want to do the motionless stuff? Or do you need to move a little?'

Disconcertingly he continues to look at me. There is a small smile on his face.

'I'm fine for now,' Amber says, but her trembling voice betrays her.

I fidget a little on my chair, accidentally brushing against Jake's thigh. He looks at me with mild amusement and I redden.

For the first time I notice other people in the room

have been affected too. Shirts are open at the neck. One woman with her white hair in a bun and surprisingly youthful pink cheeks has taken her foot from a sandal and her toes twist repeatedly around the leg of her chair. People are drawing in an urgent, almost frenzied manner. A man in front of me, about my age, drops his pad to the floor. He retrieves it hurriedly and places it on his lap to conceal a very obvious erection inside his baggy cords.

'Jesus,' I whisper.

Jake stands and indicates that I rise too. I follow him in numb silence as he moves amongst the class, quietly making encouraging comments, his long artist's fingers sliding softly over sketchpads. I can't help but be aware of his scent, the warmth of his body, the gentle authority of his voice.

Then, from the four-poster I am sure I hear Amber moan. Her head is back against Greg's chest now, her predicament apparent to everyone. She is on the point of orgasm, but trying her best to hold back.

Silently I leave the room.

I rush along to the bathroom in need of coolness, of sanity. Outside the window the trees sway with reassuring calm, the centre bath gleams; stoic, solid, pure. I splash water on my face. It's as if I am extricating myself from a dream; not a bad one, but one that has grappled too much with my senses. In the long mirror the light through the trees dapples my hair with gold. My cheeks are pink with sunburn but something else too. My faded tan looks more intense, my skin looks touchable. I touch it. But it's my eyes that have really changed. The blue of them gleams; gleams and lives as if I have seen a hundred worlds in a day.

I lift my dress and rub myself until the separate trees pulsate and thicken as one, until the white of the bath is fluid and softens to a cloud in front of my eyes. I press and rub my clit until I feel Jake Fitzgerald's cock inside me, slow and hard and demanding. I rub myself till I come, shuddering and moaning aloud and not caring if anyone hears.

When I stand outside the room again I am sure that everyone has gone. The silence is so intense. Relieved, I push open the door to collect the folder of work notes I have left. The first thing I see is Greg's face as he kneels on the bed. Behind him the sky is now filled with dark clouds and I wonder at the swiftness of this change. Greg's wig is off and his dark shadowed eyes and long lashes gleam like demon's under the spikes of his hair. He no longer wears the ballet skirt. His brown torso and thighs are bare but for Amber's gold body snaked around him. Her shoulders and head are flung back on the white satin and her auburn hair cascades over the side of the bed. Her face, upside down, seems dead, mask-like. She is silent, they both are. He fucks her without expression, but he fucks her wildly so that her body bucks, almost bounces off the bed. He holds her wrists to stop her falling. They pound together rhythmically as if to some silent chant in their heads. Only one or two of the students are still trying to draw. Most sit fascinated, pencils clenched in fists. There is something compellingly joyless as he crashes so hard into her I am sure that she must break apart. He is fucking her like the devil.

Jake appears at my side and thrusts a drawing towards me. Then he claps his hands.

'Stop,' he orders as if a ringmaster at a circus. 'Apart. Now.'

Instantaneously the two models disengage, pelvis from pelvis, thigh from thigh.

Finally, with almost perverse gentleness, as if the snake-woman has become the fragile doll, Greg lifts Amber from the side of the bed. Jake switches on the tape again and the honky-tonk piano rises garishly around the walls. The students stand and make to leave, now chatting softly and easily among themselves. In front of the gloomy window, spattered now with soft rain, the satin bedcover undulates like a fluid snow-drenched mountain.

'Oh darling, yes.' Greg's voice under the cover is warm, almost as if he is in love with her, though I know he isn't.

'Bastard, oh you bastard.' Amber says the word in the same tone that Greg says 'darling'.

With the students gone and their chairs askew, the large bare window with its smoke of clouds, framing the luxurious dishevelled bed and the unseen but obvious passion of its two occupants, the room seems more like a theatre. Jake and I are the awkward separate spectators.

Then, as if suddenly bored, Jake starts to rearrange the chairs like a school caretaker while I glance down at his sketch.

It is a single figure. The limbs are Greg's, the hair unmistakably Amber's. The face, and I stare at it a long time, is mine.

She appears to be airborne, her hair streaming behind her, her strong boy's limbs rising to the sky. Far behind her are trees, a balcony and two open shutters.

I sit down heavily. Jake comes over. He holds a corner of the drawing while it trembles in my hand.

'Well?' he asks softly.

'It's grotesque,' I say abruptly to hide the quiver in my voice.

There is a flash of pain in his eyes but quickly his expression works itself into a smirk.

'Glad you like it, Larissa.'

He reaches into his shirt pocket for a cigarette and smokes, ignoring me. We sit there for a few icy minutes as the honky-tonk gets more ostentatious and, in their frenzy, the couple in the bed dislodge their opulent coverings to the floor. Then they writhe like two large insects under the grey sky until they too fall over the edge in ecstasy.

I stand in front of the oval mirror, examining my thirty-seven-year-old face, my naked breasts, my arms, my

71

reasons for staying. Outside, the sky has turned almost white; yet another mood change.

Tonight we are to have dinner together, Greg, Amber, Jake and I. Jake had thrown the invitation over his shoulder, a lazy afterthought as we all walked out of the door while the honky-tonk petered out. 'Be there, Lara. It'll be fun. We can talk.' As if we ever could, Jake.

I lie back on my lightly embossed bedcover, gazing through the open shutters at the white spaces between the trees.

'Lara. Are you there, Lara?' The urgent but hushed male voice makes me jolt upright. I look around the shadowed room. I see my startled face in the mirror. My heart thuds.

'Lara, please come.' The little boy appeal from this morning. The voice is not in the room.

I rush outside to the balcony forgetting my nakedness.

I half expect to see a garishly painted face, the provocative pose of a woman determined to get what she wants, but instead, Greg stands uncertainly, one foot on the bottom step, dressed in white shirt and jeans.

'You'd better come up.'

He takes the steps two at a time.

'I suppose I shouldn't be so presumptuous as to ask if you were waiting for me,' he says looking at my nakedness.

'No, you shouldn't.' I smile and quickly grab his hand to lead him inside.

I wonder whether I should switch on the golden-shaded lamp by the bed to relieve the gloom, but somehow the darkness suits my mood. We stand watching each other by the long mirror.

'Lara, what's wrong? Why are you looking at me like that?'

The hand that has been caressing my shoulder, cupping my breast, travelling further down, stops.

His face is now scrubbed clean. He looks so sincere, so innocent. There is no sign of the demon I glimpsed two hours previously.

'All these changes in you. It's unsettling.'

'Oh come on. I told you about the modelling.'

He puts his arms around me when I shiver.

I watch us in the mirror. I feel as if we're in a film set.

'No, I mean . . . even at lunchtime with Jake and Amber. You were like someone else; authoritative, older. *And* you practically ignored me.'

Without warning he bends down and lifts me up into his arms. He carries me over to the bed and sets me on his lap. Then he switches on the golden-shaded lamp and we sit in a circle of yellow light, like a spotlight on a stage.

'You don't get it, do you?' he says softly, caressing my nipples. I find his apparently uncertain touch arousing. I roll my thighs towards his crotch. He seems not to notice.

'Look at you now. You're different in this light, a goddess of warmth and mystery.' His fingers move absently down my body. I quiver. 'And this morning you shagged me with your beautiful golden arse bobbing in the sea. Very different to the Lara that blushes and stammers in front of the great J F.'

His hand has settled between my legs. His middle fingers are barely moving but he is touching my clit almost as if by accident. I feel as if my cunt is being kissed by a breeze.

'I was stoned,' I whisper, my hand on his chest, my nails in the spaces between his shirt buttons. Against my thigh I feel his cock rock hard in his jeans. But his face gives nothing away. He covers my face with tiny reverential kisses ending with the soft, dry meeting of our lips. I think I must be leaking on his thigh. I begin to lose control. I push myself more onto his hand, trying to part his mouth with my tongue. He draws back; looks at me seriously.

'You were another Lara, one that spoke to me with her cunt and not her inhibitions, a tantalising powerful woman. You can do it again. You can do it for Jake.'

'I don't want Jake, I only want you,' I lie, out of my mind with the need to come.

Suddenly he takes his hand from between my legs. I glare at him, twist fully round like an animal in attack and make a frantic grab for his cock. He catches my wrist.

'Good, now you're getting angry. But you must learn to savour it, control your passions, optimise them. Then you will hold all the power.'

Our brief struggle has left me straddling his thigh. My clit throbs against him. It takes all my willpower not to rub myself against his leg. He looks at me with tolerance, benevolence; like some kind of messiah who has delivered his message to the ignorant and is waiting for the enlightenment to dawn. Yet I notice that his erection has not yet subsided. It reminds me of twenty years ago when Steve tried to teach me to master and control my passions. But what *he* really meant was to give him a blow job first.

'OK, tell me. What do you want me to do to you?' I try to make my voice offhand, bored, but the intensity of my frustration and anger burn through the words.

And again I glimpse the hurt child, but swiftly he changes to little-boy-daring, reaching up and raising my hair with both hands above my head.

'No, darling. It's what I can do for you,' he says. He lets my hair fall, rises and takes my hand. We leave the spotlight and stand before my wardrobe. I watch, perplexed, as one by one he takes each dress, each scarf, each of my long summer skirts and throws them, ostentatiously, onto the bed. How unexciting the colours look – neutral pale tones, like a mountain of snow going to slush.

As Greg rifles through my shameful pile of clothes I fight off the urge to go to my tiny bathroom to escape a looming sense of depression and to finger myself to orgasm. He selects a white skirt and a long gold scarf that someone gave me as a Christmas present and I have never worn. He draws them into the air like a conjuror pulling rabbits from a hat.

'These will do for now,' he says. 'You must sit, Lara.'

He all but frog-marches me in front of the mirror and with a firm touch of his hand on my shoulder makes me sink to the rich-toned oriental rug on the floor. I sit naked and cross-legged like an escapee from a dream about a magic carpet.

'Open your legs,' he says and, seeing my expression, explains, 'It's part of the transformation. Reinforcement therapy, I think they call it.'

'God, Greg, I don't know where your head is half the time.'

'You and me both, darling,' he murmurs and for a second he looks solemn before he gives me his take-on-the-world grin. He kneels, straddled over my spread legs, his knee nudging my clit, as he pulls my hair off my face and secures it with a clip.

'Make-up, you must have some surely?'

I nod towards my bedside table. 'In there.'

Once more I feel desolate when he takes his knee away and goes to fetch the large make-up palette Stace has given me but which remains barely touched.

He smears his thumb disdainfully over the one eye-shadow that I ever use.

'Winter beige, now there's a surprise.'

'Oh, Greg, just get on with it will you.'

He nestles his knee against my crotch again and I close my eyes in bliss.

'Now let's see if you really are one of the great untouchables.'

'One of the what?' I ask absently.

He leans over me to paint my lids, his cotton shirt swishing gently against my nipples as his lower thigh presses harder into me.

'J F's words, not mine. What you and his wife had in common apparently, pretty women who look as if they'd cry rape if you made a move.'

I stop his hand in front of my face, digging my nails into his wrist with fury. As if in spasm, his knee jerks against my cunt.

'That's rubbish,' I gasp, 'Jake doesn't know me well

75

enough to say that. Christ, he didn't even recognise me the other day.'

'Maybe it wasn't that he didn't know you but that he wanted to know you differently,' Greg says quietly.

With infinite tenderness he lays me back on my magic carpet. I lie with my pulse racing as he glosses my lips, frowning to get them just right. I am pinned beneath him, overwhelmed by a cocktail of emotions. I reach up and hook my fingers inside the top of Greg's jeans. How dare Jake talk about me like that and why the hell didn't he tell me he was married?

I run my hand down the ridge of Greg's cock, cupping his balls inside his jeans. Just a momentary flicker of his lashes betrays his feelings. He sets the lipstick brush carefully back in the palette.

'At the risk of repeating myself yet again,' I say, unable to prevent the bitterness in my voice, 'would you fuck me now . . . please.'

'Not yet,' he says. 'Not until you're ready.'

He pulls me to my feet and stands behind me as I gaze at the woman in the mirror. She has sultry eyes, full lips; she has cheekbones like a catwalk model.

'My God, I'm beautiful,' I whisper.

'You always were. But now you see it.'

He allows himself a triumphant smile and lets my pinned-back hair rest on his shoulder. His fingers slide around my waist, down my abdomen and rest in my pubic hair.

Then he dresses me in a way that I have only ever been undressed before.

He fastens my button-through white skirt at the front, not the side, leaving all the buttons below my crotch undone. Then he smears some cherry-coloured blusher from the palette onto his fingers.

'Lift your skirt,' he says.

Kneeling in front of me he proceeds to work the red powder from his fingers into the inner lips of my cunt.

'Oh Jesus, that feels good.' I put my hands on his silky

hair. His lips are so close. I want him there with his mouth.

'Oh, Greg, please.'

He doesn't reply but strokes colour between my legs until my juices wipe his fingers clean. Then with his hands firmly on my thighs he kisses me softly all around but not quite on the place he has just painted. My legs begin to tremble.

'You're driving me crazy.'

He smiles but says nothing.

Then he stands and proceeds to massage the blusher into my already erect nipples. This is more than I can bear. I run my hands around his back, down his hips and try to push him against me.

'You're not giving me enough room.' He grins and leans back, tilting his pelvis and his obviously hard cock rests near enough my wet lips to make me squirm towards him.

'Stand still!'

The hard slap on my buttocks makes me gasp with indignation, but something else too. My pelvis jolts forward clashing momentarily with Greg's erection and the aftershock of the hot tingle of his hand spreads deliciously through my abdomen and culminates in the now familiar ache of desperate anticipation. But I bite my lip and don't complain while a trickle of juice escapes my pussy. I wonder if it's tinged pink like rose water.

'Don't worry, Lara, not long now,' he says softly. 'Almost there.'

As if taking pity on my obvious need for release, he takes his tinted fingers from my nipples and lightly caresses the orbs of my breasts. I glance down and think how wonderful they look, their centres accentuated like rosebuds. Another trickle escapes me.

'That's the trouble,' I whisper. 'I *am* almost there. You keep doing things to make me on the brink of coming. And each time my longing gets worse. My make-up's running, if you know what I mean.'

'Therein lies the secret,' he says, winding my gold scarf

around my shoulders and tits in the sheerest halter neck style. 'Withholding orgasm as long as you can makes the final moment of release incredible. That interval between initial arousal and culmination of desire should be exquisite and transforming.'

He kisses my nipples through their golden casing.

'You see, Lara, the more time you spend savouring your sexual arousal the more you will get in touch with your sexual psyche. Then you'll have no inhibitions. You will be able to manipulate your sexual allure – even in front of the great J F.'

I gaze at him in astonishment.

'Well then, fuck me.'

And he does.

Standing at first, one hand behind me, he pulls on the golden binding around my breasts so that my back arches and the netting of the chiffon chafes my nipples deliciously. With the other hand he frees his cock and inserts it into my wet pussy. He moves very slowly at first, bending his knees slightly so that the root of his cock massages my clit.

'Oh. That's *so* good.' I close my eyes as he retreats slightly then fills me up again.

He squeezes my buttocks so that my thighs press against his and simultaneously tightens his grip on my scarf, increasing the pressure on my nipples. I spread my legs more to maintain my balance though I know he won't let me fall.

'I want to come,' I whimper as the power of his slow strokes begins to increase.

'Well you can't,' he says tightening the gauze on my chest so much I'm sure it will split. 'You're my slave girl and if you can't withhold orgasm I'm going to make you come again and again until you can't bear it any more.'

This is all he needs to say.

With one hand I grab for the small of his back. The other slides down his hips to force him harder against me. The swiftness of my action takes him off guard. He loses his balance and we topple together onto the rug.

His arms cradle my back as we stumble, but he is unable to control his lower body which crashes hard against mine as I fall; legs splayed, knees bent. His cock slams into me with such a force that I slide a couple of inches up the carpet and after a second of immense pain am convulsed into the most intense orgasm I have ever had.

'Jesus. Oh, Jesus Christ.'

He lifts my back. I'm still anchored to his cock.

'Lara, are you alright?'

'I want my punishment,' I breathe before half fainting back to the rug.

And he fucks me slowly then quickly; rolls his hips then stops; butts me softly for a while then slowly and deep and quickly and hard; and I come; and then again. I feel like I'm the bud of a flower blasted open then dissolving its petals into the air, then going into itself, then opening and flooding the whole universe with my colour and essence.

'Please. Please, no more,' I whimper on the point of passing out with the bliss of it all.

Then I see his face above me tense ferociously then release all his tender years as he allows himself to surrender to his own orgasm.

Afterwards, he lies for a while with his head on my heart. Outside, the sky is blue-white, drained, devoid of the day's energy. It is evening and we never saw it coming. Greg rests his hand on my breast and from time to time wets my nipple with his mouth. The wine-red bud glows through its golden veneer. For some reason I think of a baby nestling and can't help but hold him hard all the more.

Greg and I walk hand in hand along the corridor away from the west wing. Under the splintered regal light of a candelabra I feel suddenly unsure. Greg has insisted I do the minimum to fix up my post-coital appearance, repainting my lips and re-teasing my pinned up hair being deemed all that is necessary. My skirt is rumpled and neither of us has washed. My thighs are still glazed with rose-coloured come.

'God, just look at my nipples. I really can't . . .'

He touches the painted tips lightly through their golden film. He looks proud.

'Look I just can't. Jake and Amber will know what we've been up to.'

'Exactly,' he replies, but relenting a little, adjusts my scarf enough to give me another layer of netting through which my nipples are only just visible.

'And just what *have* you been up to, Larissa?'

The loud voice startles me. Jake has his back to us as he holds a bottle of wine in front of the door to the seventies room. The familiar mocking note in his voice unnerves me.

'Greg has been painting me,' I say lamely.

Greg grips my hand tightly and I know it is not for support.

When Jake turns around, the half-amused expression dies on his face. He stares at me and I feel the light splatter like gold on my hair and on my opulent costume; on my whore's face and body. I feel myself grow taller in my high-heeled sandals. I am back on my magic carpet with my legs open, being shagged like never before. I feel my naked pussy throb again as I boldly meet Jake's astounded gaze.

'Are we going somewhere, then?' I ask nonchalantly. I let go of Greg's hand and walk assuredly towards Jake.

Wordlessly he swings the door open for me.

'We're eating in here,' he murmurs and, as I pass, recovers himself a little.

'Nice work, Greg. You've done a good job there.'

'I aim to please, boss,' Greg says cheerfully and nips my backside as we enter the eery sienna light and shadows of the well-remembered room.

A small table ornately set with candles and flowers has been placed in the middle of the rush matting. At the window end, Amber sits with the blossom tree now strangely somnolent behind her and the flames of the candles in front licking her make-up-free face.

She wears a simple cotton dress – the kind I usually favour. Her hair is in braids. She looks, and the realisation stuns me, like someone's wife.

'You are very nice,' she says grudgingly and pours herself a large glass of wine from the several bottles on the table.

I sit with Greg on one side and Jake on the other. At a mischievous glance from Greg and the pressure of his hand on my thigh under the table, I open my legs, coming into swift contact with the knees of both men.

'Oops, sorry.' I give Jake a wide-eyed glance which he returns with a look of surprise that quickly turns to a quiet smile.

'Wine, Larissa?' he asks in a low voice. He does not attempt to withdraw his leg from mine. Yet neither of us press further. We keep contact but no more. This sensation is strangely thrilling coupled with Greg's continued caressing of my inner thighs under the table. I start to become wet and find it very difficult to maintain my decorum.

We help ourselves from the variety of fish dishes laid out in the centre of the table. The intoxicating sea smell and the rubbery, slippery texture of the slivers and chunks excite me further. I drink very little yet I soon start to feel exuberant as the pale sky deepens and the bloom-laden tree rustles against the glass. In the candlelight, I watch the contours of Jake's older face while he eats, drinks, smokes and tries not to look at me. Watching his dark, shadowed eyes and soft facial lines makes a heady pastime combined with the excitement of Greg's young knuckles buried inside my pussy hair. I long to put my hand under the cloth to feel if Jake has an erection.

'Put some music on ... please,' I ask and I see him flinch.

'What would you like?' he asks, playing for time.

'You choose, go on.'

He rises and turns quickly towards the stereo system. Amber is searching in her bag for cigarettes and doesn't notice his obvious erection. As he rifles through some tapes and CDs Greg digs his hand into my knee and, with an inclination of the head, indicates that I should rise too.

I stand immediately behind Jake, letting my breath heat his brown neck where his hair gathers in curls above a white T-shirt.

'Shall I help?'

This close to him it's hard to convey the offhand sensual drawl I intend. The familiar nerves rise. I force myself to brush my hand against his cock as I pretend to examine a CD.

He turns his head and looks into my eyes for a long time. I succeed in holding his gaze for several seconds until I am forced to blink as I feel something sharp in the corner of my eye. The blinking does not stop the irritation. He reaches slowly to my eyelid and dislodges something there.

'An eyelash,' he says as the pain goes and a welling up of salt water escapes my eye.

He runs his thumb carefully under my eye make-up. I am light-headed. I feel as if the two of us are alone in our own space and time.

Abruptly, an over-shrill voice carries from the table.

'So you know this house well, then, Lara?'

The quality of Amber's tone makes me wheel around to look at her. Jake, unperturbed, chooses some music and squats down to put it on the system. Amber's face in the candlelight looks pale. She is smoking furiously. During our meal she has drunk a lot, talked little and eaten less. I know I should say something friendly and placatory to her, but I don't get the chance. Dramatically, with her whole body quivering, she downs almost a full glass of wine in one lusty ferocious gulp.

'And Jake,' she continues. 'You two have the history, yes?'

The bitterness in her thick accent turns to menace. This

time Jake turns, too. I hear him sigh. But I can't let him go, not straight back to her, not while I stand here with my painted face and aching crotch. I think of the controlled demonic fucking I witnessed in the afternoon and something of the devil rises in me, too. I put my hand on his shoulder as he turns to leave me. I dig my nails in. He stops in surprise. Then slowly and deliberately I run my hand down his back scouring him through the white cotton. I take a deep breath and force myself to say calmly, 'God, no, we're like brother and sister, aren't we Jake?'

There is a pause while the music on the stereo creeps into the start of a ballad that used to make me cry.

> *Reach for my hand and take me*
> *We'll go higher than the sky*
> *Warming tears as they come down*
> *Swallow them inside our ground*
> *And we'll stay close forever*

Jake sits beside Amber and lights her cigarette. Now the table seems bigger, our collective intimacy diffused. Greg is looking at me curiously but I pretend not to see, concentrating on drinking and smoking with an ease and contentment I don't feel. The room seems very warm.

'Does anyone mind if I open the window?'

Amber in her naivety has taken my summary of the relationship between Jake and I at face value. The colour is back in her cheeks. Jake, having picked a sheaf of notes from an adjacent table, has gone through with her a very full programme of modelling for the coming weeks. Placated, she nods her head at me pleasantly.

'Go ahead. It is hot.'

Greg watches me walk to the window. Jake ignores me completely.

I perch myself on the windowsill and let the tree blossom caress and graze and stab my bare back as the wind rakes it. I drink my wine and tell myself I don't care. I look down at my rose-pink nipples, hard in the

83

breeze; as hard, yet soft too, as the myriad buds on the branches which frame me. All is deception. Greg grins and gives me a thumbs-up sign.

In silver thoughts and golden dreams
The future runs in magic streams

I feel utterly alone.

Jake and Amber are sitting very close on the corded sofa. Greg is lying on the rush matting apparently meditating. I remain by the window.

'You must have had some real good times here all those years ago,' Amber says pleasantly. Now she bears me no malice but, inside the darkness of my make-up, my thoughts are heavy too. Suddenly I want to compensate for all those years I have been continuously sweet and deferential, and scared.

'Indeed, there were some incredible times,' I say airily clutching the stem of my glass so hard it's in danger of breaking. 'Remember that corset I wore, Jake, that wine-coloured thing with all the bones digging into me. We were guzzling beer with all those people. The corset was under my normal clothes and none of them knew and it pressed into my abdomen so much I had to keep going to the loo every half an hour.'

I laugh lightly, falsely.

The look he gives me is not one of distaste or the veiled excitement which I anticipate, but one of anger, as if I have betrayed him. Amber glances between us, now in a state of drunken confusion. Half-drunk myself with a mixture of power and exhibitionism, I move to get the bottle of wine and for some reason decide to refill Amber's empty glass. Jake puts his hand over it. I look at him with defiance but can do nothing more, while Amber sinks back into the sofa in a cloud of lethargy and disinterest. Jake takes advantage of our locked glance.

'Why don't you, Larissa –' he says with a steel in his voice that makes my blood run cold '– try a little posing for us tomorrow, seeing as you're so into corsetry and showing yourself off.'

'Fucking great idea boss.' Greg, in one agile move, goes from lying flat on his back to sitting cross-legged, wide-eyed with excitement. 'She's a natural, I told her.'

Amber rises unsteadily and glances at us all from behind her hair, her tall beauty beaten down to a gangly childishness. A picture of Stacey comes into my mind when I've been unnecessarily bitchy to her because Steve hasn't phoned or sent any money. I swallow hard as Amber goes for the door.

'I retire now. I have a lot of work to do tomorrow.'

She musters all the dignity she can, but her voice is thick with misery. The door closes softly behind her and Jake looks at it. Then he snatches the bottle of wine from me and fills all our glasses to the brim.

'A toast,' he says crashing his glass so hard into ours that all our wine splashes together like drops of blood onto the floor. 'Who's like us and who would want to be!'

Greg and I are walking on the grass verge around the house heading back towards the balcony steps. I eagerly breathe in the cool black air as if to wash away the images of the previous few hours.

'It went well tonight.' Greg is carrying my shoes with one hand. The other is slipped contentedly around my waist.

'Yes,' I say quietly, thinking that he's really far too young for me. I feel oddly nervous. I shiver. 'It must be really cloudy. I can't see the moon and it should be nearly full.'

Greg rubs his hand up and down my arm. 'I told you we should have gone back along the corridor but would you listen?' he says in a friendly way.

'Did they divorce?'

'Who? What are you talking about, Lara?'

'Jake and his wife. He's not still married is he?' Suddenly all the details seem important to me. My mind is miles away, years away.

'Oh they didn't divorce. She's dead.' Greg stoops to pick a small white flower and place it between my breasts. It falls away almost immediately.

'How did she die?'

There is a light scurrying in one of the bushes: a fox or similar, something trapped or terrified.

'Well, the talk is she was on drugs. It was years ago. He tried to get her off it, even locked her in a room: the cold turkey thing. She couldn't hack it though. One night she threw herself out into the garden.'

I stop with my foot on the bottom of the balcony steps. Greg stumbles against me.

'Lara?'

I look upwards to where the green shutters, now black, seem to swing a little too much in the light wind. I spin around and look behind us as if we are being followed. But there is nothing but the sea of white rocks that is the gravel and the bushes growing in on each other like a wall. Above them the sky suddenly lets me glimpse the white disk of an almost full moon through the haze. Then, just as swiftly, it is black again.

'Lara, for Christ's sake, what's wrong?'

'Come up with me. I've something to show you.'

Jake's drawing of the boy/girl/woman falling through the air lies on the bed. I sit beside it trembling. Greg kneels on the floor, looking at it. Then he glances at me and begins to laugh.

'You think he's cast a spell on you or something. Oh, darling, really. It's just a sketch.'

He picks it up, examines it more closely. 'And a fucking good one at that,' he murmurs.

'But, Greg, don't you see? This has to be the room she was in. It's the only one with a balcony. And he's had steps put in. They were never here before. Why has he given it to me?'

'Probably because it's the only half-decent guest room

in the house and the steps mean you have a certain degree of autonomy,' he replies matter-of-factly. Then realising my distress he drops the piece of paper and puts his arms around me.

'Look, don't you trust Jake?'

'There was a time I'd have trusted him with my life.'

'Well, then.'

His hands move down to my waist, my abdomen, and rest just above the skirt buttons between my legs.

I sigh, all at once feeling ridiculous in the costume of my alter ego or whatever Greg is trying to convince me it is.

'I'm going to have a shower, get rid of this gunk on my face.' I slide forward but he seems reluctant to relax his hold. 'I'm really freaked around here, Greg. I don't know what's going on.' I put my hand over his, gently push him away.

I'm halfway to the shower room when I hear him say, 'You might consider that it's *you* that's freaking you out. Truth is only a matter of interpretation, you know.'

Oh, fuck off, I think.

I undress as I walk, discarding my gold scarf on the floor. It looks like an iodine-soaked bandage with its two rosy spots like the seepings of a wound.

I pass the locked cupboard and reach for the shower room door.

'Can I stay, Lara? Just for a while. Until you sleep?'

This voice, I think, this young plaintive voice will always turn my head. 'I'd like that.'

We are curled into each other, my back to his stomach, as one creature in our satin womb. I don't want to look out at the night. I just want this solace to go on.

'I used to do this with my sister when we were small and things in the house frightened us,' Greg whispers, his warm breath on my neck, his hands crossed over my abdomen.

I imagine him a tiny doe-eyed boy with his sweet hairless limbs clinging.

'What things?'

'Oh, nothing. It was a long time ago.'

'Everything's a long time ago,' I murmur.

The smell of our bodies and our pasts are cocooned manageably around our solidarity.

'Make love to me, Greg.'

'A variation on a theme of "Fuck me at once Greg"?' He bites my shoulder playfully.

'Absolutely.'

He barely has to move, as if the connection's there, waiting to be met. His cock burrows between my open legs, comes slowly inside me, so hard and thick I feel every millimetre of his progress until he is in me up to the hilt, his root rotating languidly on my clit. The rest of our bodies don't move. We cling to each other while our pelvises dance and rise and bind together.

'Oh, God, Lara. I feel like I'm going to heaven.'

He begins to shudder and I quiet him with my arms as if he was a child.

'Can I come, too?' I whisper as I sense in his beautiful controlled movements a desperation.

He kisses my neck. 'Yes.'

And I do, my whole being clawing and fighting and sinking and rising in ecstasy, although I don't believe I make a single physical movement.

Chapter Four

*T*oday, the sky looks as though it will never rain again. The trees are filled with sun and barely moving, but for the occasional rustling and yielding in their brightness, as they give shelter to an errant bird.

It's ten in the morning and already the sun is hot on my shoulders. I'm wearing a camisole Greg has given me; it's crisp and white, a part of the modelling costumes. In it I feel like a virgin and a whore. Most of my other clothes have been taken away to be altered and dyed. He has permitted me the bright-coloured skirt I first arrived in: 'I like the idea of juicy flowers splattered around that lovely juicy arse and clit. I want you to wear nothing underneath. As it brushes against you I want you to think of me'

Every step I take I feel the silky material caress my skin, and I think of Greg and the previous day. I feel as if a layer of me has been peeled away. It's a good feeling, but scary too. Shedding skins may liberate, but skins also shield the vulnerable and today I feel buoyant but vulnerable as well.

Even the front of the sombre house looks alive and full of summer. Today, with the sun so blazingly intense, the windows on its craggy old face gleam like the eyes of the rejuvenated. I feel the sun tease my skin; warm my daintily encased breasts; tease my nipples; slide like a warm bath over the thin material masking my thighs and raw awakened clit. I think of Greg's expert prolonged wonderful shagging and his clever quick fingers on make-up brushes, sponges, through scissors, inside my cunt. I turn around grinning hugely and not caring if I'm seen, although it's unlikely. Early afternoon seems to be the time when the cars and bikes bring in the outside world. Then suddenly, as I gaze contentedly at the twinkling eyes of the house, something occurs to me. I crouch and scribble on my pad. 'Mask', I write and 'veil' and 'trick of the light'. Then I rush round to the rear of the house and survey the calmer greener glow of the windows there as they wait patiently for the sun to transform them too. From some distance I look at the stained glass of the summer-house. Halfway down, the glass is vivid with light as the sun climbs in the sky. But the colouring on the lower half is soberly dark, inhibited-looking. I write on my pad: 'Tinting of windows or alternative screens'.

Exuberant that, at last, my turgid intellect is emulating my more open spiritual and physical self, I cross the grass to the low bench outside the summer-house to drink the mineral water I have brought.

'How much longer, you asshole and bastard? This is not the most comfortable position.'

I catch my breath. The voice seems near but somehow muffled. Then I notice the door to the summer-house is slightly open.

'Just about there, sweetheart. Open wide as the good doctor said.'

I know I should move, but I'm curious. Sliding to the end of the bench where the coloured glass curves around to the front of the structure, I peep through a tiny droplet of clear glass; a raindrop on a petal in the flamboyant design.

Jake is standing at an easel painting animatedly. Amber is stretched out on the hammock with her wrists bound above her head. She is also tied at the ankles. Her

90

legs are apart and there appears to be something, a pillow or cushion, beneath her so that her hips are raised. She wears a sheer, toga-like garment which exposes one of her heavy golden breasts and slopes across her abdomen and off over one thigh.

'Verrry pretty.' Jake lays down his brush to light a cigarette. 'Give me a few more pubes though. Oh sorry, I forgot. You can't.'

He walks over to a small stool beside the hammock. With the hand not holding the cigarette, he moves some of the white material on her lower body aside. Then I catch my breath as he runs the tips of his fingers over her stomach and around the edges of her sex lips. I see her bent legs rock slightly.

'Don't keep doing that. I need to pee.'

'Oh, poor, poor Amber. Is this better, angel?'

I bite my lip as with the side of his thumb and the heel of his hand he begins to massage between her legs, still casually smoking the cigarette. Involuntarily, I move my own clit slightly against the rough wood of the bench.

She moans faintly, 'That's nice. That'll stem the flow.'

'And this?' he asks, dropping his fag-end on the floor and bending down over her legs to put his face to her cunt. I see his head move slightly back and forth as he licks and kisses and inserts his tongue inside her.

'Ooh, yes. That's really putting in the plug.' Her body begins to buck and strain against her shackles.

He lifts his face from her abdomen, lightly caresses her auburn pubic hair.

'We can't have you getting too greedy,' he says briskly, 'Now you're nice and wet for me I should get to work.'

'Bastard! You are my lover. You can't tease me like this. Get back down!'

'I am one of your lovers, *you* are one of mine.' There is a cold note in his voice. 'Besides, you're a model. You must always exercise will power and self-control.'

'And you're a bastard and I'll piss in your face if you give me any more grief!'

Through her indignant tone I hear sadness. I think of her fear and jealousy the previous evening

'Promises, promises.' Jake grins and rises abruptly, whipping off his unbuttoned shirt and hurling it across the room as he walks back to the easel. It slams into the window just where I peer through, his lighter or some other hard object knocking viciously against the glass making me start. I glance guiltily around but there are no signs of life either in the serene façade of the building or the quiet, sweet-smelling garden. The only one that is likely to be around is Greg and I know that my 'peeping Tom' act would only amuse and perhaps arouse him.

'Fucking hot in here.'

Jake is standing facing the window in front of me. I duck my head back but not until I catch a glimpse of him wiping sweat from his strong tanned chest. I notice with delight that he is slightly hairier than he used to be.

'Let's get down to business.'

I watch his broad shoulders tilt and tense, the muscles on his arms firm and stretch, as he washes and teases and carves his impression of the imprisoned Amber onto the canvas. For several delicious minutes I imagine that it is me who is posing, that he has anchored my legs far apart and threatened to shag me unconscious if I don't behave for him. My hands, like Amber's, would be bound and I would be helpless as he bit, nuzzled and sucked my pussy. I would be unable to squirm with fear and ecstasy, so unrelenting would my bonds be. Then quickly he would let his cock go free, thick and hard, to plunge into me until I felt faint with his relentless fucking and the cumulative effect of numerous intense orgasms. I move my naked clit once more on the warm harsh wood. Then I am jolted back into reality, remembering that I am indeed to pose, not just for him but for a whole class, this afternoon. Waves of panic seize me. I stare with a dry mouth at Amber's smooth, svelte, young woman's body and imagine myself dressed similarly. Without the aid of Greg and his full assault on my psyche making me believe I can carry off such a feat I feel myself

shrink back into Lara, single mother and recent entre-
preneur who is helpful and reliable and very nice and
not in the slightest bit sensual. Oh Christ. Perhaps I
should tell Jake that I'm ill or overworked – I really have
to start on my ideas for the house or I'll fall behind
schedule. But I know I won't or, more precisely, that he
won't let me. Jake Fitzgerald is determined to have some
fun out of me this afternoon.

I watch in a fog of numb dismay as Jake energetically
completes his painting, occasionally pausing to bark,
'Keep still' at the completely motionless and exquisite
Amber.

Then I see her quite distinctly move so that the skewed
diamond shape of her opened legs rocks slightly.

'Damn it, Amber. Do as you're told!'

The blood rushes to the surface of my skin. I don't
think I'd like him to talk to me like that.

'Please, Jake.' Amber's thick Germanic accent sounds
weak, almost childish. 'I *really* need to pee soon.'

'That's what you get drinking all that coffee this morning,' he says in an offhand way, using his thumb to
smudge away some detail at the top of the canvas.

'I had the colossal bastard of a hangover,' she says in a
bitter tone.

'And whose fault was that?' Jake wipes his brush on a
rag and stands back to survey his work.

'Yours, asshole,' Amber snarls, but there is a note of
desperation in her voice which Jake seems oblivious to.
'You and your soldier sprite, that Laura.'

'Nymphet martyr and her name is Lara, Larissa if you
correlate it specifically to the definition, and nothing is
going on between us. She's practically my sister-in-law.'

He says this in a weary tone which brings a lump to
my throat. Yet I can't help wondering why he discussed
my name with her at all.

'I'm not sure, oh, I don't know,' Amber says in confusion. 'But I do know if you don't untie me soon I'm going
to have the accident in this toga.'

Her voice is now shrill with need and I'm astonished

93

at the way Jake is responding. I have always known him to be complex and irritating, but I have never known him to be cruel. But now, as I watch this girl struggle increasingly for control, I feel an urge to go in and untie her myself.

'Go ahead, then,' Jake says indifferently, picking up a tiny brush and crouching in front of the canvas. 'It's just sheeting anyway.'

Under my skirt I cross my own legs tightly in empathy with Amber's predicament.

'Are you fucking kidding?' Amber almost screams at him now. 'Gregor'll be ape-shit if someone pees in his costume. You are such, such an asshole and I never, never forgive you if you make me wet myself.'

This seems to get through. Jake looks at her in surprise as if he has just grasped the urgency of her plight, puts down his brushes, crosses over to the stool and proceeds to untie her ankles.

'Greg's a bit of an old queen about these fucking costumes anyway,' Jake says in a churlish voice as if trying to excuse his prior indifference.

'Jealous,' spits Amber, drawing her knees up to ease her discomfort.

'What?' Jake stands to release the ties on her wrists.

'You're jealous,' she repeats wriggling now as he starts to undo the rather intricately tied constraints. 'He gives one to your nymphet and you're jealous.'

'What would you say if I told you there was a large knot in one of these things?' he responds mischievously.

'You asshole,' screeches Amber aiming both feet at Jake's groin and just missing her target as he moves swiftly out of the way.

'OK, OK, point taken,' he says and, inexplicably, his tone changes to the gentle one that used to turn me weak all those years ago. 'Almost there, sweetheart. Good girl.'

He rubs her abdomen gently, murmurs something sympathetic as he feels her fullness, then offers her a gallant hand to help her to her feet.

Now that she's standing, the toga looks longer and

more cumbersome. Making small sounds of displeasure she gathers it up as she makes for the door with hurried steps and a reddening face.

Jake reaches down to the floor to retrieve his cigarettes from his shirt pocket and, as he comes up again, I see a flash of pure devilment in his eyes. When Amber struggles past him, her face strained with discomfort, he draws back his hand and whacks her backside.

She lets out a yelp and runs forward as fast as she can.

Mesmerised by the whole scene it takes me some seconds to realise that I will have to move or be discovered. I leap up and scurry around to the back of the summer-house just before Amber flings back the glass door and rushes outside lifting high the burden of her costume.

I hear her sigh blissfully as she relieves herself beside a bush muttering, 'Fucking asshole bastard, pig pig pig.'

A swish of her toga and the easier sound of her footsteps signal her return to the summer-house. For a moment I tell myself it is wrong to spy, then I creep back to the end of the bench and peep through my fortuitous dewdrop.

Jake is sitting on the hammock smoking, still bare-chested, his legs casually apart. He appears relaxed, almost boyish; daydreaming. I wait for Amber, now tall and erect, with her equilibrium restored to go into attack mode, but she doesn't.

With a strange excitement and a little jealousy I watch her approach to him soften with each step. I am amazed by this. She, so close, can see something in his eyes that I can't even guess at.

She towers over him, then bends a little and, for a second, the luxuriant curtain of her hair obscures my view. I see her fingertips settle in his hair, a gentle caress. Then quickly she moves back as if a sudden weight is on her and I think Jake must be leaning, or have somehow fallen, on her chest. I shift on the bench, trying to get a better view, trying to hear if anything is being said. No words are exchanged. But there is something in her powerful stance and his abstraction that makes me believe they are involved in something that does not need words.

She falls to her knees and he holds her head. This time I see his expression clearly. It is the one of infinite sadness, the new expression that he never wore two decades ago, but which I have glimpsed fleetingly over the last couple of days. From my distance and shabby exclusion I wonder at this portrayal of grief, the way he seems to want to hide from the dazzle of summer, relishing the gloom behind the coloured glass. I think of his wife and how much he must miss her.

'So, angel girl, you tell me. Am I to be punished?' The odd neutral quality of defeat in his voice startles me.

'You are my big bad Jake and I will punish you.'

Amber's voice has lost the sulky little girl quality that she turns on and off at a whim. This is a more astute, decisive Amber who knows when she has been given power. Nonetheless, she has a strange look on her face. It's almost as if she is frightened.

'What must I do?' There is a faint feverishness in his voice. He tilts her face back to look right into his. He looks serious, yet entranced.

'I think first you must lick me all over.'

They change places. She lies back on the hammock with her legs trailing the floor while he settles himself astride her and proceeds to remove her thin cotton wrapping very gently, as if peeling a dressing from a wound. Then he bends over her and, from her closed eyes to her chin, to her long neck and down, he works with his mouth, brushing her with his lips, letting his tongue lap around her earlobes, kissing her softly, then hard, on her own lips which she struggles to keep closed. By the time he is down to her breasts, cupping each one tenderly before running his tongue around her nipples, then kissing them harder and sucking that new hardness, I see her legs rise in response, till the pads of her feet move with barely controlled frenzy on his clothed hips.

'You big bad bastard but I love you so much, I really do.'

When she says this he stops for a moment, tenses, but then continues.

His head moves rapidly across and down her lower body, while her fingers, enmeshed in his curly hair, strain tighter as her ecstasy grows. He buries his face between her legs while her knees rise higher and her legs open wider.

'Now, you stop now!' she cries unexpectedly, digging her nails into his scalp to draw his head up.

Unconsciously, I am clutching the wood on the back of the bench so hard that my own nails are in danger of breaking. I'm amazed at her self-control asking him to leave her at such an advanced stage in her arousal. I can't imagine that she must really want this.

She moves forward on the broad swathe of cloth. So does Jake, sitting nearly upright and keeping the hammock steady with his strong arms.

I'm reminded of his words of two evenings ago, 'You can't shag on that thing, it has been tried.' I feel ugly and inadequate.

'Is it my hand you want? Do you want me to rub you till my bastard fingers are cramped and numb?'

I can't see his face but the tone of his voice chills me. I can hear the undercurrent of excitement there but also something else: distaste, not for Amber or the situation, but for himself.

'Not yet!' Amber speaks the words crisply, entering into the spirit of their game, and it occurs to me that she might, after all, want to get revenge for Jake's earlier attitude to her.

'First, you are to be in *my* hands,' she says in a tone of low relish. 'Unzip!' she commands.

I'm not surprised to see the hardness of Jake's cock as he frees it under her avid gaze. But I am utterly astonished at what happens next. Drawing her arm far behind her, Amber suddenly lunges forward with the flat of her palm swishing sabre-like through the air. She strikes

Jake so hard across the cheek that his head moves to one side.

'Jesus Christ!' I put my hand across my mouth.

The next blow comes immediately, in a similar fashion, from the other side. Jake's head jerks the other way.

'Now,' Amber manages to say, trembling with effort and something else too, 'you must tell me what you are being punished for.'

'I am a bastard to women. I am no good. I make them suffer and therefore I have to suffer.' He finishes the last words lamely.

Amber gets off the hammock and stands, her face and strong shoulders bathed in gold by the sudden sinister intrusion of a block of sun.

'Kneel!' she demands and, though the haughtiness in her voice seems authentic, I notice something curious. As the sun shines in her eyes I see that they are filled with tears. She drops to her knees in front of him and takes his penis in her hand. For a minute or so she caresses him gently, her fingers working from the root to the tip of his cock. He has a look of almost pained rapture on his face.

'I deserve everything I get,' he says in a husky voice.

Amber takes this as a cue to change tactic. Sliding her hand under his balls she squeezes as tight as she can. I see him wince.

'More. I need to suffer. Please.'

She squeezes again. Then she twists his poor flesh as if wringing out a cloth. He doesn't cry out or buckle or try to extricate himself from her touch although he is shuddering and his face is contorted.

'Have you suffered enough?' This time I can hear, quite clearly, the distress underlying the authoritarian harshness.

'I can never suffer enough for what I have done.' He sounds almost haunted. 'Punish me now, please.'

Amber removes her hand from his hard penis and bends over to take him in her mouth. Again she begins by sucking him slowly and tenderly, her body swaying softly back and forth as he holds her head. Then, either prompted by some unseen gesture by Jake or because she has precognition, Amber lifts her face from his cock and, baring her teeth like some madwoman, lunges down to deliver a series of bites all the way down his shaft. This time he does cry out, partly in pain, partly in degradation, but mostly, I suspect, in pleasure.

'Harder, harder, bite clean through it and I'll never hurt another woman again!'

Suddenly I'm aware that I am shuddering with a strange sickening excitement. I am also wet between the legs. Unable to help myself I pull my skirt from beneath my hips and settle my clit on the very edge of the rough bench.

Amber continues to nip and gnaw at him, moving her mouth up and down, gripping onto the root of his cock as if wanting to squeeze the spunk from it. But after several minutes during which I am sure Jake must be on the point of orgasm she suddenly lifts her mouth and says in a voice now undisguisedly tearful.

'Don't you think you've been punished enough now, Jake?'

He looks down at her as if seeing her after a long absence. 'Ah, sweetheart, I've made you cry. I didn't want to do that. You do what you see fit, whatever you need to.'

She chokes back her tears and puts his penis back in her mouth. This time her head moves rapidly and he holds her shoulders as she works her mouth expertly around his cock. Almost immediately his body tenses, he throws his head back and, just before releasing his seed, pulls her head from his cock. I see the sudden spurt of white which splashes and trickles on her hair and face to run with the remains of her spent tears and some fresh ones too.

'Why do you never let me drink you?' she sobs in a broken way. 'You deny me your seed always, always.'

'You want too much from an old man,' he replies in a

tone of light jocularity, but one which is tinged with sadness.

They're still kneeling on the floor and he picks up the unravelled toga and proceeds to wipe the tears and semen from her skin as if she is a child with a dirty face.

Then he lies back on the rough floor and, using his body as a resting place, holds her on it. Ashamed and desperately aroused, I rub myself frantically on the harsh edge of wood between my legs and bite my lip to stop my cries at the swift fierce climax.

Now the faces on the pictures on the wall are vivid with a sun that is now lighting up the top half of the room with obscene brightness. And all the painted mouths that smile seem to be laughing at me and at my exclusion and all the eyes that are dark with melancholy seem to know and are content to conceal the secret sadness behind the scene I have just witnessed.

I sit sipping, hardly tasting the coffee I have let go cold, gazing around at the absolutely spotless, twenty-years-out-of-date kitchen, wondering what it is that makes Jake preserve so slavishly the settings from his past.

Then I look up as he comes in from the noon sun, alone, with shirt unbuttoned, a faint sweat on his brown skin and the familiar mellow smile back in place. I can't meet his eyes. I am unable to reconcile his easy manner with the troubled soul I have just glimpsed.

'Aren't you going to eat?' He sits opposite me at the small table. 'You have a long afternoon ahead of you.'

'I couldn't eat.'

'Don't tell me you're nervous,' he says mischievously. 'Not after last night's little exhibition. Imagine letting them believe I had a teenage girl trussed up in agony for my own pleasure. Really, Larissa.'

I blush. 'I know. I'm sorry. I was a bit . . . out of myself last night.'

His expression softens. He reaches across the table, touches my hand. 'That's OK. We all do it from time to time.' He laughs. 'God knows, we need the release.' I glance into his eyes and think for a moment, he knows. He knows I saw everything this morning.

But then he says quickly, 'Anyway, I think you'll enjoy modelling immensely. Don't look so worried, sweetheart.' He raises my hand to his mouth and brushes his lips over my knuckles. 'Haven't you always been able to trust me?'

His eyes shine. I think, yes, Jake, but that was then. Maybe I don't even know you any more.

At two in the afternoon I leave my room, wearing a bathrobe, and walk along the shadowed hall like a woman about to be executed. Greg has told me to meet him so he can dress me, but I'm sure he hasn't said where. I walk leadenly towards the room with the four-poster bed, pausing only to glance out the window when I hear the terrifying sound of light-hearted chatter and laughter rippling through the summer afternoon.

The students have gathered, smoking, leaning against their cars splashed bright with sun. Some are showing each other their sketches made the previous day. Fingers are pointed, small admiring sounds made, but also shoulder shrugging and more laughter which I, in my heightened state, take to be of a taunting nature. Wait till they see me, I think.

'Oh God, I can't do this,' I whisper to the brazen carefree heavens.

'Yes, you can, darling.'

Greg comes up behind me and slips his hands around my waist. I rest my head on his shoulder, glad of the support.

'I'm petrified.'

'You'll relax into it. Don't worry, I'm an expert at getting models to loosen up.'

'Don't tell me,' I say weakly, 'it's your thing.'

He takes my hand, leads me into the bathroom and locks the door.

Scraps and lengths and squares of material, raw and in made-up costumes, lie in an exquisite heap in the middle

101

of the floor. Two large make-up boxes sit at either side of the sink.

'Is it alright for me to get dressed in here?' I ask doubtfully. 'What if other people need to use the ... facilities?' I finish up surreally, like an old schoolmistress.

'There's a bog downstairs they can use. Anyway, this isn't just where you're dressing. This, dearest one, is to be your stage for the next few hours.'

I look around in alarm: the large tub, the sunken bath, the huge marble seats and a few thick towels; no hiding place. I had at least imagined I could camouflage myself in the folds of bed linen.

'But what will I wear?' I ask hoarsely.

Greg begins to sort through the bundle on the floor.

'Jake wanted you naked ...' he says cheerfully.

'Oh no!'

'... But I said we'd get much more mileage from the session if you were clothed, at least partly.'

'At least.' I sit down on the edge of the bath feeling quite faint.

'He took some persuading, he's an awkward sod when he likes to be. In fact, he's been more of a stubborn old fart than usual. I'm wondering whether our little business relationship is running its course.'

'He called you a queen this morning,' I mutter to the deep unwelcoming hollow of the tub.

'Now, what can you wear?' Greg lifts, examines and discards into the air length after length of vibrant cloth. The marble floor is like a sea, crazily strewn with snakes.

'That one!' I leap up from the bath. A bundle of silver satin has been exposed in the diminishing pile. Greg picks it up, looks at it doubtfully.

It is very old, edged with lace and has tiny seed buttons, a long, slightly tatty, but still magnificent Victorian-type gown.

'Well I really don't know,' says Greg doubtfully. 'It's certainly nothing like what J F had in mind.'

'I just don't think I'd feel comfortable in anything else. Besides isn't it *your* job to organise the models?'

'Yes, alright. We'll need to make some adjustments though.'

He brushes my hair till it gleams, then perversely backcombs it until it looks as if I've slept on it for a week. He paints my face sparingly so that my cheeks are radiant and my eyes shine. My complexion looks like satin.

I gaze at myself in the bathroom mirror. 'It's not the look I'd have imagined with that dress.'

'Well, I was thinking earth mother meets whore extraordinaire – a more mature compelling look.'

I'm not sure whether I'm being insulted or not.

'I used to have fantasies when I was seventeen about wearing a dress like this . . .' My nervously garbled words are smothered by the dress being pulled over my head. 'Steve would carry me to bed and put his hand up my skirt.'

'Who's Steve?'

'My ex, Jake's brother. Then he'd say . . .'

'Fuck! It's too tight.'

'. . . Then he'd say, "I'm going to undo each of these tiny buttons very slowly and kiss each of your nipples until you're wild with anticipation . . ."'

'Fucking good idea. That'll get round it.'

'What are you talking about, Greg? Please, listen to me. I need to talk otherwise I'll pass out with fear.'

'Sorry, my darling.'

I watch the two of us in the mirror. He kisses my neck. I do look like a sort of earth-mother-whore. The dress is neat on its capped sleeve shoulders, tight at the waist and flowing and generous below and . . . completely open at the front. I stare at my small exposed breasts in horror.

'Tits out for the boys, Lara. It's the only way. It won't fasten. Don't worry, you look amazing.'

Before I can draw breath there is an urgent knocking on the door.

'Greg, two minutes to go. I've a lot of people here. Are you ready, man?'

103

My face in the mirror freezes in alarm. Greg gives me a reassuring smile and goes to open the door.

The students troop in one after another, carrying stools and pads and pencils, smiling cordially at me while I stiffen in a kind of shocked grimace.

Jake comes in and bangs the door shut. I jump.

'Right, people back – back against the wall.'

Once again I am reminded of a ringmaster and his animals at the circus.

Having settled everyone, he comes forward to examine me. He looks me up and down as if I am a tailor's dummy. A variety of expressions – mild surprise, perplexity, exasperation – come and go in his face. Finally he frowns and takes Greg aside. The spatterings of conversation among the students become more sporadic. A dozen pairs of interested eyes home in on me standing in my frozen idiocy. I glance down and notice a six-inch tear at the foot of my dress. I wonder if anyone has noticed. Someone has. Falling to his knees in front of me, Jake takes either side of the material and rips the dress right up the front. His eyes are level with my naked pubes. There are one or two ripples of laughter from the back of the room and I glance across at Greg who reddens. Jake gets to his feet. He winks at me.

'Much better, Larissa, don't you think?'

I am speechless. Greg grudgingly agrees.

'Right, let's go.' Jake walks briskly back to the students. 'Set her up.'

'You'd think I was a pack of cards,' I mutter as Greg takes me by the hand across to the window. A large wicker chair has been placed in front of it.

'Sit with one leg draped over the side,' he says softly. 'That's right, but lean back, look languid, well shagged. Give them a slight self-satisfied smile.'

I glance over his shoulder at the row of watching students. The man I saw yesterday with the erection is now jiggling change in his corduroy pocket. The earnest young woman with the deep frown and plaited hair is doodling on a tightly held pad. I realise that several of the women are younger than me. I look down at my open legs and knickerless crotch, my small breasts, my unpainted fingernails which start to tremble on the silver satin.

'I can't look at them at all,' I hiss at Greg. 'I can't or I'll throw up.'

'What we want here is emotions, sense of personality. Remember she's not a piece of meat.' Jake is walking back and forth in front of the class looking slightly bored.

'Turn your head at an angle,' whispers Greg. 'Stare at the marble. Yep, fine.'

'Would you mind telling me how we can do fucking emotions if we can't even see the model's fucking face?'

I wince and colour; stare like a frightened rabbit at the swirling blue and green, wishing it was a vortex that would pull me in.

'I figured she'd make a far more enigmatic subject in profile. She has a slight sneer in her mouth . . .'

I twist my mouth vaguely at the manic wall of sea. I think how wonderful it would be to drown.

'. . . The emotions should come out in the tensions of the body muscles. It'll be a bit of a test for everyone.' Greg finishes glibly.

'Well folks, Mr Landsdowne has decided it part of his remit to set you a little test. I suggest you get on with it.'

The sound of Jake's footsteps slapping down on the marble comes nearer until I can see him out of the corner of my eye, about five feet away from me, sitting cross-legged on the floor, sketch-pad in hand. With my distorted vision I am convinced he is glaring at me.

I hold the position for a short period, perhaps about ten minutes, but it seems to stretch interminably. Thankfully, my trembling ceases and a state of transfixed shock sets in as I dimly sense the frenzied scratching of Jake's pencil. I think of Greg's instructions to look 'languid, well shagged' and know I have failed miserably.

Unexpectedly, just as I feel I might pass out if I have to stare much more at the encroaching wall of seething ocean, Jake rises and claps his hands.

'OK. That's enough of that. All change.'

I raise my leg back over the chair. It feels heavy, alien to my body. I put my knees modestly together as I feel Jake's eyes on me. His sketch is on the floor and I notice he has drawn me naked anyway.

'Is that the session . . . finished?' I ask.

'That's it started.' He is actually frowning at my naked breasts.

'We need to get theses nips hard,' he mutters. 'That was a warm up. Do you feel warmed up, Lara. I have to say you were a bit wooden.'

I rise and walk furiously towards Greg who is arranging mattress-like blocks of foam inside the sunken bath.

'What now?' I whisper.

'In the tub.' He looks at me almost apologetically. 'The goddess rising from the ocean or then again maybe drowning.'

He puts the last bit of foam in place and kisses me on the cheek.

'I'm drowning,' I say flatly.

'Bad as that, my darling?' He brushes a gentle hand over my hair and face.

'We're going to have to mess you up a bit for this.' The shock of Jake's voice behind me makes me jump.

I feel his hand on my shoulder, then, quite harshly, he turns me away from Greg to face him.

I gaze at him breathlessly as he runs his thumb and forefinger around the collar, the shoulders, then down one side of the front of my dress, his hand grazing my nipple. I am angry and amazed but, despite myself, I begin to feel a warm glow of excitement. Then I realise that it is only the dress that concerns him. His dark fervent eyes are tracing a path down the satin seams, not my body.

'Ah! Here,' he says suddenly and, with one crude movement, rips the material where it is thinning from the neck down about ten inches, completely revealing my right breast.

The girl with the plaits nudges her large-busted friend

and they both giggle. The buzz of conversation ceases completely. My face blazes. Jake seems unaware of my embarrassment.

'What are you doing?'

He squats and makes another large hem-to-waist rent in the material.

I gaze imploringly at Greg. His eyes are burning.

'I think you guys should take ten minutes,' he calls back to the class.

With the three of us left in the room and Jake now pulling the cap sleeve suspended to a flimsy scrap of the remaining material back off my shoulder, Greg stands close beside him.

'Go easy there, boss,' he starts in a fairly affable tone but when ignored continues darkly, 'She's not a piece of meat, remember.'

Jake glances from one to the other of us then says quietly, 'Sorry, Lara. I didn't mean to be rough with you.'

He turns, walks to the window, pushes it right open and stands smoking, looking out.

I am trembling from annoyance and apprehension.

'Do you want anything?' Greg picks up a heavily beaded lilac shawl and wraps it around my shoulders, although it is warm in the room.

'Just to get out of here,' I whisper, trying to laugh.

Both of us glance over at the unmindful Jake as if we are involved in some kind of conspiracy.

'I'll speak to him if you like,' Greg murmurs. His voice and his eyes are kind but there is a hint of regret there too.

'No, fuck him! I won't be intimidated at my age.' I take off the shawl and throw it away theatrically. The weight of the beading carries it across the room. It hits Jake on the shoulder then falls. He brushes off its impact as if brushing away an insect.

'Besides, I don't want to screw up your session,' I finish weakly.

'Here.' He hands me some bottled water and two small

brown tablets. 'Herbal tranquillisers. Just to take the edge off.'

For the best part of ten minutes Jake has been working my limbs, my torso, my hair and my face as if I'm a rubber doll. I've been sitting, kneeling and lying on my stomach with my lower leg raised. He has piled my hair up and let it fall back again. Every touch has been mechanical. No eye contact has been made at all. I am annoyed, yet I am aware of his strength, the ease with which he flips me from my side to my back and I feel the first stirrings of arousal between my legs. If only he would look into my eyes. He's piled up the foam layers until it appears that I'm sitting on some kind of volcano construction. Then he has taken them away and made me kneel, peering over the side, so that I must look as if I'm about to crawl out of a hole.

The herbal pills are having an odd effect on me. I don't feel relaxed. But I am experiencing a sort of light-headedness, a vague feeling of nausea and the sensation that I might drift into a kind of nervy sleep at any moment.

Greg has been talking to the rest of the class, looking at their first sketches, to fill in time, becoming increasingly on edge the longer Jake is taking. Finally, glancing at his watch, he walks forward.

'Shouldn't we get started?' he ventures cautiously.

'But I don't think we're saying anything, yet.' Jake looks at me doubtfully.

'Perhaps we should have Lara lying on her side to start off with. Just let them use their imagination. They're still at an early stage.'

Contrary to my expectations Jake doesn't argue with this. He looks at my now cross-legged form and says quietly, 'Maybe you're right.'

Greg puts me in position, on my side, one leg bent and raised, the strip of torn satin Jake has made snaking between my thighs.

'Alright?' he whispers.

'Sort of.'

The truth is I feel dizzy and disorientated, wishing I hadn't taken the pills on an empty stomach. However, the faces of the students near the wall are pleasantly blurry. I take a deep breath and focus on a point in the middle of the room.

'OK, everyone forward!' Jake's rather exasperated yell startles me into alertness.

I look up in alarm as he and Greg lead the advancing army of students and their barrage of chairs towards me. 'This'll make it work, a better view,' Jake says with satisfaction.

They settle themselves in a semi-circle about eight feet from me, Jake at one side, Greg at the other.

Almost immediately, as the hub of activity quietens, I begin to tremble. I stare fixedly at the brown brogues of the man with yesterday's erection, but the arm supporting my head judders, my chin quivers, my bent leg twitches violently. To disguise it I move my thigh, quite visibly, further in.

'Jesus Christ, Lara! Don't you think we've wasted enough time? Just hold the damned position.' Jake steps fiercely towards me.

'I can't.' l hear the feeble croak of my voice and stare miserably at the small tear in the knee of his jeans as he stands, now about a foot away. His breath comes in loud furious bursts. At the side of his leg, the round-faced woman with her white hair piled high gives me a small sympathetic smile.

He bends down so that our faces are level with each other. For the first time that afternoon he looks straight into my eyes. From the corner of my vision I see Greg rise.

'Would you mind telling me exactly why you agreed to do this if, as you say, you "can't"?' On the word 'can't' he contorts his voice into a sneering feminine imitation of my own.

'That's not fair, Jake.' Greg is now sitting on the edge of the bath. He puts a protective hand on my shoulder.

'It isn't you know,' the round-faced woman peers over Jake's shoulder from a slightly misty near distance.

'Damn right, it isn't.' I hurl myself upright, rocking on my soft bed and almost falling forward onto Jake's shoulder. I manage to stop myself a few furious inches in front of his face.

'I had no choice but to do this. *You* wanted it to be some humiliating little entertainment where you would be the great master and I would be some grovelling sycophantic prop in scanty knickers. You have made a fool of me and jeapordised the class. You love your little power games, don't you Jake? Well this has backfired and shown you up as a thoughtless selfish bastard!'

All through my speech various shades of surprise and anger have come and gone in his face. I have refused to let him interrupt although he has tried several times. But on my last venomous outburst his expression changes. All passionate feeling drains from his features until he looks dazed and saddened. He lowers his eyes then rises, turns to Greg and says evenly, 'Maybe you could take over for a while.'

He walks from the room searching the usual pocket for his cigarettes. My mind flashes back to the morning when I watched him in the lurid gloom of the summer-house with Amber. He hates himself, I think, as the white-haired lady gives me a rather eccentric thumbs up sign. The two young girls smile and murmur their assent; most of the men look vacant, bemused or embarrassed.

Half an hour later and the class is sketching contentedly. I'm lying once more on my side, with a slick of material between my legs and my breasts exposed by the tatters of satin. I'm also wearing a blindfold of organza, the ends of which are long as ropes and are wound around Greg's wrists. He lies behind me.

'It was the "power games" speech that did it for me,' he whispers cheerfully.

With the blindfold in place, I am no longer intimidated by my audience. I can retreat inside my head and inside the wonderful sensations softening my tense body and ravaged spirit.

'But what exactly do you want us to draw?' queried a raw-faced youth, as Greg shamelessly pulled off his shirt and trousers and knelt beside me, organza strip held aloft like a banner.

'Whatever you fucking like, chief,' he'd said, settling himself behind me with the whispered words, 'Wiggle your arse and give me a hard-on.'

For about five minutes we have been lying quite still but for the building pressure between my buttocks and his firm abdomen and rigid cock. I have the urge to reach back and touch him, make him touch me, at the front. The herbal medicine is now working perfectly and I melt against him, my consciousness ebbing into momentary half-sleeps against his chest then sharpening in tiny bursts of pleasure at the growing urgency in our bodies.

'Are you getting wet?' he whispers.

'Mmmm, yes.'

Suddenly I feel a slight grazing sensation around my clit. I think at first that Greg has inadvertently pulled on the strip of material between my legs. Then I feel it again, the satin tightening and moving through my lips pressing, then leaving, my clit.

'Is the model supposed to be smiling like that? She wasn't before.'

I am certain that the well-spoken, but rather excited, voice belongs to the man who had yesterday's erection. I am also sure that he is beginning to get one now, sensing what is happening to me. The thought of him becoming more and more aroused till he loses control excites me even more. I become warm and swollen between the legs, the soft expectant ache spreading through my lower body.

Then I feel the palm of Greg's hand clamp hard against my cunt. I gasp, wondering if this can be seen by the students. I hear the man with the erection clear his throat. A couple of people shift in their seats.

'Don't let it show in your face, Lara. Remember, keep in control. And absolutely, definitely, do not come.'

Greg's barely audible murmur has a cold demanding edge to it and for a moment this is enough to still my growing arousal. But, as his firm hand begins to work alternately with the rhythmic massage of my clit by the now exceedingly taut band of satin, I find it almost impossible to keep my face immobile, my voice silent and, with my exquisitely tortured body writhing and craving his, I feel my juices seep, then leak copiously into my satin strap, soaking his expert fingers. The only way I can prevent myself pulsating towards climax is to bring to mind images of Jake naked and humiliated being slapped and bitten by Amber, while some other torture deep within him darkens his already sorrowful eyes.

For what seems like an age, I maintain my rigid position, while inside me colours of yellow and red flood alternately, then in unison, while I climb a mountain, then quiver a while on a plateau; while stars on the point of explosion suddenly melt. Just when I think such seething ecstasy can't be borne much longer and I must will myself to faint, I hear the door open and the sound of Jake's slow, loudening footsteps come nearer.

As they do, Greg's hand and the friction of the satin strip slowly cease.

I hold my breath, dazed by a mixture of fear, excitement and expectation, waiting for one of them to speak but there are long black seconds of silence until, to my astonishment, I hear Greg say in a curt over-officious manner, 'Right Lara, change of position.'

I feel him flip me over onto my back. The already tight band around my head tightens more and the long, gauzy trails of it are snaked deftly around my wrists, my arms are drawn smartly above my head and the ends of the strip are attached to something. When I stretch out my quivering fingertips I realise that I am anchored to the taps.

I can almost smell the tension in the room. There are

scattered whisperings and murmurs. I can hear someone's nearby breathing. I sense that Jake is very near.

When I feel Greg's first touch on my inner thigh, I spread my legs, my overwhelming desire for gratification together with an impossible fantasy planting its seed in my mellow psyche, overtaking my few remaining inhibitions. I keep thinking Jake has never seen me open my legs like this and I open them further. The wet satin is lifted from my cunt and the tip of a hand, hard and purposeful, enters me and I shudder. A mouth wets and caresses my hard nipple and I moan, unable to help it.

'OK. That's it folks. Time up now, class dismissed.' Jake's voice is calm and businesslike, betraying no sign of emotion.

A veiled clamour rumbles through the students, but soon I hear chairs being scraped back. Greg's thumb begins a slow circular massage of my clit and my hips squirm in growing abandonment. I hear the man with the erection quickly croak, 'excuse me' and walk hurriedly from the room. I wonder whether he has already come in his trousers or is rushing to the downstairs loo to bring himself off.

I rub my foot on Greg's lower back as his tongue licks then thrusts its way into my cunt. A window is flung open and the sound of trees and the warm smell of summer fill the room.

'You too, Greg. You've done enough for an afternoon.' Jake's even voice with just a slight edge on the last words stills Greg's tongue in me.

'No!' I protest, but my voice sounds far away, dreamlike. I feel very dizzy.

Without another word I sense Greg leave me. A breeze passes over the wetness of my damp body. In the quiet of the rustling trees the door closes.

I pull on my shackles. My heart starts to thud; irregularly, loudly. The wicker chair is being scraped along the floor towards me.

'Who is it? Who's there? It's you Jake, isn't it? Isn't it? Untie me please. Please I'm scared . . . I feel sick.'

Suddenly my distorted senses tell me it's not Jake or even Greg that now sits watching me on the wicker chair, but someone who is going to harm me, perhaps the man with the erection. Any minute now I'll feel his spindly desperate body crawl into me like some death-bestowing insect. Or worse, he might want to punish me for acting like a whore. Oh Christ, when will the first blow come?

'Please,' I wail. 'Please, I can't stand this. Say something.'

Then I feel him move over me, feel and smell the warmth of his body as, after a moment's hesitation, he comes to lie beside me and wrap his arms firmly around my upper body. I feel the outline of his shirted cigarette packet on my breast. My near hysteria exultantly moves into a choking gasping half-laugh.

'Thank God, oh, thank God.' My wet face is buried in his neck.

'I'm sorry, Larissa.' The only words he says, just once, in a quiet husky voice.

He doesn't untie me, but supports me with his arms. My naked leg snakes around his hard, clothed thigh. I know my juices, the juices caused by another man's touch will stain him. For a while, as my post-crying shudders cease and his mouth lies motionless in my hair, I drift into a kind of half-sleep where the scented sighs of the trees makes me feel again every charmed summer of my life.

Then I feel his lips move, touching my brow, lingering mysteriously on each of my shielded eyes. There is a short, slight tickle of a kiss on my nose and then his mouth covers mine so perfectly I believe I have been waiting for it forever. His kisses are soft as a child's then hard as a demon's, wet and nourishing, then hot and teasing. He kisses me until I feel myself dissolve.

His fingers travel their soft, knowing, desolate journey from my neck to my nipples as they strain towards him, to my wet, hot, needy cunt and back. And down and back again. In secret acquiescence neither of us speaks, but my lower body twists and rises to be nearer the firm

114

power of his thigh, my clit throbbing towards his cock, craving its fulfilment and the ecstatic moment of delivery. He holds me so gently in my bonds, but his body tells me he wants to fuck me as he has never done to anyone before.

Finally, when his hand is drenched with my moisture and the wave of pleasure he is sending through my body comes faster and deeper, I thrust my pelvis urgently towards the rigid outline of his erection. Then he stops. His fingers rest. His breathing quietens as if he has a lifetime of thinking to do before slamming his cock between my legs. I wriggle, I moan, I sob. I wish desperately that my hands were free and I could just reach for him and put him there. Please, please release your cock and fuck me.

After an eternity, the arm supporting my upper body moves abruptly lower to encircle my waist. Before I realise what's happening he has me firmly in his power and, when his fingers tenderly, then firmly, lightly, then pulsating with varying degrees of finely tuned pressure, come for my clit, I am helpless. For perhaps about a minute I try to follow Greg's instructions about controlling my arousal. I revisit the sad, the disturbing vignettes of my life, I bring to mind once more the pain in Jake's eyes that morning, but this time the memory bestows me with a terrible poignant desire to kill that hurt. But I must withhold orgasm so that he gives me what I want. I need, long for, his cock so much. Inside. Inside. The word whispers through my head like the breeze in the trees. But still he coaxes me so sweetly, so deftly, so irresistibly, and I am getting weaker, drowning in my bliss. I feel I will float off and that the only thing keeping me in the tangible world is the strength of his embrace and the genius of his touch. He kisses me again, just once, softly, but simultaneously inserts the top of his thumb inside me, rolling the ball of it hard over my clit. It's enough. I feel my head jerk back, my bonds tighten and pull, my hips and open legs heave in spasm towards him as the waves of pleasure inside me rise to a crescendo and crash into sweet blackness. Then everything is dark and fading fast.

I push myself up groggily on my soft support. The windows are firmly closed and the sky beyond the trees a shade or two darker than I last remember seeing it. My white towelling robe has been tucked in around my body. My silver dress has been removed and my bonds are gone. I examine my wrists. There are no marks. I glance around the room. Apart from my foam bed I could almost believe the afternoon's events have never happened.

Chapter Five

*I*t's midsummer's day and a small bush beneath my balcony, shy and nondescript since I arrived, has now burst into red bloom. And so it has joined the ranks of the elevated, the ostentatious flowers scattered around the garden showing their true colours as June deepens.

Greg and I are to drive to the beach. I wear a dress of dark pink cotton, dyed and altered so it adheres closely to my body as I move. I look in the mirror and brush my lengthening summer-kissed hair with satisfaction. But the sun is changing position in the sky and the mid-morning shadow creeps into my room. I stretch out my foot and dip it into the black light. I paint my mouth determinedly pink as familiar twinges of restlessness and unease threaten to surface. My days now are usually good. My body, for so many years starved of a man's touch, is now sated; feels stronger and more glorious inside Greg's desire. In the evenings he comes with candles to banish all the ghosts that lurk within these walls. He adorns me in lace and silk, paints my face. Then we talk and lie and kiss and suck and pound each other raw until my mask is dissolved in our passion and my fine costumes and sleek underwear are discarded like gift wrapping on the floor. But in the deep of night I lie alone watching the moon between the trees. An owl hoots desolately as if in premonition or the shutters bang unexpectedly, despite an apparent lack of breeze, and I crave a man's arms to cover my nightmares, his cock to drive away the demons. And the man is not Greg.

When the knock comes on the door I drop the hairbrush. I gaze at the door handle, puckering my dress with clenched hands.

'Who is it?'

'The Grim Reaper. Who were you expecting, darling?'

Greg comes in wearing a pair of old cut-down jeans and no shoes.

'I figured there was no way you'd let me drive your car so I thought I'd come as *'au naturel'* slave boy. Here!'

He throws me a peach and walks out to the balcony. I follow him, hand him back the fruit: I have no appetite.

'I've just done my lipstick.'

I look down at the red-flowered bush. How sad that it's the only flowering plant this side of the house; a show-off on it's own.

'OK, what is it? Bad night or something?' Greg puts his hand on my chin and turns me around to face him.

'It's Jake.'

'Quelle surprise.' He places a segment of fruit at my lips so I'm forced to accept it.

'Yesterday evening I wanted to talk to him. So ... he was alone in the kitchen, Amber wasn't there ...'

'Which would never do!'

'Oh Greg, shut up. It was about the work, the plans for the house ...' I say this too vociferously. He raises his eyebrows, leans back against the railing and smirks. 'I need his input. I have to arrange dates for the electrical work, the decorators. He was just tidying up. Fanatically. I think he does much more of the housework than he lets on. Hand maidens indeed ...'

'Which is entirely relevant to the point you are about to make.'

'The point I'm about to make is that he wasn't interested. Didn't want to look at any of the drawings, barely listened to what I said about the lighting. There was a box of old photos on the worktop. All he said to me was, "Do you think it's time for a clear out, Larissa?"'

Greg wipes the juice from his palms on the front of his jeans. He looks so young, so guileless, I can't help but smile.

'Jake's like that with everyone, Lara. A great guy when he's in the mood. But then he detaches himself, checks out. It's just the way he is.'

'But I need his agreement, Greg, not this, "Do what you like, Lara".'

'That *is* agreement. The guy's giving you his consent.'

'Oh, honestly, Greg.'

'Oh, honestly, Lara.' He comes close to me, puts his hands on my buttocks presses me to him, rubs his cock, already semi-hard, against my front.

'The reason,' he continues, 'that you're pissed off, is that since he gave your pussy such a delicious seeing to, finishing what I started, by the by . . . since then, there's been no other action.'

'Greg, come on . . .'

'How was it you put it? He made you come so intensely you fainted.' He waves his hands theatrically in the air.

'I didn't say that at all. I fainted because I hadn't eaten all day and you gave me those hellish herbal things.'

'Excuse *me* for being a mate.' He puts his hand inside my dress and reaches between my legs. 'Nice one. No knickers. Horny bint.'

'Oh fuck off, I thought we'd be swimming.'

'Fuck off yourself. *Can* I drive?'

'No.'

We take a detour to the beach, driving into the country then looping back. The fields smell fresh and the sky is radiant. It has been a dazzling fortnight weatherwise.

Greg smiles at me from time to time, reassuringly, saying nothing, as if he knows the darkness inside me. I think again of my encounter with Jake. How desperately I wanted to see his admiration, his delight as I arranged sketch after sketch, fragments of sky and sea in all their poignant moods onto his spotless worktop.

'Students at our old college are going to make them, paint and finish them, the lot.' I was breathless as I gazed into his blank eyes. 'Screens, you see. You can lower them and raise them when you want. It'll change the whole house.'

'Not the whole house, Lara.'

His eyes were dark in the evening light.

'No, I realise which rooms you want left,' I'd said quickly, my mouth dry.

'Ah, poor Lara.' His expression softened and his hand was on my cheek. 'I'm sure a few weeks of bringing a new world into my run-down home will be good for your soul. I'm not sure, however, that the magic will work for me.'

From the pile he was sorting, he placed a photograph, carelessly, on top of my work. It was black and white, dented by his thumb. It was a girl, alone against the clouds, in silhouette. Suddenly the thrill of anticipation of weeks of creating the sky and experimenting with paint as bright as sunshine, evaporated.

Greg leans forward pressing the 'on' button of the cassette.

> *You're a girl from a different world*
> *Can't wait for you any more*
> *Flash your eyes then let me be*
> *Send kisses from your door*

'What the fuck's that?'

I smile to myself, remembering. 'Before your time, my child.'

'I'm sorry, Lara. I didn't mean to offend you.'

I glance at Greg. These chinks of boyish insecurity in his bravado are perhaps what I like most about him. That and . . .

I reach across and thrust my hand inside the leg of his shorts.

'Jesus!'

As usual he becomes erect almost straight away. I slide my fingers along the shaft of his cock, gripping it slightly at the end and then caressing it tighter on the way down before cupping his balls.

'You're becoming the assertive one,' he murmurs, head back on the seat, biting his lip.

I take my hand away to change gear. When I put it back I feel the oiliness already on the tip of his cock. I rub my thumb and forefinger against and then inside his foreskin.

'To what do I owe this little delight?'

He reaches down and unzips himself. His cock springs free.

I move my hand quicker and harder until he begins to arch his back.

> Open your arms and set me free
> Don't need you any more

'Variation on a theme,' I tell him and pull over.

I lift my skirt, stretch my thigh over his leg, rub myself on his knee. I know by his closed eyes and light grimace that he is trying not to come, trying to relish the moment. As the music rises I think of that long ago summer, masturbating on my handbag strap imagining Jake's cock thrust into me, Steve driving as if possessed, oblivious to my damp knickers and determination not to squirm. How I wanted to come. Desperately.

Now I stroke the silk of Greg's hair, and work his shaft for all I'm worth.

'Let go, angel,' I whisper, partly for him, partly for that unhappy teenage girl. 'Let it all go.'

Almost immediately he groans and judders up towards me and back as a hot blast of come drenches the front of my dress. His head falls forward onto my breasts. I am still massaging my clit on his knee and getting wetter when he looks up at me with a reverential gaze which renders me motionless.

'What?' I smile at him, bewildered. To my astonishment I see tears in his eyes. 'Greg, what is it? Tell me.'

'Just your voice. The way you spoke to me just now. It reminded me of someone.' His voice breaks a little.

'Greg. What? Please.'

But quickly he recovers, pushes me gently off him, kisses my nipples through my semen-soaked dress and says brightly, 'Tell you what, you don't half give a good hand job for an old lady.'

Greg is like a child on the beach, grabbing my hand and dragging me into the sea while we are both still dressed.

We stand thigh deep in the waves and he caresses me through the tight wet cotton.

I try to settle myself on his thigh as he presses my hips against him, but the wet band of material won't yield.

'Dear, dear. Does poor Lara need Greg to give her a little orgasm?'

He tries to raise my dress as we laugh and sway in the unpredictable swell.

'Lara can wait,' I say in a firm voice. 'I want to get out of this dress and go for a swim.'

I convince myself that the deeper, colder water will calm the flickers of desire within my body. My fervent nights and days with Greg have made me realise that denial of quick fulfilment and build-up of desire do indeed result in the best orgasms.

We return to the foam where Greg discards his shorts and carefully lifts the dress over my head. Tiny rivulets of red-pink water trickle down my body and into the ocean.

He traces his fingers down their path: the rosy streaks on my shoulders; my breasts; my abdomen; my thighs. I shiver.

'You're like a water-colour running in the rain,' he says softly.

My dress and his shorts are lapped by the edge of the

122

waves, moving closer together with each fresh wetting until, deserted by the tide, they lie quite still on top of each other. I gaze at them a moment, pleased. Greg smiles and takes my hand.

'Come on. Race you.'

He swims more energetically than I do, more courageously. But I keep up with him and we don't stop until we are far out. Then he lies back and floats at peace with the brilliant sky and the roll of the sea. I tread water breathless and apprehensive. The shore seems a long way off.

'How deep do you think it is here?' I find it hard to keep the anxiety out of my voice.

'Don't know. There's a sharp dip around these parts though.' He flips himself into an upright position beside me. 'You're not scared are you? You've been deeper than this in the sea pool.'

I begin to swim back towards the shore.

'I know. It's just the vastness of the ocean. Not knowing what's underneath.'

He draws level with me. 'You sound like Celine.' He swims on his side his face averted.

'Celine?'

He begins to move faster through the water, speaking quickly as if forcing, punching out the words.

'My stepsister. She came to live with us on the coast . . . Fucking terrified of the water, Celine.'

'Greg, hold on.'

But he slices ahead through the water as if it's a race, or as if he's being chased. I catch up as he is wading through the shallows. I touch his shoulder.

'You were telling me about Celine being terrified of the water.'

He sits down heavily in the foam, breathing harshly. He presses his fingers against his eyes as if clearing water from them.

'Nothing to tell,' he says airily, 'I taught her to swim, that's all.'

* * *

Our clothes are draped over the bulky dune grass to dry in the noon sun. We make our own towelled niche in a small parting in the thick tall green. For a while we sit neatly, side by side, gazing contentedly out to sea. Then he squeezes the salty sea from my hair, strokes the wetness from my skin and massages sunscreen into my back and shoulders, and my breasts, paying special attention to my nipples.

'Can't afford to hurt these little treasures,' he whispers, circling them again and again with the gentlest touch. I lean back against his shoulder letting my thighs fall open as his fingers lubricate the skin inside my legs and up towards my sex lips. Then his thumb strays inside their moist folds. He slicks it back and forth a couple of times.

We fall back and against one another. I wrap my leg around his waist and his erection slides against my clit.

His embrace is very strong, urgent; he has one arm around my back, drawing me to him so close that I can't move anywhere but further into him. His other arm cradles my head. He kisses me hungrily, parting my lips. He seems much needier than usual, less in control. But I am becoming quickly aroused and I don't want it to be over too soon. I want my lower body to ache with desire while he speaks to me, maybe stroking my wrist, looking into my eyes. I want to have to force myself not to squirm, when we sit side by side, our legs touching then pressing together.

'You're clingy today,' I murmur, when his lips leave mine for a moment, when he moves a small way back to gaze at me, smiling.

'You're complaining, are you?' His eyes are warm, teasing.

I reach down and caress his balls.

'Course not,' I whisper. 'It's just what happened in the car. It seems to have had an effect on you.'

He moves further back from me, just a little. He is still smiling, but his eyes shine less. Suddenly, instinctively I make a connection but don't stop to ponder whether I should pursue it.

'It's Celine isn't it, your stepsister? I reminded you of her and it's upset you.'

Abruptly, we are apart. Greg sits swaying slightly, his hands clasped tight in front of his knees. I notice that his erection has all but subsided.

'Look, I'm sorry. I've obviously said the wrong thing.'

Without looking at me he twists around and reaches into a basket containing some food. After groping around he produces a bottle and a corkscrew.

'Open that will you?' he says quietly.

While I remove the cork he looks around as if expecting someone else to appear on the deserted sand. Finally he looks towards the sky.

I hand him the bottle. He drinks deeply, closing his eyes before handing it back to me. A group of gulls hover over the receding ocean, moving neither up nor down, circling aimlessly.

'I'm not really into this sort of thing,' he says at last, looking down at the grooves our bodies have made in the sand, 'I'll make it brief. Celine is a few years older than me. I was about nine when she came. She was twelve, thirteen, something like that. My mother and her father – *not* a good combination. He was such a shit, Lara. Celine and I joined forces to devise ways we could dodge his temper, for all of us. I've two younger sisters as well, you see. That's how the dressing up started. The land of make-believe.' He gives me a quick apologetic smile, almost meeting my eyes but not quite.

'Oh Greg . . .' I stretch my hand out, but he doesn't take it. Instead he reaches for my other hand and the bottle.

'Give it here, you!' Once more the cheeky grin is radiant on his face, the sad little boy inside scuttling back to the past.

He takes a small drink and snuggles closer to me, putting the bottle dramatically to my lips.

'Seeing as you're so determined to play truth or dare

125

instead of letting me give you the rodgering of your life, it's your turn now – the life and times of Lara and J F.'

'Oh forget it, Greg, I've given you chapter and verse of 1979 – teenage angst and staring at the ceiling with my legs apart wondering if I smell down there. What else is there to say?'

'How about, what you're going to do next?'

I sit in silence contemplating this, drinking too quickly. I mull over the times I have seen Jake in the last fortnight: a couple of encounters in the garden, passing each other in the sunlight, lingering awkwardly, then going in different directions; the two or three meals we have shared, all four of us, him with Amber, me with Greg. All *so* comfortable and friendly. As if I was the Lara of twenty years ago, Jake is kind, half-amused and sometimes plain dismissive.

But then I've caught him looking at me or, more precisely, we have been caught looking at each other. Underneath my glistening eye shadow, my glossy lips, inside the sensual wrappings Greg has created for my body, I gaze at him with a desire that is primitive and unadorned. For a moment our eyes lock. Then Amber speaks or the music changes and the spell, which almost worked, fails, and he squeezes Amber's thigh or whacks her bottom. She, delighted, kisses his neck and I glance down at my whorish veils and I wonder.

'It's not going to happen, Greg,' I tell him matter-of-factly and knock back some more wine.

We lie on our sides facing each other. He raises his knee and buries it between my legs.

'It will if you stop behaving like a schoolgirl every time you come within six feet of him. There's no point dressing like a tramp if you're going to act like a virgin.'

I tighten myself around his thigh forcing my lips against him. 'There, slave-boy. Go to work.'

'See what I mean,' he says working his muscles subtly between my legs. 'You would never speak to J F like that.'

126

I blush at the thought. 'But he intimidates me, Greg. He always has done.'

'Then you, my darling, are not doing what you've been taught. Focus on what you want *him* to do for you. Seduce him, woman.'

I close my eyes and drink more. The sun is hot on my body, Greg's fingertips graze my thighs and buttocks and my pussy leaks on his knee. I think he might be right.

'Smart little bastard, aren't you?' I breathe as he hits the spot once or twice and I fall right back on the sand.

'And you, dearest, are too drunk to drive and . . .'

'Oh, Christ . . . Greg, I forgot!'

The realisation propels me upwards but in a swift strong movement he pins me down with his knee jammed between my legs. My arms are spread and held at the wrists.

'And besides, you are a fantastic lover,' he concludes.

'Am I . . . really?'

He laughs and comes down to lie beside me, wrapping himself around me. 'Yes,' he says softly, 'you're very . . . very caring.'

Then, because I'm embarrassed by the compliment, or because I've had too much wine I say foolishly, 'God, you make me sound like your mother . . . or your sister.'

I feel him freeze immediately. My head is on his shoulder. I can't see his face. The sound of a motorbike, maybe more than one, comes into earshot, louder, very near, then growls away again.

'Why did you say that?' His voice is distant. His body disengages from mine.

He lies back on the sand, looking upwards. His eyes seem too dull to be seeking the sky. I am over him in an instant stroking his face, kissing his brow. He doesn't even look hurt. He looks absent. I'm annoyed with myself and worried, but most of all I have a desperate need to bring him back to me.

So I lay my body over his, as if a shield, placing one hand behind his head. I stroke his hair over and over, the

127

way I used to a long time ago with Stace when she was a child. I plant kisses gently all over his face.

'Whatever it was. It's in the past. You're with me now. You're a good person Greg. You're wonderful, lovable, special. Look what you've done for me. You deserve to be happy.'

Eventually, as my mouth moves softly over his, I see his eyes flicker.

'Wonderful, lovable, special,' he says, 'I'm honoured.'

'You should be. I intend to honour you.'

I travel down his body slowly, kissing and caressing him, at first to comfort, to ease his hurt. But then, with my hands harder on his chest and my lips sliding over the soft down on his lean dark torso, I know I want to arouse him, to make him need me desperately. I run my tongue around the area of his navel. His hands, light and uncertain on my shoulders, press harder.

'You do think I'm special, don't you Lara?' he asks in a heartbreaking voice.

'Yes, my angel, I do.'

I stroke his balls gently and massage the flesh behind them. His fingers tighten in my hair. I kiss the tip of his cock. For the first time ever it rests flaccid on his abdomen.

'I don't think I'll be any use,' he says with a rueful laugh.

'You're thinking of her, aren't you . . . Celine?'

I rub my chin against his cock, unthreatening, playful like a puppy. He hardens slightly.

'When I told you we'd hold each other when things got bad in the house . . . it was more than that . . . eventually.'

'I guessed.' I insert the tip of his cock in my mouth, suck it once or twice, withdraw. Now he is semi-erect. 'It's alright, though,' I whisper.

He raises himself on one elbow to look at me as I take him in my mouth again. He tastes of sea and baby soap. I swallow him up to the hilt, slide back and lunge at him harder. Now he is fully erect. I withdraw and rub my thumb back and forth on the tip, my fingers gently squeezing the shaft.

'Is it, though, Lara, alright?' He looks at me eagerly. I smile and nod. Then he looks like a child who has been given full marks for his homework.

'Jesus,' he says, falling back, 'you're so wise.'

Now I suck him fervently, flicking my tongue over and around his foreskin, digging, then releasing, my nails in his thighs, letting my hair brush over his chest.

'You're so beautiful,' he says in a choked wondering voice. Then timidly, 'Would you go on top? Celine used to like to. No-one has since then.' There is a silence. 'I was sixteen,' he whispers, as if he can't quite believe it himself.

I spread my thighs wide and lower myself onto his erection. I move myself on him, slowly up and down, gripping him now again with my internal muscles. When his hard body meets with my clit I feel small jolts of pleasure. I try to minimise them.

'She told me it was wrong. But I knew it wasn't.' His voice shakes with the emotion of his memory and the anticipation of his orgasm.

I bear down on him harder and faster. I feel as if I'm on horseback flying towards the sky.

'The way I see it,' I gasp, 'there are many times it is right to share our bodies, for affection, for security, for just not being alone.'

Now frenzied and ecstatic as if I've made some tremendous discovery, I have to force myself to slow. I grind my clit against him, simultaneously tightening my inside muscles as hard as I can.

'Oh, Jesus,' he groans.

I throw my head back to the sky, preparing myself for an amazing synchronised orgasm but I don't see the sky, I see the dark naked torso and surprised frozen expression of Jake Fitzgerald.

He stands about six feet away at the side of the long grass, his shirt slung over his shoulder, absolutely still, watching.

For a second only, I stop, wondering how long he has been there. But then my passion takes over, my need to save and exult my confused young lover.

I move myself up and back then let myself lunge hard down on Greg, feeling his cock thrust deep inside me. Again and again.

But as the hot sky bobs I never take my eyes off Jake.

'You can never take away the past ... Those you hurt ... that hurt you back. But ... you can learn from it ... you can learn ... to be ... more ... compassionate.'

On the word 'compassionate' every nerve in my body vibrates in climax and Greg pulls me to him as he too comes violently. When I glance skywards again, Jake has disappeared.

Greg falls asleep with my head on his chest. Although part of me, the peaceful, self-protective part, wants to stay with him, my niggling restlessness, my unfulfilment wins out.

So I cover him with a towel against the unrelenting sun and put on my damp and clinging pink dress. I walk towards the sea. The tide is right out and I have to walk some distance. A breeze has risen, cooling the air, and, as I walk at the edge of the surf, I imagine I hear faint and taunting voices. I realise I must still be quite drunk and decide I should walk until some clarity returns.

I move fiercely through the foam as if I'm going somewhere, as if I know my mission. But in the greater pounding of every step, nothing can dispel my mind's picture of Jake Fitzgerald's sombre handsome face. I make a vow to myself. I decide I either go to him soon, grab his cock and order, not request, him to fuck me or I instruct the work on his house to be finished as quickly as possible and I leave and never make contact with him again.

A flurry of water displaced by two warring birds a couple of feet into the sea rises up and drenches the front of my dress. My face is showered in coolness and I sober up momentarily.

Then the sound of female laughter, definitely not in

my head, filters through the air. I whirl around to see an unmistakable splash of red hair next to a mass of black rock. Without thinking further I walk determinedly towards the scene as if *this* is my mission.

There are three of them, in varying stages of inebriation. Amber, naked and in honey-skinned splendour leans against their stone niche with her foot inside the unzipped fly of Jake's jeans. He, propped on one elbow, lies on a multi-coloured rug drinking copiously from a bottle of whisky. Kneeling neatly at his side, wearing nothing but a tiny pair of white shorts, is a small elfin-faced brunette. She holds Jake's erect cock shyly in her hand. She looks about sixteen years old and glances up at me with slightly glazed green eyes. All three of them regard me with good nature and no surprise almost as if I was expected.

'Hello there, I'm Melanie.' The young girl has a child-ish, faintly Scottish accent and tiny perfect white teeth. Whether it is the age I assume her to be or her easy cordiality I feel inexplicably incensed . . . and jealous.

'A hand maiden, I presume?' I glare down at Jake, wishing I hadn't consumed so much wine.

He grins at me cheerfully and the two girls break into ostentatious giggles. 'Ah, sweetest Larissa. My dearest nearest . . . almost . . . sister-in-law. Why don't you join us? Now I have such a glorious hard-on. . . . pity to waste it. What do you say, Larissa?'

I stare at him in utter astonishment. I realise that it is the first time I have ever seen him so completely and resolutely drunk.

Amber smiles at me, takes her foot from his balls and, in a proprietary manner, kneels at the other side of him.

'He's so amazing, don't you think, Lara?'

'Amazing,' I murmur.

'Drunk as the skunk and still capable of such beautiful erection.'

Then, as if taking a child's hand from a toy that belongs

131

to her, she encircles Melanie's tiny wrist and makes her lose her grip on Jake's cock.

'Beautiful,' Amber repeats and, prising his jeans further down his bronze thighs, proceeds to cover him with her large glistening mouth. I feel my face burn in the heat and my nipples stiffen under my wet dress. I glance into Jakes eyes. He looks intently at my breasts.

'Mmmm, wet sundress competition,' he murmurs then, in a louder raucous tone, his voice faltering as Amber's crazy red hair moves more frantically over his abdomen, 'Now, don't . . . be a stranger, Larissa. Come and join . . . party.' He holds up the bottle. 'Have . . . drink with me.'

My first inclination is to turn and walk. I have a sense of foreboding, but I also can't help feeling a terrible, deep excitement.

As if in a trance, I kneel beside the elfin-faced girl, who good-naturedly takes my action as a cue for her dismissal. She rises and stoops on the sand to find her bag and some cigarettes. Jake looks purposefully at her small tight bottom and then into my eyes.

I hear a soft rushing noise in my head as if I'm about to faint, yet I know I won't. Never before have my senses seemed so sharp, so heightened. I stare into Jake's hypnotic glittering eyes, drag my gaze to his warm sensuous mouth; his tanned faintly lined brow; his beautiful cheekbones. Even though it's Amber who has his long hard prick in her mouth and Melanie who now sits behind him, her thighs spread and her surprisingly generous breasts cradling his head, it's as if they don't exist, as if there is only Jake and me. I am the one sucking him to orgasm, the one with her fingers in his sleek, dark curls. And now he looks at me as if he knows it. Abruptly he reaches down and, with a gentle but definite movement on her forehead, makes Amber take her mouth away. She retreats, hurt and surprised, looking from him to me and back again.

I feel breathless.

'You want to, don't you, Larissa?' he says then, but his

132

voice isn't warm. It is strangely sober and slightly bitter as if I have unwittingly wronged him.

'What?' It is all I can think of to say.

Still staring at me in an unfriendly way, he hands the nearly empty whisky bottle sideways to Amber and stretches out his hand to cover mine, which rests on my damp lap. He presses down a little so that I'm touching the top of my pussy with my own fingers.

'You want, Larissa, to reach out and touch my cock. Then, you want to take it and ram it into your moist little pussy.'

Melanie has left Jake and now sits smoking, cross-legged with her back to the black stone. My face blazing, I glance at her. She looks uncomfortable.

Amber cradles the whisky bottle as if it were a baby, the edge of tears starting in her eyes. 'I think you have had too much of the whisky, you asshole,' she says, trying to make her voice light-hearted, but unable to mask her nervousness and distress.

Abruptly, he swings around to snatch the bottle from her. 'I think I'll be the fucking judge of that.'

Large luminous tears well in her eyes.

Jake drinks deeply while we all wait, frozen. 'Well, Larissa,' he says sarcastically, 'tell me if it isn't true.'

'What isn't true?' I fight to make my voice clear, unwavering. Determinedly I hold his gaze. You're beautiful, I think. I want you. I really do.

'If I were to put my hand up that pretty little wet dress to seek out your pretty little tight pussy, I would encounter your pretty little wet panties wouldn't I? You sit there with those big trusting novice nun's eyes and all the time you're wetting your pants for me. Well,' he pauses, 'aren't you?'

He looks at me triumphantly. I can't think of a single thing to say. I can't move. Then Amber bursts into loud sobs and buries her head in her knees, wailing 'asshole and bastard'. Jake doesn't even glance at her. Melanie gets up and wraps her arms around the rocking inconsolable form. I think how incongruous they look, the tiny elfin creature comforting the tall big-boned weeping girl.

'There, pet, there,' she whispers in a soft knowing way that tells me, despite her looks, she is a lot older than sixteen.

Jake has now lost interest in me. Satisfied and uncaring of the upset he has caused, he sits up, looking casually straight ahead and tilting more whisky into his mouth. Our faces are less than a foot apart. Behind us a seagull flies very close and settles on the rock behind his head. It seems to be looking pointedly at me. Suddenly I remember Greg's words, 'Seduce him, woman.' Breathlessly, I watch my hand steal out very slowly and cover his now semi-erect penis. His head jolts around in surprise. My heart beating so loud I'm sure he'll hear, I stare fixedly into his bemused eyes.

'I'm not wearing any.' My voice is clear, unfaltering.

'What?' The whisky bottle loosens in his grip. His mouth working itself into a smile has stopped uncertainly.

Amber stops sobbing and both girls watch.

'I'm not wearing any knickers,' I repeat and smile, squeezing his cock. 'I rarely do these days.'

Slowly and firmly I move my hand back and forth, the full length of his shaft. Twice. He is brick hard. A small amount of come glistens like a dewdrop on the tip. A couple more times, quickly now, I slide my hand till he groans softly then closes his eyes.

Then, disconcertingly, the seagull rises from its perch, thrashing its wings furiously and cries into the sky as it leaves us. It sounds angry. Without knowing why, I feel shocked and frightened. With all my strength I dig my nails into the hot thickness of Jake's cock. His upper body jolts towards me with pain and astonishment and, amazed at what I've done, I jerk backwards a little but not before Jake's grip on the bottle loosens sufficiently for it to tilt and deposit a small lake of whisky into my lap. I watch and feel the coldness and weight of it; feel it begin to seep through my dress and sting the soft skin around my cunt.

'You vicious little bitch!'

I rise, giddy and terrified, the whisky running from me, some trickling down my legs to the sand, some falling on his chest. I run blindly along the sand sobbing and stumbling, calling out Greg's name. Overhead the seagull screeches, heralding my crazy path. Then Greg is coming towards me his shorts streaked with fruit juice and sand, a look of shock on his face. He stares at the wet patch on the front of my dress, tightens his arms around me when I collapse on his chest.

'It's OK, Lara. You're safe now. What's happened, darling? Tell me what's happened.'

'Jake.' I manage to gasp.

He holds me at arm's length. 'Lara, what did he do? Where is he now?' He looks around furiously, gripping my shoulders. 'Lara, what did the bastard do to you?'

He looks so comically agitated and murderous that my tears turn to half-hysterical laughter.

'Oh Greg, it's OK, really. He didn't do anything. It was me. It was actually quite funny, I suppose.'

He looks at me suspiciously, not understanding. He wipes the tears from my face. I steady my breathing.

We walk back up the sand towards our refuge in the dunes. I feel tired. I rest my head on his shoulder.

'Could you do something for me, angel?'

'Anything. Name it.'

'Could you drive the car. I want to go . . .' I almost say 'home' but the realisation that I can't remember what home feels like causes a new tightness in my throat. 'I want to go back.'

'Of course, my darling,' he whispers. 'It was always my plan.'

We both try to laugh but neither of us quite manages.

He drives more carefully than I had imagined, stealing little glances at me from time to time. Once more we take a longer route back. Dark clouds now roll across the blue

135

sky, colouring the green and yellow fields deep and lush. The hot air feels oppressive.

'Thunder forecast,' Greg remarks, running his hand over the drying wet patch on my skirt.

I smile weakly as if this is good news.

'I'm glad that's only whisky,' he says, rubbing the top of my thigh almost respectfully. 'I didn't know what to think when I saw the state of you.'

He frowns. 'I would have killed him you know, Lara. Even though he's bigger than me I would have . . .'

'Oh, Greg, I told you . . .'

'No, I can't bear that, men intimidating women. I saw too much of it, you know . . . before.'

I reach across, touch his knee.

'Oh, sweetheart.' The brief painful flash of his early years leaves his face. 'Tell you what,' he says brightly. 'If I'm a good boy, can I lick it all off?'

'Only if you're very, very good,' I say and turn my face to look at the vivid youthful crops, afraid that I'm going to cry again.

My room is hot and airless despite its afternoon gloom. Greg helps me out of my dress and, from my wardrobe, selects my one virginal, long white nightdress.

'You need the comfort,' he says and turns back the sheet of my bed.

But he doesn't join me and I don't ask him to. For a while he sits on the bed, smoothing the sheet over my shoulders and breast, touching my hair. The sky is very dark between the green trees. Occasionally, I think I can hear distant thunder. I close my eyes. Behind them, everything feels very hot and gritty.

'You want to be alone, don't you?'

I open my eyes, try to read his expression, look for signs of hurt and rejection. But all I see in his hazel gaze is wisdom as if I'm looking into the eyes of the tender and knowing mature man he will some day become. It makes me sad to think I won't know him then.

I nod, reach out and clasp his hand.

He grins and he is a boy again.

'I like to think I know women quite well,' he says with disarming self-assuredness.

'It's your thing.' I smile at him.

'I'll go and get you something to help you sleep.'

'There you are my darling,' he says, returning with a closed palm and a large glass of water. 'You'll have some pretty odd dreams after the wine you put away today but you'll crash out big style after.'

'I'll drink to that.' I swallow the two large mud coloured tablets.

We share a brief, almost chaste, kiss and I wonder if I've lost him as a lover. I look into his eyes.

'Thanks for today, Lara,' he says quietly. 'What you said about Celine. It made things clearer.'

'I'm glad.' I sit up and put my arms around him; smell again the sea, the soap, the fresh boyish sweat. 'Does that mean you won't want to shag me any more?'

He jumps to his feet full of energy, his eyes shining. He looks as if he's about to break into a jog.

'What the fuck do you think, darling?'

I don't sleep after he has gone. Every time I close my eyes I see Jake's face. I feel my hand on his cock, see the strangeness in his eyes, then the harsh drunken mockery. Then I think of him twenty years ago. He could never be cruel then. I think something must have hurt him very badly for him to pass on that pain to other people.

After a while I feel more relaxed. I vaguely ponder my situation. I decide that things are irretrievable between Jake and me. I came here with an impossible dream and now I'm going to have to let that dream go. But then I hear his words again, 'You want to Lara', and I am angry. *You* want to Jake, only you can't admit it. I will the image of his face, the smell of him, the touch of his hand on mine to go away but it won't. I lie on my back and breathe in the stifling dark sweet air. When I think of you I want to open my legs. The way I felt when I was seventeen and the way I still feel now. I lift my white gown to my waist and I spread my thighs, letting the light satin caress me, then I lower my hand. I feel his touch, his artist's hand that plucks like magic any hidden deep secret within the soul and puts it on canvas. I slip my other hand under my ribboned bodice. I stroke my nipple. It is his hand, his mouth making me arch my back to him. I move my fingers hard, urgently, against my clit. I can't wait for him and the pleasure he sears through my soul. I can't wait for you. I can't, I can't. Wracked in sweat and twisted sheets, my body shudders into orgasm and I drift into sleep with a ribbon of white lace tight between my legs.

It's raining and I'm running through the trees. But I can't escape. He's catching me up. My white dress is heavy with rain and slowing me more. My breasts, my thighs, my cunt, are plainly on view but frozen and tight with fear. Then all around red blooms rise grotesquely from squat insipid bushes growing bigger all the time, their mouths open wide to suck in all the air. I'm breathing fast but there's nothing left to breathe. The sky's roaring. I slip on the wet grass and my nightdress tears as it catches on a low branch. I'm trapped. Above me, the holes of sky between the trees are judgmental as eyes. You whore, you whore. Then it is his eyes, those dark menacing eyes that I once loved and trusted so much, leering over me.

He stoops and tears my dress. He's laughing; a panel up the front rips. My cunt is exposed. From my neck to my navel his hand fells the cotton as if it is tissue. I scream. He laughs more. He was once kind to me but he doesn't remember. I push myself hard against the trunk of the tree. Still he laughs, comes for me. I scream again.

Then I am sitting up, half-conscious in bed. Outside, I hear intermittent explosions and a constant hissing, rapping sound. My room is nearly dark. One shutter is closed against a rind of demonic sky. A far-off tree dances. Then, in growing horror, I watch as the other shutter comes slowly towards me and in the dark the outline of a woman in a deep pink dress and gold sandals forms against its black frame.

I crouch against the scattered pillows and the hard wall, shuddering all over and shrieking my fear into hot dark air. Then, in the short time it takes my warped senses to recover sufficiently to realise that what I am screaming at is my own dress rinsed and hung on the slatted wood to dry, I am alerted by something else, something less theatrical but infinitely more frightening. Someone is trying to get into the room.

I stare, paralysed, at the door handle. I blink a couple of times doubting myself again. But I'm sure it's not moving. I force myself off the bed towards it then realise that the frantic sound of metal being twisted and rattled against wood is not coming from the door to the hall but to my side. The slim wooden door next to the shower room is vibrating wildly. I scrabble back against the bed, but not before I glimpse the splintering of wood and a hand clawing through the open, ragged space.

I half tumble, half roll over the dishevelled bed taking the silk sheet with me. He barges into the room, stumbling against the wall, grabbing the bedstead for support. He is still naked to the waist, his hair is rough, tangled as if he's been asleep. I smell stale whisky from where I cower on the floor.

'Jake,' I whisper, but he doesn't answer.

Even in the deep gloom I can see the glitter in his eyes as he stares down at me.

Panic-stricken, I stumble to my feet and make for the shutters to the balcony. But the catch has dropped and my hands shake so much I can't open it.

I hear his breath behind me then his arms come around my waist so tightly it knocks the air from me. He lifts me straight off my feet and, with tremendous effort, whirls me around and carries me kicking and struggling to the bed.

'Jesus, Jake, please,' I whimper as he deposits me heavily onto the rumpled mound of silk. My head falls sideways between the valley of parted pillows. One falls over my face. I am plunged into soft blackness where there is no air. Then I feel his weight on me, his thighs pinning me down.

'You're going to calm down, do you hear? You're going to calm down. Then you're going to sleep.' His voice sounds crazed and haunted.

My overwhelming terror invests me with a sudden superhuman strength. I knock away the stifling black of the pillow and force myself upwards, my hair wild over my face so that I see nothing but patches of his bare chest. I lunge for it with my nails. Two streaks of red appear almost like a cross, glistening.

'No, don't do this.'

He sounds imploring now. I think suddenly that he's more afraid than I am. With all my might I extricate one of my legs from under his and slam my foot into his abdomen. His body, weakened by shock and fading alcohol, falls back sufficiently for me to escape. This time I manage the catch on the shutters and fling them apart. My pink dress dislodged on its hanger, sweeps up and out into the seething rain.

'You're not doing this to me, Victoria. Not again. I won't let you.'

He staggers out into the curtain of wet as I make for the balcony steps. I turn, amazed, my fear evaporating.

'What did you say?'

We stand with three feet of teeming rain between us. He stares at me as if I'm an apparition, begins to wipe the running wet from his eyes.

Then he takes a step towards me, stretching a hand out to the saturated strands of my hair, as if he doesn't understand what they are. Still unnerved and uncertain, I take a step back.

'What did you call me?' I ask again.

He stands still, shakes his head once. 'Christ,' he whispers. 'Oh, Christ.'

Then he half-turns and stumbles towards the balcony railing and vomits into the rain.

We stay like that for several minutes, Jake bent over the balcony, increasingly drenched and beaten down and me, motionless, gazing and wondering as the rain drums through my dress. Soon it diminishes and the sodden trees once again come into focus, the sky behind them white and drained. I go over to Jake's stooped form, treading my dress into deeper pink pools on the shallow flooded floor.

I put my arm tentatively around his shoulders. He doesn't straighten up or look at me. Instead he gazes down at the sea of stones, washed white and clean.

'You have no idea how sorry I am, Lara,' he says.

He fetches some thick towels from the large bathroom and hands me one almost shyly. Our drenching has sobered him. He seems reticent but somehow anxious to make amends.

'I'll go somewhere else if you want to change,' he says quietly.

I laugh.

'I would have thought you've seen enough of my body over the last few weeks for it not to be a shock.'

'The circumstances are slightly different, don't you think?' he says almost formally. Then, in a lighter tone, 'Christ, do I have a headache.'

'You'll have a chill too, if you don't get out of those.'

I put my hand on the top of his saturated jeans. He looks down at it a moment, then over at my bedside table. 'Do you have any aspirin?'

'Yes.'

'I'll get out of these then.'

He goes round the corner to the shower room.

When he returns I am sitting on the once-more lush, smooth bed, wearing a towel around my body and one turban-like around my head. I have tidied up and no sign of the recent traumatic chaos remains. He is also wearing a towel around his waist and the scene strikes me as almost comic, apart from the darkness in the room and the shutters that have drifted closed.

I switch on the gold-shaded lamp as he sits with me

on the bed, close but not too close. We avoid eye contact. I rub my foot with the towel. I am aware that he is watching me. I glance sideways at him. His hair is still wet. I long to dry it.

'I could really do with a cigarette,' he says at last. 'I've no idea where I've left mine.' He laughs shortly.

'I have some down here.' I reach into my cabinet. I feel his eyes on my back.

'I only smoke when I'm stressed,' I say to the floor.

I hand him the packet, a lighter and a couple of aspirins. 'There's some water over there.'

The towel loosens slightly around my breasts. Quickly I tighten it.

'Are you now, Lara ... stressed?' His voice seems clearer. When I turn to him he is looking right into my eyes.

'A little.'

He lowers his eyes, takes a cigarette from the packet, offers one to me. He flicks the lighter and, as I bend to take a light, my towel comes away from my head and falls down his arm. He raises his other hand to save my hair from the flame.

We smoke for a minute or two looking at each other, not uncomfortable but not at ease either. Just careful, subdued, accepting of where the drama of the day's events has left us. I begin to feel quite sleepy, probably as a result of Greg's tablets, I want to open the shutters, but the moment doesn't seem right. I look around, trying to keep alert, wondering where we go from here.

'It really is a beautiful room, this, have I said?'

Jake breaks into prolonged laughter.

'What?' I watch him, relieved. I start to laugh too.

'Only you, Larissa, could say such a well-brought-up, middle-class thing as that – after I've pinned you to the bed in some drunken hallucination, after you've clawed me to bits . . .'

I glance now at the cross I've scoured on his chest and put my hand to my mouth and giggle. He puts his arm around me and takes the cigarette from my fingers and stubs it out.

'My God,' he whispers into my hair. 'Whoever said we were older and wiser?'

'Not me Jake.'

Then, suddenly, I'm afraid of the closeness of our mood and my cheek on his chest.

'I'd like to dry your hair,' I say shyly.

I kneel on the rug between his feet and rub his dark curls back to softness. This time the towel around my breasts falls away with no warning. He spreads his hand across my breastbone, vaguely rubbing the flesh there as if in contemplation. His little finger touches the top of my naked breast.

'I want to go to bed,' I whisper.

He stares at me. I hear his breathing.

'I mean to sleep,' I say quickly. 'One way and another it's been a hell of a day.'

'I know.' He strokes my cheek. 'I'm sorry.'

My nipples harden. I feel the tiny flickers of desire start inside me. I wriggle a little back on my heels. He looks down at my restless thighs.

'Lara . . .' he says softly.

'Could you open the shutters please,' I say, in a faltering voice, 'I'd like to see the sky.'

He rises and I gaze at his beautiful back as he walks across the room. He flings the shutters apart and the sky is blue, late afternoon blue. The trees are refreshed and content and glisten green. The world is reborn. As he returns to me, a tiny bird settles behind him on the balcony railing. My eyes fill with tears.

'It's beautiful,' I whisper, looking out.

He takes my hand, helps me to my feet, switches off the gold-shaded lamp.

'You want me to stay, don't you?' he asks quietly.

I can't speak. I nod instead.

I lie on his chest and he cradles me in his arms. Neither of us attempt to kiss or touch the other. When I lift my thigh over him it is only to get closer. He looks at the ceiling, not particularly preoccupied, but drained. I want to give him some words of comfort, but as I gaze at the blue sky my head seems woolly, the world seems to recede.

'I feel as if I'm going to fall off the edge of the earth,' I murmur.

'Then I'll just have to hold on to you, won't I?' He wraps me more firmly in his arms.

'Thank you,' I whisper and tumble somewhere, with him coming too.

I sleep soundly with images of Jake flitting through my dreams. Jake walking through a forest of rain, arms reaching to me for shelter. Jake on the beach carrying me through the surf. He settles me down in the shallow foam and lifts my pink dress above my waist. When he enters me, the sea comes too, lapping my hips, taking back all our juices. Jake in the seventies room drinking wine with me at the candle-lit table. He slides his hand under my golden dress and makes me come as the organ music rises and pink petals from the tree float into the room like confetti.

When I awake the sky is late-evening pale. I can't remember why I feel happy, then I feel Jake's chest beneath my head. He smiles down, watching me.

'Haven't you slept at all?' I ask.

'Bits and pieces. You kept soaking me into wakefulness.'

'What?' I hardly dare look at his face.

'Don't worry, Larissa,' he says gently, 'I adore women dribbling on my chest.'

'Oh God, I thought you meant . . .' I stop, flustered, suddenly aware of the damp stickiness between my legs across his thigh. I also realise that he has an erection.

As if sensing this he moves slightly away from me and says ruefully, 'Even at my age I wake up with a stiffy, I'm afraid.'

I hold my breath then move my hand down his chest, his abdomen, and daringly caress the tip of his cock.

144

'No, Lara,' he says immediately. I colour and with-draw, curling away from him.

'God, I'm sorry.'

He pushes himself up against the pillows taking me with him and resting my hot face on his shoulder.

'I want to tell you something,' he says, glancing out towards the quiet sky. 'I didn't think I would, but I want to tell you about Victoria.'

'Your wife.' I run my fingers over the solemn set of his chin. It is slightly rough, shadowed.

'Who told you?'

He looks at me with a trace of alarm and I withdraw my hand.

'Greg told me a little,' I say carefully. 'It was here, wasn't it, in this room, that she . . . had her accident?'

'That was the *grande finalé*, when the silly bitch threw herself over the balcony.' He turns to me in a sad, wondering way. 'Just to get away from me, Larissa – that's why she did it.'

I can't stand his pain. I half cover his body with mine, stretching my thigh over him, my arm across his chest, rubbing his shoulder. I kiss him lightly on the neck. He doesn't object. Neither does he seem to notice.

'That can't be true. I'm sure it isn't. It must have been the drugs.'

'The drugs,' he says shortly. Unexpectedly he tightens his grip around me with his free arm. 'The drugs were merely the end result.'

'I don't understand.'

He sighs, reaches down to the bedside table, finds a cigarette. Through the cloud of smoke he begins his story.

He is years away, a world away, recounting in a flat voice the traumatic incidents of his marriage. The parties where Victoria fell down stairs, passed out in people's gardens. The time she took his car and drove it off the road at dawn, crashing it through the long grass to the sand. 'I found her sitting cross-legged by the shore, a joint in hand, gazing at the waves, the car buckled and embedded in a sand bank, twenty yards off.' The time

145

she set fire to the orchard. 'I was painting, the trees, the sky, and the house in the distance. She seemed quite happy, sitting stringing beads – she used to make jewellery – then I went back to the house to make a phone call. When I came back she was standing in this ring of fire, smiling, fascinated. She'd taken some acid and I didn't know. The canvas, easel, all the fucking paints scattered at her delighted feet. All because of me, Larissa,' he finishes in a dark tone, stubbing out his cigarette savagely in the ashtray.

Both his arms come round me, his hands absently rubbing the small of my back. We are silent for a short while. Then he rocks me gently against him as if it is me who needs comforting. One knee is raised, allowing my open legs to straddle his thigh. With mounting excitement and growing shame I realise that the soft rhythmic movement is causing my clit to rub against him and I am getting wetter and hotter. I move a bit, but unconsciously he clamps me to him with his lower leg.

'I still don't see how it's your fault.' My voice quivers. I want to know the answer but I also want him to stop arousing me . . . if he doesn't mean it.

'Why don't you ask me why I married her?' he says suddenly. The rocking movement ceases. He presses me hard against him as if I will try to escape. Unable to stop myself I move my lips once or twice on his leg.

'None of my business,' I murmur, snuggling into his neck.

I brush against his cock. He is semi-hard. He turns my face to look at him.

'I married her, Lara, because she was shy and uncertain and very sweet, quite in fact, like you.'

The way I used to be, I think, bearing my clit down on the top of his thigh.

'The kind of girl I used to avoid. Because they unsettled me and I fucked around too much.'

Christ, what if I come against his leg and he doesn't even notice?

'But she thought she was pregnant and she was scared

and I married her and I still fucked around. I was only twenty-five, with two or three prizes behind me. I spent a lot of time in London; fast cars; parties. She preferred it here, looking after the house. But she got lonely. Then, when we had people round, she started to smoke dope. It relaxed her. But then it took hold. It was everything – acid, uppers, downers then finally the big one. I wasn't even around enough to notice until it was too late.'

He lights another cigarette, offers me one.

'I'm fine,' I say.

'You're flushed,' he mutters. He searches my face. 'Sweetest Larissa,' he says casually and puts my head back on his shoulder.

I bite my lip to try to quell my desire. He must know I'm wet, I think. He must feel it.

'I don't think you're right Jake, to blame yourself. Addiction is . . .'

'And what would you know about it?'

His voice is cold. I feel his embrace loosen slightly.

'Well nothing first-hand but . . .'

'Precisely.'

'. . . But you can't go on punishing yourself for the rest of your life.'

'That's exactly what I intend to do.'

His words bridle with such self-recrimination that I push myself off him, stare into his eyes.

'The Jake twenty years ago that shagged everything that moved has turned over a new leaf,' he says softly.

I blink, shake my head, smile bemusedly.

'I don't shag anyone now, Lara,' he says in a sad final way. 'No penetrative sex. My punishment.' He laughs awkwardly.

I fall back on the pillows.

'My God,' I whisper.

Ironically, he chooses this moment to lie over me, gently pulling me further into the bed, stroking my brow and touching my hair as if I was fevered.

'So you see, sweetheart. That's why I've kept my

distance. Not because I don't desire you, not even because I don't want to get involved...' he breaks off, gives a dry laugh '...though there is that too. But because I can't give you what you want, Lara.'

I gaze up at him, feel, somewhere against my lower body, the nuzzling of his erection, feel the need in my pelvis to rise up to him.

'I think I should be the judge of that,' I say hoarsely.

'Lara.'

'Jake, I'm wet for you...'

'I know, sweetheart, but...'

'It's midsummer's night, Jake Fitzgerald.'

He smiles into my eyes. I pull his head towards me and kiss him.

Then, quite by accident, I feel the tip of his cock nudge my lips. I reach down and grab it, open my legs. Then I look into his eyes and see the desire but also the uncertainty, the conflict.

'On your back, Fitzgerald.'

I caress him gently at first, running my fingers up and down the length of him, feeling him harden more, waiting for him to stop me. He doesn't.

'You have the most fantastic touch, Larissa,' he whispers.

I move my leg over him, straddle him once more, nestle my cunt on his thigh which trembles now as his excitement mounts. I stroke his balls, massage behind them, slide my finger along the ridge of skin. For a moment I stop there, remembering Greg's words on prolonging ecstasy. Then I dig my nails in, rub him there, return to his cock.

'Lara, you're driving me wild.'

'You like?' I lean down, whisper against his neck, as I work his cock furiously.

'I like lots,' he groans, simultaneously sliding his hand beneath my pussy. I slow my hand on him as he moves his fingers in small circles around my clit.

'My God, but you're a wet little girl,' he murmurs as the first drops of pre-come escape his cock.

'You were right when you said that this afternoon,' I breathe. 'I got wet at the sight of you when I was seventeen and I still do now.'

He frowns. I work him faster. He clutches my cunt and I shudder.

'I was a bastard for saying that to you, Lara.' He moves his fingers slowly, gently as if trying to make amends. I feel as if I am throbbing into his hand, as if he will feel my cunt beat like a heart. There is a soft womb of clouds in the light night sky and I feel as if I will melt into it.

'You are *not* a bastard, Jake Fitzgerald,' I say, my voice trembling as I sit on the edge of orgasm.

He looks at me once with an expression of utter gratitude and jerks up towards me with his hand slamming against my clit and we both come.

The hours from night to morning never really darken. We drift in and out of sleep, sometimes waking to kiss, resettle one body against the other, hold each other tighter. We don't come apart till dawn. At five in the morning I lie and watch him sleep. A shaft of pure yellow sun lights up his peaceful face and enriches his dark hair. For a moment he could be the Jake of twenty years ago.

Then I rise and go out to the balcony. The world is green-gold and new, the air so fresh and pure it takes my breath away. Then I hear Jake call my name from the bedroom. He sounds anxious and confused. When I call back to him he comes out, still half dazed from sleep. He puts his arms around my waist, kisses my neck.

'I was afraid when I woke and you were gone. It's hard to forget sometimes.'

I turn and kiss him.

'Why *did* you put me in that room ... and then sleep in the adjoining one?'

'I wanted to be able to look out for you, if you ever

149

needed me.' He hesitates. 'I suppose I could move somewhere else.'

'No, don't do that.' I run my fingers through his rumpled curls. 'I do need you.'

Chapter Six

*A*s lush June turns to sizzling July, Jake and I act as if we are having an illicit affair. He thinks no one knows, but of course, I have told Greg. It is decided between us that my pink dress hanging over the balcony will signal to Greg that it's OK for him to visit. For four nights after midsummer it remains in my wardrobe. On the fifth morning Greg, Amber, Jake and I are having an awkward late breakfast on the kitchen courtyard. I am dressed in high heels and make-up for a meeting in town. Amber sits in a rumpled T-shirt, her gaze shifting between her own perfect nails and Jake's face when she thinks he can't see. When she raises her eyes it is plain she has been crying. Greg tries to keep a semblance of conversation going but there are many long silences, relieved only by the summer noises of birds and insects. I am so unnerved I ask Jake for a cigarette with my coffee.

He glances at me sharply.

'You're not nervous about seeing these contractors are you? I could come with you if you are.'

Amber shifts her chair noisily on the gravel.

'I've been going to meetings on my own for a quite a while, thank you. Besides, I thought you wanted me just to get on with it. You weren't interested in the plans.'

Then I look pointedly at Amber and back at Jake again. He frowns, not understanding.

Greg tries his best.

'I've made the most fucking amazing costume for you my darling, all feathers and fur, toning in with your glorious hair.' He pulls his chair beside her and clasps her hand. She doesn't look up.

'And what more could a girl ask for?' Jake remarks in a vaguely camp tone that I don't altogether like.

'I don't want any fucking costume.' Amber is close to tears.

I lose my nerve. 'I'm going to get some fresh coffee.' I rise and glare at Jake. 'Speak to her,' I mouth and he looks at me blankly.

I stand by the percolator desperately trying to imagine another voice outside other than Greg's.

It's another hot day. Already I feel the perspiration start under my marigold and flame dress. My underwear is very brief and sheer, clinging to my damp body. As the aroma of coffee rises into the stifling air I think of Jake tumbled between my sheets with his mouth on my cunt. I think of his expert fingers and his searching sensual lips. Already I feel a new dampness start between my legs.

As if conjured up by my thoughts, I am suddenly aware of the scent of him behind me, a woody linseed soap-tinted scent. Before I can turn I feel his arms around my waist, his hands stealing down my abdomen, his fingers between my sex lips, pressing my clit through the thin material of my dress.

'My goodness, Larissa. You really must stop fantasising about me when I'm not servicing you. You're ruining your underwear,' he murmurs against my neck. 'Then again you're the perfect height in these heels, beautifully on par with my cock. I could just slip it in under your dress and . . .'

I spin around. 'But you wouldn't, Jake,' I say sharply.' 'Remember you don't . . .'

'Sweetheart, what's wrong? What's upset you?' He runs the back of his hand down my hot cheek.

I sigh. 'You're supposed to be out there talking to Amber.'

'Why?'

He puts his hands on my hips; presses me against him. He is very hard. I feel my mouth go dry.

'For God's sake, at the very best she feels neglected. At worst, she's desperately in love with you.'

He reaches around me to collect the coffee jug.

'Christ, women,' he says, wearily. 'Amber's a young girl. They think they're in love, they get over it. I thought you might still just remember that feeling, Lara.'

We head back to the garden. He uses one hand to carry the coffee, the other to fondle my backside.

Amber hardly gives him a chance to sit down before her eyes flash across the table. I am directly opposite her. I can't decide whether her look includes me or not.

'So where have you been these past nights anyway, for fuck's sake?' she says in a surly but nonetheless frightened tone.

Jake lights a cigarette slowly. His eyes are cool, slightly hard. He inhales and blows a large cloud of smoke impertinently close to her face.

'Who wants to know?' he says in a cold, disinterested way.

Despite the simmering heat, I shiver. Greg glances at me.

'I've come to your room a couple of times,' Amber whispers, unable to keep the distress from her voice.

'We agreed, did we not, that I would come to you?' He pauses, blows a fresh cloud of smoke between the two of us. '. . . If necessary.'

Amber gets to her feet, incensed. 'We agreed nothing you asshole,' she hisses, 'You tell me what to do. You make the fucking rules . . .'

'. . . and you break them with the usual degree of feminine obedience,' he says, smirking and throwing his

153

cigarette end across the gravel despite the ashtray in front of him.

I feel something tighten inside me. I rise abruptly, look unnecessarily at my watch. 'I should make a move.'

'You're sure you don't want any company?' Jake looks up as if everything is normal.

Amber turns quickly towards the kitchen, tears already on her face.

'I'm perfectly certain.'

Then Greg rises. 'I think maybe a touch of the old Landsdowne PR is called for,' he says with faltering joviality.

We both watch him follow Amber. I am breathing fast.

'Well that'll do it,' Jake says lighting another cigarette. 'A good rodgering from Gregor will definitely sort her out.' The edge in his voice is unmistakable.

'What's happening here?' I look down at the ground. I hear him rise and come towards me.

'Well I don't know about you, Larissa, but I feel very horny.' He runs his hand from my neck down my back and cups my buttocks. 'But seeing as you have your men in the city to meet I will just have to content myself with the idea of your ever-dampening panties as you wing your way back to me.'

When he holds me hard against his cock and kisses me for a long time I suddenly feel that I'd like to resist him. But I don't.

To sit in a straightforward monochrome hotel with straightforward monochrome men is a relief. As I go through meticulously detailed plans with a softy spoken architect and praise a self-conscious tousled-haired student for his examples of screen painting, the idea of not returning to the place of whispering greenery and unsettling passions seems increasingly appealing. The silverhaired but unthreateningly handsome man who is to co-ordinate the work on the house invites me to lunch armed with a sheaf of paperwork for which he apologises. He glances occasionally at my breasts in the cool dim restaurant but his paternal smile and sincere admiration for my ideas bring tears to my eyes. I blame them on the too fierce smoking of a cigarette. He sees me to my car and I drop the screen sample given to me by the student. The man picks it up and holds open the car door.

'You must be delighted at how it's all coming together,' he says.

I clutch my plans and invoices and pieces of sky. On the real horizon, far off clouds rise from the sea.

Another week passes and I feel as if I'm clinging to the edge of a cliff.

One morning, nervy and tired, I'm lying on the shallow ledge of the rock pool waiting for the soft motion of the water to give me peace. I feel the touch of a foot on my shoulder and sit up violently.

'Jesus Christ, Greg. You almost frightened me to death.'

He kneels beside me, patting cool water onto my brow and cheeks.

'You're so uptight these days darling,' he says softly. 'Did you expect someone else?'

'God, no.' I laugh lightly.

Jake and I have come to the pool three or four times during our liaison. He lies with me under the cool umbrella of the fragrant bushes with my legs around his back while he sucks my clit. I wrap my mouth around his cock while he rests on the stone ledge, an eager tide swelling new water around our bodies. 'You must suck me dry before we drown, Larissa.'

One memorable occasion unsettles me. We walk from the house, my head on his shoulder, his arm around my waist. We carry a blanket and a bottle of wine. All the other times we meet at the poolside, this day we go together. But we don't get to the pool. As we walk over the scorched grass of the orchard, Jake stops and looks around as if he has stumbled across an ideal picnic spot.

'This will do,' he says and makes his way through the

charred tree stumps to throw the blanket under the orphaned trees. I follow in silence.

We sit under the stunted canopy of foliage, wordless, looking at the circle of blackened and destroyed vegetation, so eery and tragic as it is, an island in the abundant greenery and within earshot of the immortal voice of the sea.

We open the wine and drink it from the bottle. Jake has his back against the tree holding me on his chest.

'You're very tense,' he says after a while.

'It's just being here ... I mean, do you come here often?'

A short burst of laughter follows.

'One of these days I'll write them all down – your little sayings.' Then his voice changes. 'Actually, no. I don't think I've been here at all since that day with Victoria.'

'Then ... why?'

'I suppose I feel like confronting some of my ghosts. With you. Is that fair?' He tilts my face back on his shoulder, looking into my eyes.

'Possibly not, but I suppose I should feel privileged.'

When he lays me back on the blanket I cling to him, moving as close as I can to his body.

'You're scared, Lara. I was wrong for bringing you here.' He sounds tired and forlorn.

'No I'm fine. Just hold me. Make love to me.'

But for the first time I am not aroused by the proximity of his body, by his hands on my breasts, by his hardness against my abdomen. I feel we are being watched, judged, that the residue of two decades ago has never left the melancholy air around us. Finally, withdrawing his hand from between my legs he lies back on his side.

'We'll go to the pool. I don't want to make you unhappy.' His eyes are troubled.

'And *I* want to make you happy.'

I take his erection in my hand, stroke him and caress him, lay him back and worship him with my tongue and my mouth. Each time I raise my head before lunging again I watch his face, the pleasure in his submission, the

156

peace in his bronze forehead. But he doesn't come. Just when I feel his body rigid beneath me, when it begins to twitch, when his hands around my head grow insistent, suddenly he manages to stop and pull away. He draws me up towards him, puts an arm around my waist.

'But what do *you* want, Larissa?'

I sink over onto my side, open my legs and with trembling fingers take his rigid cock, inserting it between my cunt and my buttocks, straddling it. Within seconds I grow wet. I search his face, see the conflict and the fear there.

'I won't put you anywhere you don't want to go.'

I rub myself against him and within seconds feel him move too. He pushes the small of my back to him so that my clit presses hard against the root of his cock.

'You're so beautiful, Lara.'

His hands frantically pummel my buttocks against him. Then unexpectedly, in an uncontrolled way, unusual for Jake, he comes, bucking against me and sending a gush of hot wetness through my legs. We fall apart and I feel his seed underneath my hips before it sinks into some dry grass exposed by the dishevelled blanket.

'I'm sorry,' he whispers, recovering himself immediately and placing his fingers between my legs.

I'm sure I can smell apples in the air, although it is far too early. I imagine I sense the presence of other people, young, carefree with a lifetime of summers in front of them. I try to stop his hand. 'It's OK, Jake you don't have to.'

But he continues to caress me, letting his fingers linger on, then leave my clit. He rubs me with long searing strokes inside my lips. And I look up at the proud meagre boughs of the remaining trees, see how their baby fruit is growing and surrender to orgasm.

Greg and I swim out a little way but I feel weak and soon want to return to the shallows.

'I'm not sleeping too well,' I explain. My head rests on

his body in a semblance of a lifesaving position as we swim back.

'The affair with the great J F leaving you a little jaded?' He hauls himself onto the ledge and helps me up.

'I just said I'm not sleeping well, that's all.'

We go to sit near the bushes. Even in the hot sun I tremble. He wraps a towel around me.

'I can help you with the sleeping problem,' he says quietly. 'But I think you're either going to have to get what you really want from Jake ... or bow out. I take it he's still not giving you a good 'seeing to', as they say.'

I laugh. 'No he isn't, but it's not just that. It's Amber ... and, well, you.'

His fingers come under the towel; brush my nipples to hardness.

'My darling Lara, do I really strike you as the jealous lover? I want you to be happy. In control. Really, have you understood anything I've taught you?'

I stroke his silky hair and droplets of sea trickle down his forehead. 'No, it's not *you*, Greg. It's the other way around. Sometimes Jake makes these snide remarks about you and ...'

'Ooh, I'm wounded.' He throws up his hands in mock effrontery.

'I'm serious. I don't like it. Then he's so offhand with Amber, too. Sometimes I think I don't even like him.'

'Then you're going to have to get yourself sorted out,' he says, pulling me to my feet. 'But for now you're going to bed with the aid of a little Landsdowne magic ... and I don't mean the ministrations of my talented prick.'

We walk back through the charred orchard. I feel safe here with him. I take his hand. His vigorous youthful presence transcends the spirit of the place. 1979 is just a number to Greg.

'By the way, speaking of penis supremacy,' he says suddenly, 'can I ask you something? You can lie if you like.'

I squeeze his hand. Anything he could ask about his

performance in that respect can only elicit a positive answer.

'When I fuck you, Lara, I mean really nails digging in, womb opening fuck you, do you pretend it's him?'

I don't answer. He looks at my face.

'Thought so,' he says. 'Oh well, guess it's just a rehearsal for when I get married, if ever. *C'est la vie.*'

It's Saturday afternoon, two weeks after midsummer's day, and the weather suddenly breaks. Jake has taken me into the summer-house, to paint me. He is subdued, respectful, arranging me gently on the hammock, adjusting my flimsy peach-coloured costume so softly off my breasts and over my thighs that I barely feel him. I have taken some of Greg's herbal relaxants against the instructions for daytime use. I lie back on the thick material and smile at Jake when he gazes anxiously at my face.

'You're getting very good with this make-up thing,' he remarks. 'Those slanted cheekbones, those haunted eyes.' He runs a finger along my eyebrow. 'But you're not are you, Lara, haunted, I mean?'

There is a faint rustling sound outside. A chill draught passes over me.

'What?' I ask sleepily.

'I'm worried.'

I sit up. I feel giddy and hold onto his arm. His flesh beneath my cold touch feels hot.

'I'm worried that I was right ... that our relationship ... encounters, whatever, isn't what you want ... and ...'

'Jake ...'

'Let me finish, Lara. I've been mulling over what you said about Amber. And you're right. I am being inconsiderate and selfish. So I've asked her and Greg and I'm asking you ... of course – I thought we should all eat together tonight so I can try to make amends.'

He seems to be talking very quickly but it may be an effect of the tablets I am taking. I lean forward, kiss his brow, touch his mouth.

'Sure, it sounds fine, don't worry, please.'

I sink back on the hammock. The material behind my head is soft and welcoming. I smile at him as he arranges his easel. I open my legs wide.

'Damn it,' he says suddenly. 'Where's the fucking sun got to?'

He goes to the glass door and looks out and upwards. As if not believing what he sees, he opens the door and stands outside. From where I lie I can't see the sky, but I see the garden. It's gloomy; the greens are dark and lack-lustre, quivering uncomfortably in a new wind.

'What's wrong?' Quite illogically I begin to feel alarmed.

'I wanted to paint you with the sun filtering through the coloured glass. But there's been a return to real British summertime. It looks like winter out there.'

He lights the oil lamp on the table. I glance behind me. All the garish faces are illuminated on the wall, their eyes in my direction. I feel my heart race, I wish I'd taken another tablet.

'But you look wonderful, Lara.' He turns to me with eyes full of tenderness. 'All the faces in the shadow behind, and you, opening, alive and real in front of me, like a flower.' He picks up his brush and I close my eyes. All I can hear is the rhythmic beating of the lamp flame against the air.

'Lara, wake up, sweetheart, we have to go.'

Jake is shaking my shoulder gently. When my eyes eventually open everything seems very dark. For a moment I can't think where I am.

'What's happened?'

I sit up; lean against his shoulder. My head seems very heavy. There's a crackling, hissing sound, far away.

'Nothing. It's just that it's pissing down, and if you remember, we came here at brilliant noon. We've no bloody clothes.'

'Oh, right.' I look wearily towards the bleared glass, the only source of light. It is grey and dark green and running with wet. All the chinks of coloured glass on either side are dead as stone.

'So,' Jake continues, 'I either dash back to the house and get something to cover you or we make a run for it.'

I glance around the gloomy space where the eyes of other people hide.

'I want to come with you.'

He takes off his shirt; puts it round my scantily covered shoulders.

'Damn, I forgot you've no shoes.'

'I want to come with you.' My voice sounds overshrill. He looks at me oddly. 'I'll go barefoot. It's fine,' I add quickly.

Outside, he hesitates only a second before lifting me up into his arms. Thankfully, the rain has dwindled to a heavy drizzle and he carries me the twenty yards or so to the house with comparative ease.

'I'm either finding renewed vigour in my old age,' he says, 'or you're losing weight, Larissa.'

I play idly with the raindrops on his chest, tracing my fingers through them as I used to do to the mist on the window as a child. I feel the tip of his erection against my hip. But I know I'll go back to my room and sleep alone. I might even take another tablet.

For a second he stands me in the shelter of the over-hanging roof outside the kitchen. Behind him the heads of acid-pink blooms are fat with rain. I wonder why we've stopped and then he kisses me. I feel my bones melt against his body.

He looks at my face. 'Jesus, Lara. You certainly are giving Greg a run for his money with that mascara brush. My, the glitter in those eyes. You look like you're in another world.'

At eight o'clock it looks to me as if it's already getting dark. As well as the candles on the table, Jake has placed others, different shapes and sizes, on surfaces all around the seventies room.

'This is all very nice,' says Amber in her touching, eager, best-behaved little girl's voice.

'Thank you, sweetheart.' Jake is also trying hard.

I smile out into the rain.

Greg comes up behind me at the window; puts his arms around my waist. 'What are you looking at, Lara?'

'Just the darkness.'

'Are you alright?

'I really need to get that tree cut back.' Jake stands at the other side of me holding out a generous tumbler of golden liquid. 'Whisky. I thought you might be chilled after . . . earlier on,' he says quietly, glancing sideways at Greg. 'If you can see beyond the branches there the sky is still quite light.'

I raise myself up on my toes and move towards his shoulder to look. He is right – the sky, though smeared with rain, is still sombre evening pale.

I laugh lightly. 'Somehow it just feels as if it will never be summer again.'

Amber and I are at either end of the boxy sofa. Greg sits cross-legged on the floor at my feet. Jake sits on one of the chairs at the table. We are all drinking long glasses of whisky, quickly, in nervous vivacity. Greg and Jake are discussing the following week's classes. Amber and I start a tentative conversation about hair and cosmetics.

'You are transformed in your make-up,' she concedes, after half a glass of whisky. 'It's the only thing I envy the older woman, her cheekbones.'

'Well, thank you.'

'No, but you are so slim, too,' she says quickly. 'I have the big bones. You are slimmer, too, since you got here?'

'I said that to you today,' Jake interjects suddenly. 'That you're losing weight.'

I am annoyed at his interruption. It's as though he's monitoring our conversation. I gulp some whisky; pull down the short skirt of my midnight blue dress, wishing momentarily that it hadn't been altered from its former demure knee length. I am terribly aware that Jake, having almost drained his first glass, glances constantly at my legs.

I ask if I can put some music on and rise. The row of cassettes inexplicably blurs before my eyes. I blink. For several seconds my vision clears but then quickly distorts again. I pick up a tape, any tape, and, with trembling fingers, insert it in the machine.

Behind me Greg says to Jake, 'That's OK, then? You can handle everything yourself next week.'

His voice seems subdued as if I'm not meant to hear.

They both look at me as I take my seat beside Amber.

I watch Jake's eyes in the candlelight searching my face, moving down my body.

> *Need to be your lover, baby*
> *Need to be the guy*
> *To hold you hard in the soft moonlight*
> *Love you till you cry.*

The music suddenly blares out into the subdued, slightly strained atmosphere. I turn around, try to adjust the volume from where I sit.

'I'll do it,' says Jake quietly. 'I'm going to get a refill. Anyone else?'

'Yes, me. Please,' I say quickly. The others murmur polite refusal.

When I hold out my glass his hand briefly covers mine. For seconds we gaze at each other. A look of tenderness then sadness comes into his face. I smile. Swiftly recovering himself he grins.

'Do you remember this, Lara?'

He goes to get the drinks.

'God, yes.' I look eagerly at Amber and Greg, suddenly wanting, in my alcohol-fuelled bonhomie, for them to share in our moment.

They sit closer together, vaguely expectant, polite and very young-looking.

'It was on the car cassette the first time I came to the house. Steve was driving like a madman. He,' I gesture extravagantly towards Jake and slop some whisky onto my wrist, 'was flat out on the back seat, completely stoned.' There is a ripple of quiet mirth from Amber and Greg. Jake is looking at me intently, drinking fast, his eyes shining. I wonder if he remembers massaging my shoulders that day. I wonder if he ever suspected I was rubbing myself on the strap of my handbag thinking of him.

> *To hold you hard in the soft moonlight*
> *Love you till you cry.*

The chorus begins its final refrain.

'You were wearing a little pink top,' he says suddenly, 'and a very short skirt.'

'Was I?' I bow my head over my glass. My vision blurs again.

'I think we should get the food,' Amber says quietly. 'It'll be burning.'

Jake follows her out of the room clutching his whisky glass close to his chest.

'Are you sure you're OK, darling. You seem to be a touch on the manic side, if you don't mind me saying.' Greg sits close by me on the sofa adjusting loose tendrils of my pinned-up hair.

'I'm getting slowly pissed,' I tell him, 'and I've not eaten much. I must stop that,' I continue vaguely. 'It's the sort of thing I keep lecturing Stacey about.'

'Well, whatever,' he sighs. 'Just watch it with those pills. I know they're alternative and New Age and stuff but just go easy.'

To change the subject I ask him about his earlier conversation with Jake regarding the following week's arrangements.

'And why exactly are you ducking responsibility?' I touch his cock playfully. 'Do you have plans for us, angel?'

He lowers his eyes, looks like a child who has been caught in a lie.

'I'm going away for a few days, Lara.' He looks into my eyes fearfully. 'I'm going to see Celine.'

'But that's wonderful Greg.'

Unexpectedly my eyes fill with tears.

'Well, it's your fault, you soppy old cow.'

He puts his arms around me. I smell the clean fragrance of his shirt.

I think, what am I going to do without you for a week?

We're all drinking too much. In the candleglow from the table and the splashes of light echoed all around the room, everyone's faces seem hollow and regal. Even Amber, with her fresh Slavic features, looks older and more mysterious. A woman on the cassette singing ballads in a breathy voice and the rain misting the window add to the atmosphere of significance and impending farewells.

'Candles in the rain,' I whisper, staring at the flickers of light reflected in the wet window. 'Do you remember that, Jake?'

I turn to him, suddenly needing him to remember.

'No, sweetheart,' he says softly.

From the edge of my vision I see Amber glance between the two of us.

'It was Steve's, an album.' I look across at Greg and Amber, laugh. They look at me awkwardly, apprehensively. 'God, you two probably don't even know what that is. Anyway it was some woman singer. Steve used to like to play it when we were ... shagging,' I finish, giggling. No-one else laughs. Greg smiles almost sympathetically.

'Steve, that's Jake's brother, yes?' Amber asks eagerly, as if my saying Steve's name is enough for me to transfer all my affections away from Jake.

'Yes,' I say quietly.

Then I feel Jake's hand on my knee under the table. It travels up my inner thigh. During the course of the meal I have been aware of his lower leg grazing mine from time to time. But now his touch is unmistakable, determined. He is brushing the soft cotton of my knickers between my legs. Thankfully, Amber and Greg are engaged in a conversation about their schooldays. I flash my disapproval at Jake. But he merely smiles and snakes his fingers under the crotch of my pants. I freeze as I feel him trace small circles around my clit. Despite my horror I feel myself moisten and fight an urge to bear down on his fingers. I also know Amber needs only to glance at my face and she will know.

I rise abruptly, holding on to the table, mumbling something about going to the bathroom. Jake looks annoyed, glances down at the hand now resting on his thigh, shunned like an unwanted pet.

Halfway down the corridor I hear Jake leave the room too, making some fatuous remark about getting more wine.

'Lara,' he calls softly, 'wait, please.'

I quicken my step but he is faster, his long strides, unsteady though they are, easily catching me up.

He puts his hand on the bathroom door, pushes it open.

The room smells of cool fading perfume – Amber's perfume. I wonder if she bathed there. I wonder if he was with her.

Jake locks the bathroom door behind us.

'What in hell's name do you think you're doing?' I say. 'This.'

I hardly have time to take another breath before he has me against him, in a firm embrace, one hand halfway up my skirt, clutching my buttocks to him, the other behind my neck. His fingers are hard into my tightly drawn-up hair, sections of it unravelling softly around his knuckles. His mouth covers mine urgently, his tongue probing between my teeth. I feel the hardness of his cock against my dress, massaging the opening of my lips. I force myself to fight my desire for him, compounded deliciously by the pressure in my abdomen caused by a vague need to pee.

'Jake, stop,' I protest weakly when his mouth momentarily leaves mine.

He draws back my head a little roughly so that I'm looking into his face. More hair falls away from the pins.

'You don't want me to stop, Lara,' he says quietly, gazing into my eyes. 'I know exactly what you want.'

He moves his hand to the front of my body, raises my skirt and thrusts his hand into the crotch of my knickers.

I close my eyes as he slides his fingers against my clit, wanting him so much yet somehow ashamed too.

'You give yourself away every time, Larissa,' he murmurs into my ear, increasing the pressure of his fingers on my clit. 'Oh, such a wet little girl.'

I shiver.

He increases the intensity of his caress and, despising myself, I press my pelvis towards him, luxuriating in my growing arousal which is made more intense by my gradually filling bladder. I know that in a matter of seconds I could come against his hand; I know that afterwards I'd regret it. Greg is right, I think, I have to sort this out.

With a supreme effort I force myself back from him, try to push away his hand. To my amazement his hold on me increases, his fingers inside my pants suddenly plunging into my cunt, his thumb digging into my lower abdomen.

'Jesus, Jake. Will you let me go? Please. I want to pee.'

He looks into my eyes. His own are burning, resolute. 'Do you really, Lara?' he says in a cold sneering manner.

I nod speechless and alarmed.

'Well, do it on the floor then!'

With a single rough movement that leaves me breathless, he pushes his thumb under the thin string-like fastening at one side of my knickers. It rips apart in a second and I feel the flimsy scrap of material whisper against my thighs and down my leg as it falls to the marble.

'What are you doing!'

I begin to struggle against him in earnest, my clenched fists drumming against his chest. The friction of his lower body against mine and my growing panic suddenly make

167

me fear I might well lose control. I squeeze my internal muscles as hard as I can.

'Jake I'm serious.' I start to sob as his hands come up to grab my wrists. 'Please.'

He stops. Staring at me breathlessly, he moves back, holding my wrists only loosely.

'Lara, don't cry please. I'm ... sorry. I'd no idea. I thought you were kidding. I thought you wanted it, too. Jesus I'm ... drunk. I didn't mean ...'

He turns away, dazed, wiping an arm over his face.

'I'll wait outside ... sorry.'

'No, Jake, don't ... stay.'

He turns. Stares at me.

'We need to talk.'

I take his hand then cross to the toilet. I sit down raising my dress.

'I'll turn around, shall I?' he asks quietly.

I smile. He looks so sheepish.

'Being a gentleman doesn't suit you, Fitzgerald.'

He kneels on the floor holding my hand, a gesture that strikes me as ludicrous yet sweet at the same time.

It takes some seconds before I can relax my muscles enough to start the flow.

'I've never done this in front of anyone. Not since I was about five, anyway.'

He laughs sadly. 'At least I can share something with you that no-one else can.'

'Jake, I just need to work this out. I want you. But ... this situation. I'm so confused. And, well, should I still be here anyway? The workmen start next week ...'

'This sounds suspiciously like a goodbye, Larissa.'

I burst into tears.

'Lara, no.'

He holds me against his shoulder while the last trickles leave me. 'You're not going to be upset. I'll give you time. We'll work it out. OK? Meanwhile I'll stay in the room next to yours ... Just in case you need me.'

'God ... you're incorrigible.' I laugh through my tears.

He reaches across me, pulls some toilet paper from the

wall and begins to dab the tears from my face. 'I always knew something like this would happen. The day you struggled up my driveway in those heels, clutching your briefcase. Even before that. I wanted to see you so much. But I knew the danger and I warned you, didn't I?'

I manage a small watery laugh. 'You did, Fitzgerald.'

'All finished, Larissa?'

'What? Oh, yes.' For a second I'd forgotten I was sitting on a toilet with my dress around my waist.

'Allow me, then.' He parts my legs gently and dabs me between the legs with the tissue stained by tears and make-up.

'Who says I'm no gentleman?'

He kisses me gently on the forehead.

We are just about to leave when he sees the scrap of my knickers on the floor. He picks them up, tucks them into the pocket of his jeans.

'A souvenir, Larissa,' he whispers. 'In case we don't have a next time.'

I glance out the window, hoping at least that the rain has stopped. It hasn't.

The volatility of the weather over the next week suits my mood perfectly. In the space of one day there are shower bursts, sometimes through the sun; there are blustery squalls of wind where the trees bend and writhe as if in some premature autumn. Then, often in late afternoon, the clouds part and the winds rest and a bright lonely calm is restored to everything.

I make sure I avoid Jake. He's fairly involved in the remaining classes with Greg gone so it's not difficult. I eat alone in the kitchen of a hundred memories, drink coffee by myself in the courtyard with the scent of flowers at their dizzying ripest. At night I slip into the lush sheets of my huge empty bed and curl up like some hibernating creature. I feel lower as the days go on. I have taken Greg's advice about the herbal remedies. But my feelings of restlessness and anxiety grow. So I swim a lot and walk in the gardens and, for the first time since

I came, make phone calls just to hear another human voice: to Jackie, my secretary, who assures me everything is going well and I am not needed back yet.

'Hang loose, Lara. It's all in order. We're getting the paperwork through now for the Fitzgerald job. How's that going by the way, you and the lord of the manor? I'm not wrong am I, sweetie? I did detect a certain gleam in the eye in that direction, a little frisson.'

'I'm far too old for frissons, Jackie.' Prim organised Ms Macintyre to the fore.

'Quite right too, sweetie. Go for a toy boy any time.'

'And I'm far too old for ... look, Jackie, I'll call later in the week, OK.'

I call Stacey.

'Mum, how's it going? Are you enjoying yourself. *Say* you are. You're far too *serious*, Mum.'

'Stace, how's the flat? Are you eating ...?'

'Have you bought any new clothes? I meant to say, not being funny or anything, but a bit Auntie Doris some of those button-throughs and things. Gross.'

'I *am* working, Stacey.'

'Oh and how's Uncle Jake? It must be great to catch up.'

I smile at this. Jake hasn't seen Stace since she was two. 'Uncle Jake is ... Uncle Jake.'

'Oh, Mum, *chill*. Loosen up. Get yourself a toy boy.'

I resist the temptation to phone Greg, although he has left a number. I will do it, I think, staring at the door joining my room to Jake's, when I have sorted all this out. When I'm chilled, hanging loose.

A team of electricians and joiners come to the house on Monday afternoon, several hours late, just as the sun comes out.

'Sorry darling, couldn't find the turn-off.'

A large man with an army crop and a face that seems wider at the bottom wipes the sweat from his brow and gazes at my bare midriff.

At that moment Jake, who I haven't seen for two days,

170

comes out of the summer-house looking dishevelled. Amber leans lazily against the stained-glass window casting an interested glance our way.

'I was just explaining to your wife here,' the foreman calls over to Jake, 'we lost our way a bit.'

'I am Lara Macintyre. I'm in charge of this project. Any delays or poor workmanship will be penalised.'

The workman looks slightly shocked, glances at Jake who looks startled too.

Jake shrugs. 'She's Lara Macintyre. She's in charge of the project. Sorry, chief.'

He walks away giving me a glance somewhere between amusement and disappointment.

'Well, we'd better get to it lads,' says the foreman.

'Look, I didn't mean to snap. This is my first big project.'

He glances around at the assembled men who are hot and look bored under the relentless sun. Then he looks me up and down with an almost avuncular friendliness.

'Don't worry, Petal. I think you, me and the lads'll get on just fine. I'm Spence, by the way. Big Spence to the lads.' He winks at me.

As they head back to the van to collect their equipment a boy at the end, tall, blond, very brown, drops his jacket. I go after him with it.

'Oh thanks, cheers.'

He blushes, just looking into my face. His eyes are sea green. He looks about eighteen, the same age as Stace. For a moment I really consider it as I gaze at the sweat on his tight torso, his strong boyish arms.

Perhaps he reads something of this in my face because he walks swiftly away, looking at me from under a white-blond fringe.

'Actually,' he says. 'It was my fault we got lost. I was reading the map. I'm hopeless.'

'Don't worry about it,' I call to him, 'I am too.'

The men open the doors of their van and talk among themselves. One of them says something to the boy and laughs. They glance back at me. But then they all stare at

Amber who is running over the grass wearing two strips of material across her body, the top one barely containing her bouncing breasts.

'Do *you* know where that asshole is now?' she asks as she rushes past me. The glint of suspicion in her eyes is unmistakable. I really do need to get this sorted out once and for all.

On the Wednesday night I take my first herbal tablet. It's been a bad day. Touring the house in the morning I overhear the foreman in one of the downstairs rooms saying to my blond-haired young god, 'Yep, about there, Kenny, it's near enough.'

I go in.

Kenny is perched up a long ladder inserting a fitting in the ceiling.

I smile nervously.

'Isn't that a little too far over?' I glance at the architect's plans, now a home for a flask of tea and a packet of cigarettes.

'No, no, Petal. These architect blokes are a bit up themselves. No idea of the practicalities of the job, you see, Lara.'

'Right . . . Well, I'd prefer it if you stick to the drawings . . . if possible.'

He gives me a small salute, reaches down to pick up a cigarette.

'Consider it done, Lara. Consider it done.'

From his precarious stance Kenny gives me a winning smile.

In the afternoon when the sun makes its usual dazzling and belated entrance and my misgivings about the progress of work in particular and my gnawing anxiety in general reach a peak, I decide to go for a swim.

I plough across the pool like a woman possessed. By the time I have sliced the water back and forth about twenty times, I'm ready to crawl onto the stone ledge. I stretch out in the couple of inches of ebbing water, letting it's soft rhythmic motion lull and caress me. I feel it splash gently against my sex lips. I put my fingers there, open my legs wider. I think of Jake and wriggle, I think of Greg and insert two fingers inside me, letting my knuckle rest on my clit. I think of Jake again; his strength, his tenderness, his body around mine, his hard cock that he denies me, and I can't help it. I stroke myself urgently and swiftly to orgasm. As I lie back trembling under the sky the sun leaves abruptly then reappears. A procession of clouds flies past my eyes. I think mistily, nothing stays the same, ever. When I wake up again the ledge is dry. My hair lies behind my head like wet seaweed. Strands of my fringe are stuck to my brow. My nipples sting with sunburn. My golden tan has a new rosy glow.

At eight in the evening I'm staring at the door leading to Jake's room and fighting off the urge to masturbate. I glance around the room looking for something to distract me. Should I start some sketches for one of my other projects (look to the future), rub more cream on my burnt nipples (no good, it'll make me think of Jake again), try out a new make-up look on my slightly pink face (impress my young blond electrician), phone someone (and be told to get a toy boy)? Nothing appeals. Then I spot a bottle of chocolate liqueur left after an experimental foray with Greg. I pour myself a generous glass and take it out to the balcony. It's a fresh fragrant evening and I notice how much more deep and mature the greenery has become. But here and there some of the foliage looks already tired. Glancing down at my red-flowered bush I am saddened to see that its blooms have perished. Once more it stands insignificant and alone. I gulp down the liqueur and make a decision. I will go to Jake's room. Now. I'll say, 'Fuck me', Fitzgerald. Now. And if he won't, I'll give him my departure date. Now.

I stand in front of the panelled door connecting the two rooms. Even in my present heated state of mind it seems too melodramatic to make such an entrance. I walk out to the hall.

I notice his door is slightly ajar. I tentatively put my head around. And withdraw promptly. Jake is sitting on the bed. With Amber. He holds her in a secure embrace, his mouth buried in the crown of her hair. The rest of her brazen snake-like locks fall over his arms.

Back in my room I have another liqueur, reach for one of the bottles of small brown pills, take three and curl up like a snail in my huge bed.

Friday noon and it is dull again. I sit at the kitchen table with a cup of soup I am finding hard to drink. All I can taste is salt and glutinous fibrous lumps. My mouth feels harsh. The sky outside is blank. Nothing seems wholesome any more.

My eyes are dry and groggy. I could put my head down now on the table and sleep. But I must wait for Jake, who's usually around at this time. Then he comes in smelling of coolness and grass. I can't look at his face. I concentrate on the familiar tear at the knee in his jeans. My throat tightens.

He sits opposite me.

'Lara, I've been trying to see you all week.'

'We've both been busy.'

I cradle my cooling cup. My hands feel cold.

'I'm glad I caught you. I've arranged a little surprise for you, for tomorrow . . .' He speaks quickly, enthusiastically. He seems nervous.

I look up sharply and his face blurs. I blink.

'It's not really a surprise if you've told me, is it?'

He runs a hand across his brow, although it isn't hot. He lights a cigarette and his fingers tremble.

'Well, no, but it's Saturday night, and I thought before you and Greg made plans . . .'

'Greg?'

'Yes, he's back tomorrow . . . isn't he?'

In the haze of the last couple of days I had lost track of this fact.

'Anyway, it's just a small party. I've contacted some of

the people we knew at college.' He smiles imploringly like a child trying to please.

I stare at him in horror.

'Right, well, sorry, I'll cancel. I just thought you'd like . . .'

'You thought right,' I say quickly, unable to bear the hurt and confusion in his eyes. 'It was unexpected, that's all. The work on the house is only just started.'

'We'll have it in the garden . . .'

'No, I mean, why . . . now? For me. I don't understand.'

He reaches across and grabs my wrist.

He looks at me and I know. Because I don't want you to go.

I lower my head.

'Oh, Jake . . .' I whisper.

'I see,' he says in a voice fighting for levity. 'You've made some plans of your own.'

There is silence. I hear the ticking of a clock, the first time I've been aware of one in the kitchen.

'When, Larissa?'

I swallow hard.

'Next week . . . sometime. I could come back the odd day or two to check on things. But I shouldn't have to stay . . . overnight.' My voice begins to break. I rise and make my way over to the glass doors. I press my brow on the cool window. I notice that the fat pink blooms on the bushes are edged with decay.

'Lara.' Jake puts his hand on my shoulder then on my neck. His touch seems uncertain, hopeless.

The palm of my hand is flat against the glass. I am suddenly warm, perspiring. The trees and grass, the forlorn looking summer-house, swim before my eyes. The sound of the wind in the bushes intensifies. I feel my knees weaken. I turn, brush Jake aside.

'I need to sit down,' I mutter then collapse thankfully on the bench. He crouches on the floor, his hand on my bowed head.

'What is it? Tell me what's wrong.'

'I feel . . . dizzy.'

175

'Get your head down. Right down, between your knees. That's it.'

I feel his hands stroke my hair and the back of my neck which is now drenched with sweat.

'OK, Lara. You're OK. I'll take care of you.' His very quiet voice becomes clearer as my consciousness returns.

But you won't be able to, I think, not from now on.

I raise my head, smile into his anxious eyes.

'I'm fine now. Sorry. Don't know where that came from. Probably just excitement from the thought of my party.' I laugh weakly.

'Come on, you should lie down. I'll help you upstairs.'

'No,' I say quickly, 'I don't think that would be a good idea, do you?'

On Saturday morning I'm out on the balcony sipping juice to relieve my dry mouth.

Greg bounds up the steps.

I gaze at him sleepily. It seems a long time since I last saw him.

'Oops, sorry,' he whispers glancing dramatically into the room. 'I take it you *are* alone?'

'I'm alone.'

'Oh for God's sake, Lara.'

'What?'

' "I'm alone." ' He mimics my flat tone. 'There you are again in that doomsday denim dress, no make-up and the smell of defeat all around you.'

'I am defeated. I'm leaving next week.'

'No you're not.'

He reaches for my hand, pulls me down to sit in his lap. 'You're having a party tonight, you're going to tart yourself up big style with a little help from moi, and you're going to torment J F so much that by the time you've finished with him he'll want to tear your knickers off and shag you on the lawn.'

'I wish.'

'Then, as your fairy godmother, it is my command.'

'Oh, Greg.'

It's good to laugh again, good to have him back.

'You must be sick of trying to transform me. I think I'm beyond help.'

He looks serious for a moment.

'You've helped me a lot, Lara.'

'Good God, your stepsister, I didn't even ask . . .'

'No matter, plenty time for tittle-tattle later. For now, I have to find my magic wand.'

'Greg, can I ask you something?' I wriggle off his lap, stand up. I don't want him to see my face.

'Which is?'

'These herbal things, the tablets. I'm afraid I lost them somewhere, dropped them from my handbag, probably . . . I'm sorry. But . . . I wondered if you had anything that would give me a bit of a boost. You know, help me sparkle a bit tonight.'

'I could see, I suppose,' he says in a mock put-upon tone. 'I don't know, Lara Macintyre – valerian queen.'

'Queen yourself.' I smile my thanks at him, a little uneasily.

Greg and I sip wine on the balcony as he puts the finishing touches to my hair. The night is balmy, fragrant. I've taken three of the new tablets and the world feels different. In the morning, summer was half over, a summer of dried-out flowers and tattered leaves. Tonight, new blooms appear, blue and misty-white, mysterious clusters dotted through the trees. The insect noise is joyous in the shrubbery. It is, I think, only mid-July.

'How do I look, Greg?' I swing around to him as he lets the last lock of hair settle on my shoulder. Already, from the rear of the house below us I can hear voices and music. Cars have crunched up on the gravel at the front, doors slammed, greetings made. The guests have disappeared into the house, leaving me to imagine what the last twenty years has done to them. Tonight the prospect of letting them see what I've become suddenly doesn't alarm me.

'Just ravishing, my darling . . . or maybe more as if you

want to be ravished. Come.' He takes my hand and leads me into the room so I can view myself in front of the oval mirror. Even the light in here is kind, the golden shade spilling its glow like sunset at my sandalled feet.

Greg has surpassed himself. My dress is ice-white, sheer and split in a couple of places around my legs. Underneath, my underwear is one-piece, shell pink, with the bra cut so far down that the tops of my nipples peep out. It fastens between the legs lengthways by a row of tiny buttons. Even standing I can feel their presence on my lips. I imagine sitting, staring at Jake, managing to climax just doing that.

'You look like an angel but you're going to act like a whore,' Greg says quietly.

'I'll drink to that.'

Greg and I walk around the side of the house to make our entrance. We link arms and voices hush perceptibly as we approach. It's twilight and the shrubbery is peppered with tiny electric lights. Speakers placed somewhere around the courtyard emit the light, heartening sounds of yesteryear into the warm evening. Several small tables are covered in pale cloth. Around these in groups are seated about a dozen people already loosened by alcohol and the fortuitous atmosphere. From my short distance away, I recognise only one or two of them.

'My God,' I whisper to Greg, 'Jake really has made an effort.'

'And here he comes, the man in black himself.'

Jake comes towards us. He is, as Greg says, dressed entirely in dark colours, one of the few times I haven't seen him in torn paint-splashed jeans. He looks gorgeous, slightly younger, and wonderfully ill at ease.

He looks straight at me, as if he hasn't seen Greg at all.

'You look beautiful, Lara,' he murmurs, then to the assembled guests, 'People, this is Lara Macintyre, some of you might remember. Lara's tarting up this old shell of a house for me.'

I smile foolishly, feeling like some dated celebrity that

the audience can't recall. A woman at the table in front of us rises a little unsteadily and walks towards me. A balding wiry man behind her follows apprehensively. I try to mask my surprise as the puffy features and over-dyed black hair, the podgy fingers clutching a glass, melt away to my memory of the busty Hispanic-looking man-eater I knew in first year. Geraldine Carter.

'Well.'

Her snakelike eyes gleam.

'I presume this young man must be . . . no, I'm wrong, it was a daughter you had, wasn't it?' She runs her hand down Greg's shirt as if he's a length of curtain material.

'I have a daughter called Stacey.' I tell her pleasantly, 'Greg is my friend . . . and lover.' Someone thrusts a glass of sparkling wine into my hand and I drink it thirstily.

'I never would have recognised you . . .'

'Nor I, you,' I say sweetly.

'We used to call you, now what was it, the ice maiden, the virgin queen, something . . .'

'Well, they certainly didn't call *you* that,' I say airily.

Beside me Jake smirks. I turn to him.

'I suppose Geraldine will be one of the many first years you shagged . . . eventually,' I say in a loud voice, taking in the seated company with a grin. There is a buzz of mirth and a lot of interested, amused glances.

'I . . . well, honestly Lara . . .'

'I quote, of course. You said . . .'

'I'm just going to find Amber . . .'

Jake turns abruptly and Geraldine Carter grabs her partner's hand and hurries into the kitchen, to return in minutes with her head bowed and a plate heaped with savouries clenched in a quivering pudgy hand.

'Christ, did I go too far?' I ask Greg.

'You were brilliant, but remember. It's not so much claws drawn with the women as pants down with the men.'

'I remember.'

I reach down and playfully squeeze his balls.

'Ooh, Ms Macintyre.' He rests his hand on my buttock as we walk.

I sit beside Nadia Gorman, the only person at the party who I've kept in touch with. In the year since I last saw her she's had her ice-blonde hair cropped and bears an uncanny resemblance to the tall athletic-looking man she has brought to the party, Richard.

'Mmm, Dick,' I say lowering my lashes. But I leave it there. I don't want to upset Nadia.

'I can't believe how fantastic you look. Doesn't she Richard?'

Dick's eyes rove from my legs, exposed by the two splits in my skirt, to the deep V neckline of my dress to the satin one-piece underneath, made visible by the action of the lights on the diaphanous material. I glance down my front and see the tops of my nipples.

'Absolutely amazing,' breathes Dick. I notice that he already has the beginnings of an erection.

Then Jake comes up behind my chair.

'Anyone for any more?'

I tilt my head back and come into contact with his lower body. I look up into his surprised eyes, letting the crown of my head rub against his cock.

He holds up a bottle.

'Wine?' he says weakly.

'Oh yes!' I say exuberantly as I feel the top of his hard penis rub against my neck. He sits hurriedly next to me and sets the bottle on the table.

Greg on the other side of me rises to refill glasses, with relaxed and nonchalant grace, despite the fact that my hand is massaging his slim hard buttock through his trousers.

'Well, you do seem to be enjoying yourself, Larissa,' Jake says, scrabbling nervously in his shirt for his cigarettes.

Then he realises he has misplaced his lighter. Quickly I stretch across the table to borrow someone's matches.

'Allow me.'

I extract one from the box, strike it and, leaning very

close to him, light the cigarette. Simultaneously I settle my hand on his thigh, nudging his balls.

He stares at me and inhales.

'In, Jake?' I ask him with wide eyes.

'Sorry?'

He gives me a look of pure astonishment.

'Are you alight?'

'Yes, thank you, Lara,' he says in a quiet, almost gruff, voice.

Four or five other people, mostly men, have set their chairs around the periphery of our table.

Someone has turned up the music. The light throb of rock music pulsates through the air and makes me cross my legs tight to intensify the small glow of pleasure and excitement swelling between them. I feel the pressure of the buttons around my clit. I sip my wine and smile.

'I wasn't aware you knew Nadia,' I say pleasantly to Jake. 'Unless she was another of the girls you sha . . .'

I can say this quite safely because Nadia has told me in the past that she wasn't one of Jake's conquests . . . although he had tried.

'I know Richard,' Jake says quickly, 'and I knew you were friendly with his sister . . .'

'Sister, really? I hadn't realised. I must say you look exceedingly fit, Dick. I take it you're very physical.'

Dick flushes slightly, then smiles shyly.

'Actually, I used to play a lot of rugby. Now I'm a sports physiotherapist.'

'That's fascinating. Jake always reckoned *he* was good with his hands didn't you?' I drain my glass.

Jake lights another cigarette, says nothing.

'Could I maybe ask, Dick . . . if you don't mind . . . Could you give my feet a bit of a rub? These silly sandals we girls wear . . .' I glance with false sorority at a woman who has joined our group. Tall and elegantly dressed, but with her pale red hair knotted into a severe bun and large spectacles overpowering her unmade-up face. Angela Lloyd. Even shyer than I had been at college, always dressed in long skirts and flat shoes. Both of us probably the only two virgins in the first year. Except that I wasn't – technically. I had Steve.

Dick obligingly spreads his thighs and takes my bare feet onto his chair, kneading, pressing and pulling at the joints of my feet. Although the experience is not altogether pleasant I close my eyes in simulated bliss, emitting several oohs, ahs, and mmms along the way. 'Mmm, further up Dick. I think I'm getting cramp in my calf . . . oh yesss.'

'I hope Greg doesn't mind,' says Dick in a light, but nonetheless wary tone.

Greg is discussing skin tone and peroxide with Nadia and doesn't even hear. I turn instead to Jake with rapt eyes.

'God no, Greg is only *one* of my lovers. And I am one of his.'

Jake pushes his chair back.

'Excuse me, I'm going to check on Amber.'

I glance back into the lighted kitchen, across to the fairylight-bordered lawn where two couples are now dancing rather drunkenly.

'Where is she anyway? I haven't seen her all night.'

'She's . . . not feeling too great. She's lying down.'

As he walks into the house, I picture Amber naked in his large bed and the taste of bile fills my mouth. I wash it down with a large gulp of wine.

'Harder, Dick, harder. Further up . . . there.'

By the time Jake returns, Angela Lloyd and I are gyrating barefoot on the lawn with four guys meandering between and around us. They whirl us around by the waist, grab our backsides and none too successfully try to rotate our pelvises against their own. We have perfected the art of holding onto an almost full glass of wine while boogying.

'God, but this is energising, Lara.'

Angela, knees bent spreads her legs while Geraldine Carter's balding husband tries to limbo beneath her. His head gets stuck in her crotch.

'Christ, but it's like having a bowling ball up your pussy,' she giggles.

She looks impressive, lycra-silk designer dress hoisted over her hips, curtain of hair loose about her face, heavy specs safely in beaded bag, lipgloss on, as rich and sticky as cherry liqueur.

'I must say I'm astonished at the change in you,' I say to her breathlessly as we lie back on the cool lawn, drinking wine, while the music softens and slows to more sedate folk-rock.

'Honestly Lara, this is pretty rare for me. I don't usually party much. I do Latino and Rock'n'Roll classes but hardly anyone knows. Remember I dropped out in second year . . .' She screws up her face at the unaccustomed taste of the wine. 'I became an accountant. Never had faith in my creative abilities, or any others for that matter. Do you know . . .'

She rolls over towards me on the grass giving the rest of the company a wonderful view of her endless thighs and high tight bum. 'I haven't had a shag for nearly a year.'

'Well, here's your chance.'

I manouevre her round to look at Jake and Greg sitting about ten feet away apparently involved in less trivial conversation. Greg waves. Jake shifts uncomfortably in his chair.

'You can see your knickers, the way you're sitting. You're giving him a stiffy,' Angela splutters.

'You can see yours too, you silly cow.'

And we both fall back on the grass convulsed with laughter.

Recovering a little she whispers, 'Anyhow, there's no way Jake Fitzgerald would want to screw me. You'd have had to pay him in first year.'

'We're not in first year now, Angela. But actually I was thinking of Greg.'

She blinks at me. 'But he's yours.'

'He's not anyone's, for God's sake. That *is* very first year.' We both sit upright with some difficulty, neither of aus trying to cover our underwear, despite, or maybe because of, the hostile glances we're getting from some of the female guests. 'Greg is the most amazing lover. Very energetic. I have never arched my back so much for anyone's cock . . . Anyway, time for a refill, don't you think?'

We both try to stand up, together and separately, but keep slipping with increasing mirth back on the grass. Finally, Jake rises and comes towards us, followed by Greg.

'Here comes the cavalry.' I giggle.

'Bayonets extended,' Angela snorts.

Jake has me upright in seconds despite my attempt to pull him down to the grass.

He looks stern at first but when I put my arms around his neck he shows no signs of wanting me to let go.

Greg seems impressed by Angela's slim but shapely dancer's legs as she wraps them around him while he's hoisting her to her feet.

'Very 1930s Paris,' he murmurs, running a knowing finger down her long pale thigh. 'Have you ever considered . . .?'

'You should see Greg doing the samba,' I say with sudden inspiration. I turn to Jake. 'I was just telling Angela, no-one can arch a woman's back like Greg.'

'Is that so, Larissa?' he mutters against my cheek.

As the next extravaganza of guitar rock crashes into the air Greg half-drags, half-carries Angela's long pointed-limbed form across the grass in a very impressive, if not entirely accurate adaptation of the dance. The drama and daring of this spectacle, and the sheer amount of alcohol that has been consumed persuades most of the gathering unsteadily to their feet to join them. I recognise Lisa Bryant, a former dazzling brunette, now faded and tired looking; Elisabeth Scott, once serene and smug in sheeny velvet, now with darting nervous eyes and darting nervous limbs. Twenty years ago these girls could twist and shimmy their pert barely-clad bodies into the most degenerate recesses of the male imagination. Now they shamble awkwardly as the music falls around them. They make contact with their partners for affirmation rather than effect. They are all looking forward to their next drink. In my skimpy dress, and wine-fuelled high, it occurs to me for a moment, how could you think yourself any different?

Jake and I are still entwined. He's edging me away from the rest of the crowd, away from the spattered brightness of the bushes and the insistent throb of the loudest music. His arm is around my waist, pulling on the fabric of my dress and my underwear. I feel the tiny hard buttons at the crotch of my knickers begin to press up and rub between my legs as we walk.

'What are we going to do?'

I hope my voice is soft and enticing, although I know it probably sounds inebriated and indistinct.

'Maybe we're going to see if I can make your back arch,' he says mildly.

I stop and kiss him hard on the mouth, pressing myself against him, pulling his body to me. I feel his erection grow harder against me and his embrace grow warmer. Finally he releases me and looks into my eyes. I smile tipsily up at him. We stand under the shadow of the trees at the rear of the garden. Everything is very dark and comparatively quiet. Tiny stars peek through the black fabric of leaves. In my heightened state I take this as a good sign.

'You're driving me crazy, Lara.'

His voice sounds harsh. His eyes look serious.

'Oh good,' I say, hoping that it is – that he means I'm tormenting him with desire, not that he finds my behaviour unacceptable. To test this out I start to unbutton his shirt, sliding my hand over the soft down of his chest. With the other I begin to caress the ridge of his cock, feeling it stir more through his trousers.

'Oh, Christ,' he whispers. Then, in a slow, flat tone that makes me shiver, 'Tell me what you want Lara. Has anything changed in the last week?'

He grips my shoulder and my tiny shoulder strap slides to the top of my arm.

I undo more buttons on his soft black shirt. Like all Jake's clothes it is understated and of dubious quality. But it suits him and I feel humbled that he has made an effort for me. I start to unzip his trousers, run my fingers over the tip of his cock. It's already glazed with pre-come.

'How many times do you have to be told? I want you to fuck me, Fitzgerald – standing here under the trees if need be, or in the bloody bushes as if we were a couple of kids. Christ, Jake, open my knickers and shag me in the middle of the lawn in front of everyone if you must.'

I laugh but it sounds forced. Jake isn't laughing. He takes my hand from his zip and slips his own through the front panel of my dress finding the round buttons of my knickers and massaging them deep into my sex lips. I am oddly ashamed of the fact that I am already wet.

'They move against me when I walk,' I murmur as if in apology. 'I can't help it.'

His fingers stop for a second but I'm so aroused I can't prevent myself from trying to bear down on the palm of his hand. It will take very little for me to have an orgasm but I don't want to, not like this.

Jake's arm encircles my waist. He holds me against him. I feel the soft pressure of his fingers as one by one he opens the buttons of my damp gusset.

'I have to know, Larissa, if it's me you want. Not Greg or Richard or that arsehole Stuart McNab or someone else whose cock you've never had . . .'

'That *was* Stuart McNab – that wasted-looking guy with the pasty face and the lines, who tried to put me over his shoulder when we were dancing. Whatever happened to his boyish good looks?'

'Another slave to the white powder. Don't sidetrack me, Lara, I overheard them all, "little Lara Macintyre, who'd have believed it. She's certainly making up for lost time." I just wonder what your little performance tonight is about.'

186

'Maybe that's for me to know and you to find out.'

Jake stares at me, his breath coming fast. The loudening laughter and the increasingly raucous voices drift towards us on the night air. I pull down the top of my dress, exposing my bare breasts and nipples and the sleek satin underwiring beneath them. How dare any of them judge me.

'Stop it, Lara. I'm not going to shag you out here in the open, as if you were some whore.'

'No, but you'll bring me off with your fingers, though, won't you?'

I expect him to take his hand from between my legs then, but he doesn't. I struggle against him but he moves his fingers faster. I close my eyes and try not to moan, try not to feel my clit throb, my lower body swell and burn with the urge to come. He bends his head, takes my nipple in his mouth, sucks it, then bites it to hardness.

'I don't want it like this Jake, I want to come with your cock inside me.'

'Then tell me the truth.'

He stops with his hands resting on my body.

Suddenly there is a burst of laughter and the wavering entangled forms of Lisa Bryant and Stuart McNab float towards us. The party is riotously branching out. Jake pulls me further under the trees.

He looks at me as if weighing something up.

'Maybe there's something *I* should tell you.'

He smooths down my dress and leads me towards the summer-house. Somewhere behind us Lisa and Stuart, amid a great deal of rustling foliage and laughter, are forming a liaison of their own in the shrubbery.

'Wouldn't it be a laugh if we found Jake and the luscious Lara humping in the next rhododendron?' I hear Stuart whisper.

'Do you really think she's that luscious?'

Just before the summer-house, I stop, filled with some unease, some foreboding.

'I won't want to hear it, will I, what you're going to tell me?'

He puts his hand to my face, strokes my skin, gazes into my eyes as if needing to find an answer. Then he glances up at the sky and sighs. When he looks at me again it's with his familiar expression of absence, the one Greg calls his 'checking out' look.

'What would you say if I told you Amber was pregnant?' he says then in a cold, steady voice.

I laugh – ludicrously, gazing at his calm face and the stars above him which sharpen like bullets then fade.

He reaches for my hand, turns towards the summer-house.

'Come on, Lara,' he says softly.

'No.' I can't move. 'I'm going.'

Somewhere behind us in the scraping of the bushes are the twinned sounds of hilarity and desperation.

'Where are you going, Lara?'

Again the soft vacant expression.

'To leave . . . tonight.'

I begin to shake, the haze of booze and valerian leaving me as pitilessly as a former best friend.

'You aren't able to drive. No one else can take you. Even Greg can't save you tonight.'

'You . . . lied to me. I trusted you. I've always trusted you and you . . . lied.'

'So hit me then. Go on. I won't try to stop you. Come on Lara, punish me.'

I feel very cold, as if someone has snatched the warmth from the summer, as if the trees will change, the leaves fall. Everything will become bare and exposed in an instant. I turn and open the door to the summer-house. I sit on the hammock, dragging a loose bit of sheeting over my trembling shoulders. Jake, with absurd clarity of purpose, bends to light the oil lamp on the table. A previous reveller has left a half-full bottle of wine. I pick it up, take a long invigorating drink. Jake sits beside me, playing with the ends of the sheeting in my lap.

'You don't want to punish me then,' he says in a strained flat way. 'Does that mean you don't care at all?'

'It means I care very much,' I burst out. 'It means if I

188

despise anyone, it's myself for being so stupid and naïve. Look at me, under all this.' I wave my hands around my dress and my face. 'I'm still just seventeen, trusting everyone else to know what's best. Steve . . . and you. I believed you, Jake.'

Then I watch amazed as his hands come slowly forward and he lays me back on the hammock.

'What are you doing!'

I try to move upright but his upper body bends over me. I feel him move his hand under my dress, seek out my still-open knickers.

'Jake!'

'I'm sorry, Lara, but I think you've told me what I need to know.' And he does look sorry, but somehow relaxed too, lighter.

'Amber *is* pregnant,' he continues, 'or she might be . . . but I'm certainly not the father.'

'I don't understand.'

'It's someone in town, a biker would you believe?'

He laughs shortly.

'So, why did you let me think . . .?'

'Because I had to know how you felt.'

I feel a knot of something, fury, hysteria, joy, start deep inside me as I gaze incredulously into his eyes. For a second I do indeed want to strike him or scream abuse but then suddenly I just laugh.

'Christ, what a pair we are.'

'You're worse.'

'I'm not, either.'

He lifts my skirt around my waist. It lies like snow around my abdomen. He strokes the buttons on my knickers against my clit. My thighs fall open further. He kisses me between the legs. I reach out and touch his soft curls, his eyelids.

'Stop wasting time and fuck me, Fitzgerald.'

'On this thing?'

I giggle.

'We can try.'

He reaches towards his zip and I wriggle down the

hammock towards him. The look of sheer gratitude in his eyes almost overwhelms me.

Then suddenly the door swings open and I slide rapidly upwards, sick and dizzy with the movement, glancing over Jake's shoulder.

'What the fuck's going on here?'

A slight Californian drawl. A taut well-honed body, in very expensive-looking well-cut clothes. Dark hair, greying at the front but cropped short by expert fingers. Light eyes sparkling with health and amusement.

It takes some seconds for my befuddled senses to know the identity of the interloper. When I do I can't help but smile. I rise and go towards him, wanting him to share in our joy. My dress surrenders chastely down my thighs like a virgin bride's. Jake's expression of mild irritation as he looks backwards, changes when he sees who it is. He sits up, adjusting himself hurriedly. But the look on his face as I walk groggily past him doesn't truly register at that moment – that look of anger, amazement, powerlessness that I remember from all those years ago as I go towards my daughter's father, the man who became my first lover.

'Hello, Stevie.'

He holds out his arms to me and everything becomes hazy.

The last thing I remember is my head on his chest, starting to sink as my knees give way, the mark of my rose-pink lipstick as it stripes down his designer shirt like a weal or a tribal mark, the splodge of my mouth on his pale exquisite trousers like a rosebud, somewhere near his crotch.

Chapter Seven

I know it's late by the fall of light on my bed. I'm alone in the tangled sheets, still dressed in my finery like some Christmas-tree fairy thrown into a box. I force down some water, find some painkillers and, after a moment's quivering hesitation, three of Greg's herbal stimulants. I sit back and try to remember. I can't. I have no recall of events after my collapse in the summer-house. I glance out at the hot pale sky and I tremble all over. Jake. I have to find him.

As soon as my feet hit the floor I feel nauseous but fight it back and stumble to the panelled door. Jake's room is extremely tidy, showing no signs of use either, past . . . or imminent. I rush out into the gloomy corridor, in a wave of panic, calling out his name, uncaring who else might hear me, who might still be around after the party.

'He isn't here.' The voice comes from the seventies room, a slightly preoccupied, unconcerned voice. Steve.

He is half-sprawled on the boxy sofa, still in his lip-stick-stained clothes. He smokes a small dark cigar, which fills the room with a malodorous mist, and he is studying some papers spread between his legs – the architect's drawings for the house. I wonder vaguely how he got hold of these but it's not my main concern. I sit beside him dry-mouthed and dizzy, frantically shaking his arm.

'Do you know where Jake is? Do you? Stevie?'

He looks at me with surprise.

'Last night he said he was going away with some girl, hippy-sounding name, taking her home . . .'

'Amber.' I can barely speak.

'Yes, that's it. Said he needed a break. I have to say, Lara, that I got the impression it was because I'd turned up. Call me thin-skinned if you like . . .'

I don't call him anything because at that moment my stomach lurches and I dash to the open window and vomit ice water and half-digested pills onto the thick glossy branches of the blossom tree.

Steve comes up behind me.

'I take it little Lara has a touch of a hangover.'

Down below through the wall of greenery I see Greg plant a farewell kiss on the hand of a bespectacled, coiffured Angela Lloyd.

'Little Lara's a fucking idiot.'

I turn and wail the remains of my eyeliner onto the lipstick slash on his shirt.

He sighs and wraps his arms around me.

'Come and tell your Uncle Steven all about it.'

I sit on his lap and sob out my story about Jake.

He says nothing for a while, just strokes my hair and rocks me a little. In my dazed, exhausted state I find his ministrations very soothing. Unconsciously, my hand slips inside his beautiful soiled shirt. I can't help but notice that he has an erection. I think vaguely that neither of us will mention it.

'Do you remember, Lara? This was how we got together all those years ago.'

I gaze at him, puzzled. There's a sadness, a wistfulness in those grey eyes.

Suddenly I do remember. Me, the autumn after I left school going back to tell him about my A-level result. An excuse really, because I fancied him. I was made-up to the eyeballs and mentally practising my lines. But my grade had been disappointing, not what either of us expected. I walked into his room and smiled as I told him. As he stood there appraising me, I burst into tears. He had taken me on his lap on the large oval chair he used to pose models in. On that occasion too I messed up his shirt with my make-up. That afternoon I lost my virginity to him.

'Oh, Stevie.'

I kiss his mouth once, softly. He touches my now bare eyelids.

'I always knew you wanted Jake you know, right from the word go.'

'But you too, Steve,' I say quickly, 'only . . .'

'Only I was a useless shag.'

He laughs shortly.

'It was *me*. I was hopeless . . .' I snuggle further into his chest, reach up and lose my fingers in his short silky hair.

He lifts my legs, which have slipped, a bit further up into his body. His hand, by accident, slides underneath one of the panels of my dress. His fingertips rest enticingly near my bare pussy.

'God, sorry, Lara . . .'

'Leave it. Leave your hand where it is.'

'What?'

I kiss him hard on the mouth and wriggle forward on his lap so that my lips settle on his hand.

'Jesus, you're quite wet, Lara.'

He looks at me in gentle surprise.

I close my eyes and let myself luxuriate in the slow hesitant movement of his fingers through my lips. I try not to think of Jake.

'Oh that is good, that is soooo good . . .'

'Is it, Lara?' He sounds uncertain, apprehensive even.

I open my eyes.

'Steve you mustn't be scared of me. I'm not seventeen any more. I want you as a lover. Today, this minute I need you, Stevie. And I think, somehow, you need me too.'

He reaches up, strokes my unbrushed mussed up hair. Christ, I must look some sight.

'You're beautiful, you know that.'

I laugh, a little shakily. 'Cut the bull and fuck me senseless.'

I sit astride him rubbing myself on his designer-clad erection.

'You don't mind if I leak a little on your Italian couture?'

'You do what you want, my sweet.'

He runs his hand down my dress, pulls it over my head, moving his cock against my pussy. Then he kisses my nipples, cupping my breasts in their shell-like coverings as if they're precious things. I begin to press myself harder into him.

'Stevie, could we ... could I take you inside me?' I whisper. 'I feel close to coming and I want to hold on a bit, slow down.'

He gazes at me in admiration.

'My God, you've changed, Lara. I remember when . . .'

'So do I . . . I need to be in control, Steve.'

I lift my hips and he slips down his trousers. I can't help but notice the sizable stain I have made on them with my juices on the lipstick mark.

'I'll owe you a fortune in dry-cleaning bills.' I giggle, straddling his cock and inserting the tip into my wet pussy.

I slide down onto his root and he fills me with his hardness. I resist the temptation to push my clit against him, although the urge is almost unbearable. Instead, I begin to squeeze him as hard as I can with my internal muscles, release, then again tighter, a sensation that Greg has assured me is irresistible to any man. It has the desired effect.

'Jesus, that is unbelievable.'

His head falls back on the sofa, his eyes closed. He looks so tanned and healthy, suddenly young again. I lean forward to remove his shirt and, in doing so, change the angle of penetration. Steve bites his lip as his cock is forced forward, deeper inside my abdomen. I hold it there awhile, massaging my clit lazily on the base, running my hands over his brown hard shoulders, his tight abdomen. Just gazing at his gym-toned firm body is making me feel flushed and desperate to come. I slide slowly up and down his shaft. He pushes up, meeting me. I move more rapidly, digging my nails into his chest. He grips my buttocks. His head falls on my breast.

'Oh, Lara,' he murmurs. 'Sweet little Lara.' There is a note of loss, of regret in his voice. I move myself more urgently. I look at the tree, at its encroaching green mass almost seeming to fill the room. Then I close my eyes to stop seeing Jake's face in my mind. Suddenly Steve slows.

'Can you still have babies?' he whispers.

'What kind of cheeky question is that?' I gasp. 'I'm a good few years younger than you, don't forget.'

He looks up at me.

'Unless you want to take a chance I'd better put something on . . . Do you, want to take a chance?'

I stare at him.

'That's how we got Stacey, remember?'

'I think I'd better put something on.'

His voice is quiet. He seems far away.

I move off him as he reaches down and takes a condom from a flawlessly tailored pocket in his trousers.

I can't help but laugh.

'Christ, Stevie, you're either a complete optimist or you're incredibly organised.'

'I like to think I'm both,' he says seriously and, for a moment, I glimpse the old pompous Steve. But instead of irritation I feel a strange affection for that young, headstrong guy who only wanted to please me and so often failed.

Suddenly I no longer want to sit astride him, driving him insane with the skill of my frenzied lovemaking. I no longer want to prove myself.

'I'm going to lie on this sofa and I want you to take me slowly and gently,' I whisper.

I almost add 'like it should have been then.' But if I have changed, then certainly he has too.

He lies at my side on the brown cording. At first we are content to hold each other, kissing and caressing with no urgency, but then we look into each other's eyes and it's as if it's the first time, as if we've never made love before. As he gently brushes my clit and takes my nipples into his mouth I feel a tremendous sense of wonder and anticipation. I take his cock in my hand, nudge it against my hungry pussy.

'Little Lara,' he whispers and slips himself so carefully inside me it seems that he thinks I might break.

As he fucks me slowly, making longer and more lingering contact with my clit, I feel myself sink into a hazy bliss. My ebbing hangover and the lack of food prolong this dreamlike sensation and it's not until his body moves more urgently against mine, until my pelvis rises and pushes towards him that the image comes again – behind my closed eyes it is Jake I see, Jake's body I feel, as we drive each other to orgasm.

For a while we lie in silence, listening to the wind fill the tree, watching sunlight come in splashes through its shivering green veil. I am lost in my thoughts of Jake and I believe, suddenly, that Steve is too.

Finally, too cold and desolate to continue such fruitless imaginings I jump up.

'I don't know about you but I'm desperate for a bath.'

He looks at me uncertainly.

'With me, you mean?'

I laugh. 'Why not?'

He gazes about the room at the charming outmoded furniture, the half-burned candles, the russet Autumn 79 walls and his eyes fill with reminiscence and sadness.

'Why not indeed,' he whispers.

I fill the bath while Steve walks around, stroking the marble walls, admiring the beautifully sculpted chairs, the way, as he says, that it feels like being contained in the centre of a waterfall.

'A man of conflicting visions, my brother,' he remarks.

I go to him, slip off the robe he has borrowed from Jake's room. In it he looks thin and boyish.

'It's why you came, isn't it, Stevie; to see Jake again?'

He doesn't reply but takes my hand as we go into the scented foam of the sunken bath. We lie at either end, our legs touching, not sexually, but comforting.

'The day I got back from the States I bumped into that hellish woman with the black hair and rough skin, the one with the weasly husband.'

'Geraldine Carter.'

'She seemed surprised I didn't know you were here. She told me about the party and I thought I should make an appearance.'

'But you really wanted to see Jake, not me,' I persist.

I move round, slide down in the warm water beside him, stroke the wetness from his brow.

'What's it about, Stevie? Maybe I can do something.'

He looks into my eyes, then away again as if ashamed.

'When you told me earlier about Jake's wife, how he feels he must be punished . . . you thought I didn't know he'd been married . . . but I did. I always knew.' He looks at me solemnly and, beneath the water, puts his arms around my waist. 'I should have come to see him . . . after she . . . after Victoria died.'

'Why didn't you?' I say softly.

He sighs, holds me a bit closer. My shoulders, out of the water, shiver.

'The first thing I thought when I heard was, how typical. Reckless womanising little bastard, and now some poor girl's topped herself because of him. Only I didn't know the full story. I hadn't even met Victoria. I had no idea, but I made a judgement . . . I was wrong.'

I shiver again and he rubs my shoulders.

'Jake made the same judgement . . . if that's any consolation.'

We wrap ourselves in large towels and go and stand on the balcony. The trees on either side of us are restless. Down below in the kitchen courtyard the tables are clear and the lights are gone from the bushes. I picture Jake clearing up early in the morning, smoking copiously and glancing at his watch. Amber, well-slept and fresh-faced, sitting in a pretty dress, watching him. I close my eyes against the whispering garden that seems soulless without him.

I turn to Steve, snuggle against his shoulder. He puts his arms around me and holds me very tight as if knowing my pain.

'I want to make it up to him, Lara. When I see what's happened here, half of the house gutted, half of it left as it was, his paintings in the summer-house . . .'

'But he's making an effort now. He's got me here to sort things.'

'He still wants some rooms unchanged though. It's eery . . .'

'Where did you get those plans, Steve?'

Suddenly I feel threatened, unsure, seventeen again.

'They were lying around in the sitting room. I'm sorry, perhaps I shouldn't have looked.'

Christ, I think. I'm forgetting things. I don't know what I'm doing any more. I smooth his damp ruffled hair. 'It's fine Stevie.' I hesitate. 'What did you think of them anyway?'

My pulse races. I find it hard to meet his eye. The omniscient teacher and the inexpert naïve pupil again.

'I think it all looks amazing. You're a very clever girl Lara Macintyre. But I always told you that.'

'And I never believed you.'

We walk back to my room, hand in hand as if nothing has changed in twenty years. I open the door and the sun has shifted position. The shutters are open but the light falls dull and heavy on the unmade bed, the scattered clothes. Another empty wine bottle has joined the one I shared with Greg the previous evening. I don't know how it got there. I slump down on the foot of the bed.

'Christ, I'm tired.'

Steve pulls back the sheets, tidies them a little.

'Get in, then.'

I slip inside. An immense rush of gratitude and relief

floods through me as my head sinks onto the pillow. Steve smiles down. I run my hand over the space next to me.

'And you?' I say, looking up.

'You want me to?'

He looks solemn, unsure.

I nod and he pulls back the covers.

I slide my leg across his thighs and he holds me quite loosely, stroking my hair warily.

'This new boyish reticence you have is quite charming.'

He laughs ruefully. 'I should have had it twenty years ago. I was a pain in the arse wasn't I, Lara?'

'I loved you.'

He runs his hand down my back, cups my buttocks, pulls me further on top of him.

He grows hard against me, but I know it won't matter if we do nothing about it.

Emboldened by the level of intimacy we have reached so quickly, I dare to ask him the question that has lurked at the back of my mind all day.

'What happened last night, later on, I mean?'

He raises himself on the pillows. 'You don't remember any of it?'

I shake my head.

'Well, after you flaked out in the summer-house we helped you up here.'

'We?'

'Jake and I. You insisted on walking, so we took one arm each . . .'

'Past everybody at the party?' I look at him in dismay.

'No, we took you round the other side of the house, although I wouldn't worry – everyone was pretty blocked by that time.'

I glance across at the extra wine bottle.

'And you both came in here with me?'

'You were determined to have another party – just the three of us.' He laughs. 'I quote your exact words as you stretched out most enticingly on this bed, "Which of my two favourite men do I want first?"'

199

'Oh God.'

'Lara, you were hilarious ... very sweet ... though I have to say I don't think Jake saw it that way.'

He plants a brief kiss on my brow.

'Then you passed out, so Jake and I had a few drinks on the balcony. It was strained between us. It was then that I really saw it, probably for the first time in my life.'

I caress his cock. Absently. Needing to touch him for reasons of solace, needing to be touched back. He runs his hand up my thigh, lightly feels my backside.

'What did you see?' I whisper, afraid.

'That terrible insecurity. He just couldn't stand the thought of needing you, falling in love with you, maybe, and me coming back to take you away from him. Ridiculous as all that is – that's the way he saw it. That's why he left.'

'I know.' I go over on my side. I tremble. I place the tip of his cock just inside me.

He slides inside me, holding me firmly against him.

'I want to stick around for a while, help you with the house. For Jake.'

'Yes.'

He fucks me hard, rolling on top of me. I cling to him as if to a rock. Then I let myself drown, heaving in ecstasy and despair. I want to stop seeing Jake's face, want to stop feeling him around me.

We lie breathless looking out at the quivering trees and the pale sky. We are connected by a loose embrace and our memories.

'When will he come back, Stevie?'

'I don't know, my sweet. I just don't know.'

Early next morning Steve and I are touring the house. A mist has fallen and only the shadows of the distant trees and shrubbery can be seen. I feel claustrophobic and anxious. I need my herbal medicine to kick in soon. Steve, in his pale expensive clothes, looks cool and at ease as we walk through the rooms. He glances at the fittings already in place and back at the drawings, smokes his dark cigar and occasionally mutters 'I see.' Or 'Yeesss, like that.' He taps walls, looks for long seconds up at ceilings, opens windows, tests railings in the wet oppressive milkiness and smiles at me fondly. Around nine-thirty he looks at his watch.

'So what's happening today, then?'

For seconds I stare at him, hazily trying to grasp what he means. Then, like a slow motion picture speeding up, I realise.

'The electricians are finishing off completely, then the painters start before noon.' I say this with false briskness.

Steve frowns.

'Bloody late, aren't they?'

'Probably lost in the fog,' I say wearily.

He wheels around, fixes me with a surprised and rather exasperated gaze.

'Well they fucking well shouldn't be.'

My heart races as I remember just that wheeling round movement, just that slickness of the wrist as he checks his watch. Steve Fitzgerald, art teacher expounding on the importance of keeping to a time framework during exams and Lara Macintyre, student, a little behind schedule in the outline drawing for her still life.

'I'll pick them up on it,' I say in a brittle voice. 'When they arrive.'

We're in the downstairs rooms at the front. Three of them have been opened up into one big area through the use of large archways. The walls are to be left light and matt, not iridescent like most of the others.

'I thought this would be a good reception area – functions, that sort of thing, if Jake ever gets into that.' I say this quietly, still aggrieved by his perceived criticism.

He walks around touching the finish of the archways, getting a feel for the space, admiring the new pale wood floor. Then, as if he knows he went too far earlier, he comes and puts his arms around me.

'This is very impressive, Lara.'

'Thank you.'

'It would, in fact, make a tremendous exhibition area. Jake could show his own works or the students' or . . .'

'Christ, you're doing it again!'

He looks genuinely perplexed. My intellect tells me I'm being irrational, that fatigue and stress and some chemical imbalance are making me react oddly, 'manic' as Greg calls it, but, emotionally, I can't seem to regain equilibrium.

'You don't have to keep giving me advice,' I say in as steady a voice as I can. 'This is *my* business. I know what I'm doing.'

I think, But you don't, you don't know what you're doing any more.

Steve smiles humbly. 'Lara, I have no intention . . .'

At that moment there is a jarring crunch on the gravel and through the misty window we watch the workmen's van judder to a halt.

Big Spence gets out and lights a cigarette while the van is being unloaded.

Steve swiftly masks the glimmer of annoyance on his face.

'Do you want to see any more just now?' I ask quietly.

He gives me a brief tight smile. 'I think we should leave it for now. I have some calls to make . . .'

At the sound of the men lumbering their equipment into the bare-boarded hall he lowers his eyes to the drawings, feigning preoccupation.

I stand rather hesitantly in the doorway to greet Big Spence.

'Lara, petal, and how are you today?'

He comes into the room, takes my hand over-familiarly, breathes asthmatically and stares at me with gleaming eyes. By the window Steve seems to be overdoing his absorption in the drawings, looking back and forth, two, three times between the ceiling and the paper in his hands. Finally he walks slowly towards me.

'The painters are coming in a couple of hours,' I tell Spence hastily. 'Everything must be completed.'

'No sweat. You leave it to me.'

He turns briskly, giving the approaching Steve a wary glance. I feel uneasy.

'Lara,' Steve says in a low but nonetheless insistent tone, 'the position of those lights won't pass regulations.'

Spence stops. Breathing harshly he turns and stares defiantly at Steve.

'Steve, we can discuss . . .' I step instinctively between them. I feel my medication take hold. Everything seems more achingly bright, sharper, more intensely threatening.

'I've spoken to your . . . to Lara about those,' Spence says, one fist shoved into the bulk around his middle, the other clenched, sticking straight down into the air. 'I told her, these bloody architects . . .'

'I'm an architect,' Steve says mildly. The coolness of his eyes grows colder. 'And I'm telling you you're going to have to comply with the plans.'

My face burns but inside I shiver as if in a snowstorm.

'Spence has a point,' I say quietly, unable to look at either of them. 'I should have given more thought to the implications . . . it's my fault.'

'Not a problem,' Steve interjects pleasantly. 'If there's been a misunderstanding you'll be compensated in terms of time and expense. Only,' he does the watch-flicking action again, 'time is short. We'll come back in an hour or so to see how it's all going.'

Then he walks calmly away leaving me with no option but to follow him.

I slam the kitchen door behind us. The first thing I focus on, in my crazy furious state, is the mess. Remains of the preparation and consumption of Steve's breakfast are strewn on three different worktops. His lipstick-stained clothes are discarded in a pile on the floor. Two ashtrays of blackened cigar butts like dead slugs flank raggedy piles of brochures and papers in the middle of the table. I remember the brief time Steve and I shared a flat when Stacey was born. I remember a lot of things that don't help my state of mind.

'Jesus Christ, look at this place. Jake will go insane when he sees it.'

'He isn't here to see it,' Steve looks at me levelly, an arm's length away, waiting.

Behind him, through the window, the mist is lifting. I hear one of the workmen whistle. Someone else laughs. The emerging bright light and vivid green is hurting my eyes.

'Why did you do that to me?' I manage to say at last.

I feel sick and murderous and underneath it all, wrong.

'I had to say something. It had to be changed. I didn't *want* to tell you in front of . . .'

'Of course you did,' I spit out. 'Any opportunity to show that stupid little Lara needs big clever Steve to keep her right.'

'That's not true.' At last his tone hardens. He moves closer to me with that familiar frown intact, steel in his eyes, one hand rising towards my body, to convince, to flatter, to control. My own arm comes back, slices the air, rises. With one swift, resolute movement I slap him hard across the side of the face.

We stare at each other for seconds. Steve rubs his cheek. His expression, no longer austere, is almost resigned. I breathe heavily unable to believe what I have done. Then I sink backward, my hands against the wall, as if he will retaliate, as if the world no longer solid will disintegrate further.

He comes towards me and puts his arms out slowly.

'Come here.'

I fall against his chest, luxuriate in the feeling of his arms around me, tightening as apologies tumble profusely and muddled from my lips.

'Didn't mean that . . . my God . . . so sorry.'

'It's OK, Lara. Really, it's OK.'

He kisses the top of my head then, very softly, my mouth as my ebbing shame allows me to look at his face.

'It's not OK, Steve. I hit you.'

'I deserved it.'

'Steve, you *didn't*.'

'Not today, maybe, but for all those other times I controlled and thwarted you. I didn't mean to do you any harm but I did. For the record,' he laughs dryly, 'you're not the first woman to land me one.'

'Oh, Stevie.' I gaze into his remorseful eyes then kiss him hard on the mouth.

'Mmmm, I'm not sure I deserved that, however.'

I kiss him again, pushing his head down to mine. I put my hand on his chest, move my lower body closer to his, run my hand down the front of his trousers. I'm vaguely aware of the sounds of the workmen somewhere in the garden. I can hear saws, wood being hammered. I can't judge how far or near. Anyone could look in the window but I don't care. Steve, however, edges me closer to the wall. He opens a couple of the buttons on my thin blouse, slips his fingers inside. My breasts are bare. He runs his hand over them, brushing my nipples. I shiver, move my hips closer, feel the hardness of him through my flimsy skirt. I slide my hand around the base of his back.

'Touch me between my legs. Please, Stevie, touch me.'

He runs his fingers up my thigh, snaking them into the crotch of my knickers. He moves his hand inside my lips, then runs his thumb over my clit. His touch becomes more insistent. I squirm a little, reach for his zip, start to pull it down.

'Lara, not here – we can't.'

His eyes shine with excitement, and apprehension.

But I need him straight away, to stop the hunger. I release his cock; begin to massage it; draw it between my legs.

'Not here, Lara,' he repeats, this time sounding faintly annoyed.

'In there, then. Now.' I look towards the large cupboard at the rear of the kitchen, now a small utility room. Something in my eyes makes him unable or unwilling to argue.

I lead him behind the thin wood door. There's a small sofa near the washing machine but I don't want to even try to make love on it.

'Here, against the wall,' I tell Steve. I unbutton my blouse, pull at his trousers.

'God, you're amazing.'

His hand is up my skirt, on my hips, tearing off the small scrap of my knickers.

I cover his mouth with urgent kisses, massage my lips on his rigid cock. I begin to swell, ache. His hands in my hair, he pulls back my head, stares at me, his breath coming fast. My knickers are on the floor, my skirt above my waist.

'Jesus, you're so hot and wet. You really need me don't you, angel?'

'Now, Steve, please.' I feel energised, alive. The workmen don't exist, the house, or Jake. All I need is Steve to give me that orgasm, to be all around and inside me. I feel as if I have an unquenchable fever.

Bending a little, he places the tip of his cock just inside me. I move down, anxious to swallow him inside me. He penetrates me slowly. I bear down harder. He fills me to the hilt. I fall back upon the scratchy raffia wall, what's left of my clothes giving me little protection against its harsh surface. But it only adds to my excitement, the grazing movement as I continue to move with him, my nails digging into his shoulders, moving down his back to push him further into me. As he drives me against the wall I feel the heat and pain in my shoulders and back intensify and melt into pleasure, join with the urgency for surrender to orgasm I feel in my burning pulsating cunt. I suddenly recall Jake in the summer-house being punished by Amber, the anguish and suffering in his expression, the shuddering discomfort of his body lifted suddenly to another dimension – ecstasy.

'Fuck me hard,' I gasp in rapture and pain. 'Fuck me until I faint.'

He ploughs into me slowly but with tremendous force. Each time he rams against my clit my buttocks slap against the wall. With each movement I lose myself further. I am damp and hot all over, consumed, but rising, too, in our passion.

'Lara, I can't hold back.' Steve looks into my face, desperate, transported.

For a second I don't recognise this man, can't remember who I'm fucking. I recognise only the feeling, the need for deliverance and transcendence. And I let myself come at the same time as him, drowning and gasping in a wave of rapture. I hear myself cry out, sob as if I'm listening to someone else.

He holds me up, clings to me as if we've been through a tragedy or a disaster.

'Ssh. Lara, it's OK, OK now.'

I start to come down, suddenly aware of the disgruntled voice of Big Spence out in the hall, very near.

'We're getting this checked before we go any bloody further. That's all there is to it, and I want her to do it. Not that overbearing git in the Calvin Klein.'

I giggle at this. Steve puts his hand playfully over my mouth.

The kitchen door opens. A few footsteps lumber in and out.

'Well I'm buggered if I know where she's got to.'

The door closes. The footsteps recede down the hall.

Steve and I adjust our clothes, whispering and laughing like teenagers.

'Shall I come with you Lara?' Steve's voice now hesitant and careful.

'Christ, no. I'll deal with them. You,' I prod him gently, 'get this bloody kitchen sorted.'

As I walk back up the hall I feel different, reborn, confident. But as the hammers start to bang all around me, muffled then sharp, as the sound of saws sing through my nerve ends and men's voices start to whisper through the house, 'She's a slag. She's an angel. She's a stupid bitch.' I am floating – and not entirely whole.

The afternoon is blazingly hot. Steve and I are sipping beer shandy in the kitchen courtyard, in the shade of the now overgrown bushes. Although I can still feel the after-effects of the morning's lovemaking – on the slightly seared skin of my back and buttocks, the muscles in my shoulders and limbs, the rawness in and around my cunt – to the onlooker we are at peace, in friendly accord, like brother and sister.

In reality, I'm drinking far more beer in my shandy than Steve is. I feel an almost jet-lagged tiredness, but know that, if I was to try to sleep, I couldn't. In a few minutes the herbs will lift my tiredness and the smile will linger when I look at Steve, I'll start to want him again. I might ask him to take me to bed. When I walk on the grass it will be fresh as May, as bright as a painting.

Just outside the shadow of the summer-house, Greg is taking one of the last of the summer sketching classes. There are less than half a dozen people now, the man with the ready erection, the round-faced woman, the girl with the large bust and her thin, self-conscious friend and the spotty-faced youth. There is no model to draw. Instead they seem to be studying the far side of the house, perhaps looking to the west wing where I sleep. I shiver when I think of them looking at my balcony. Greg, engrossed, has not yet acknowledged us. My pulse quickens. I feel suddenly invisible and fight down an urge to go over to him.

'I wonder what he's doing with them,' says Steve from behind dark glasses.

I gulp down some of the bitter drink. Who's doing what with whom? I think wildly.

The few remaining joiners are also around, over by the trees assembling a couple of last-minute fixtures. Earlier on I have met the decorators, given them instructions with polite authority on which rooms they can start on. I know I have done this but I can no longer picture the scene.

'I'm not sure,' I whisper. My hand trembles. Some beer escapes my glass, trickles between my sunwarmed breasts, dies inside the knot of my pale blue top, a large knot due to my increasing slenderness.

Steve removes his glasses, wipes sweat from his brow.

'I might go over and ask,' he says.

I smile at him, raise my foot, stroke his lower leg. Abruptly I start to feel better. Sounds are clearer, more compelling. My eyes are clean, voracious.

'Don't grin at me like that. I'm only curious, Lara. I won't interfere. It's a long while since I've taken an art class.'

I follow him good-naturedly when he rises to walk across the lawn. I sway a bit, link my arm through his.

'Steve Fitzgerald, diplomat,' I giggle, maybe a bit too much.

Greg greets us coolly but cordially, his glance not lingering on me at all. He shakes hands with Steve.

'You're Jake's brother, aren't you? We spoke briefly if a little drunkenly at the party.' He is using his sensible grown-up tone. 'I'm Greg Lansdowne,' he continues.

I turn to Steve. I want fun, mischief.

'Greg's my . . .'

'Do you want to see how they're getting on?' Greg asks swiftly with a sharp glance at me. 'I know you used to teach.'

And they leave me, the two of them, to walk in the richer grass among other people, people who now seem to eye me curiously, with no warmth.

About ten yards away I see my salvation. Young Kenny, at the border of the lawn and the rough gravel, sits on a sawn-off tree stump munching a sandwich. As I walk to him I'm aware of my slightly unsteady footing. I reflect on this vaguely. I've consumed nowhere near enough alcohol to be drunk.

I sink to the grass beside him, smile widely. He looks down at me. He's bare-chested, his golden hair damp and flopping over huge amazed eyes.

'Hello,' I whisper, parting my legs on the grass, made cool by a black cloud of leaf-shadow.

He glances at my legs in the thin clingy skirt, then looks away, reddening.

'Do you always eat alone?' I persist brightly.

'Usually,' Kenny mumbles.

Big Spence and two other men stand smoking by their van under the trees. One of them chortles. I glance over. Big Spence spits meditatively onto the gravel.

'Do they tease you Kenny?'

'Something like that.'

'How old are you?'

'Eighteen.'

'You're a virgin, right?'

From having made a half-turn towards me Kenny now turns back again, his head lowered, moodily grazing a trainer over the gravel.

'God, I'm sorry,' I reach up and touch his arm. He looks at me from beneath his fringe. 'What the hell must you think of me?'

'I think you're a very nice lady,' he says quietly.

I laugh. Somebody's mother again.

'*And* I think you're very pretty.'

This time he daringly catches my eye. I hold the gaze.

'How long do you have . . . for lunch?'

'About another twenty minutes. I usually take a walk down there.'

He gestures towards the trees adjacent to the driveway. 'Where the fountains and stuff are.'

Big Spence and his friends are watching Greg and Steve who are now standing closer to the west of the house as they study the turret. No-one is interested in Kenny and me.

'Would you like to walk there now?'

He stares at me a second then nods slowly.

We sit by a silver weed-free pond where large flowers nudge each other like lush boats. I am captivated by them, amazed that I've never come here before, either in the last weeks or in past years.

'It's another world here,' Kenny says.

I look at his blue eyes darting all around and follow them, down and up to the levels of small plateaus with tiny fountains and lonely sculptures, to the flat, obsessively tended grass, skywards to the branches of surrounding trees forming a frail ceiling for the secrets below. I feel magical, omnipotent, in my special place. I reach for Kenny's hand.

'We don't have long,' I whisper.

We make love swiftly and crudely, although I persuade myself that it is some extraordinary ritual for both of us. After his initial frightened fumbling at clothes and his reticent caresses he becomes abruptly aroused, kissing me fervently, then frantically taking out his cock to fuck me for less than a minute before pulling out and dousing my bunched up skirt in semen. Afterwards he is breathless, delighted with himself and awkward with me. He looks at his watch. I'm lying on my back watching the sun twinkle through holes in the leaves.

'Go, angel, it's fine. Just go.'

He rises and backs away from me into the dark glossy greenery, smiling, half-drunk with success.

'You're the best, Lara. Really top, ace.'

As if I was a brand of jeans or a football team.

I rinse my skirt in the pond, wring it out, let it dry a little under a far off patch of yellow sun. I lie beside it anchoring it in the world with me. I doze for hour-long minutes. There is birdsong in the world and nothing else.

Out once more into the hot light of the open sky. Vans are being packed up ready to leave. Most of the students are getting into one car. The man with the ready erection is going to drive. He looks hot, important and faintly excited. The two remaining girls are still on the lawn on either side of Steve, legs crossed towards him, one ample and one small but charming cleavage glistening underneath his eyes. He is expounding on some point by waving a pencil and moving backwards and forwards in his seat, oblivious to their rapt attentiveness. Greg is sitting shirtless and very brown in bleach-spattered shorts, drinking a beer. He rises as I emerge from the shadow of the trees.

'The joys of perspective.' I giggle, taking the bottle from him.

'How's that?' He looks at me curiously.

I incline my head towards Steve.

'That's how he won me over. Those strong arms coming over my shoulder standing so close I swear I could feel the heat from him. Then he'd just point out all the mistakes on my drawing.' I laugh again, take a long draught of beer. 'You just look *so* incredibly desirable, my angel. You don't fancy taking me behind a tree and shagging me witless?'

'I thought someone had already done that,' he says quietly, looking somewhere above my head toward the deathly silent house. I'm suddenly aware of the wind, coming out of the trees, hissing, seeming cold.

'What are you saying, Greg?'

'I'd just like to know if you're happy.'

'He's not that much younger than you, you know. Anyway, how about you and Angela Lloyd, you and Amber, you and countless other . . .'

'I'm not judging you, darling,' he says wearily.

He runs his hand down my arm as if I'm cold. I drink more beer.

'You don't have to be a big brave girl in front of me.'

'I'm having the time of my life, I'm having great sex with different guys, my career's going well, the house is taking shape . . .' I break off breathlessly. We stare at each other. Greg has a small smile on his face. Behind us on the lawn one of the girls giggles, the other joins in. I turn wildly and watch Steve luxuriate in their youthful mirth. He glances up at me, waves and turns his attention back to them. I feel old. I thrust the bottle back at Greg.

'I'm going up to my room.' I turn away, but he catches my wrist.

'Wait, Lara . . . please.'

He goes over to Steve, says something, walks back to me. They all look at me from the lawn as if I'm in some sort of cage.

212

'What did you say to him?' I hiss at Greg as we walk round the side of the house through the green tunnel.

'Said I was going to take a break, could he see the girls off. He's an OK guy.'

'Don't you think he's a control freak? Always butting in?'

'No. I asked his opinion, as it happens. He knows his stuff. In fact, he seems a lot easier to get on with than his brother. Speaking of which . . .'

'There's nothing to speak of. Jake's gone and I've a job to finish. End of story.' The fragrant gloom of the tunnel is suddenly claustrophobic.

'Oh, Lara . . .'

I kiss him hard on the mouth.

'I take it you did come with me because you wanted my body?'

He says nothing and walks ahead of me out of the green dark so I can't read his expression.

I close the shutters in my room although the sun has moved far on.

I slump down on the bed.

'Christ, I'm exhausted.'

'You said, it darling,' Greg says quietly, sitting beside me.

'What's that supposed to mean?'

He plays with the frayed edges of his shorts.

'Steve was just saying you were a bit prone to over-work, getting stressed out, even at college,' he says hesitantly.

'So you and my ex were having a little chin-wag about me. Did you also compare notes on my blow jobs?'

'You're getting paranoid Lara. I only want to help.'

'What'll help me most is you getting your prick out and ramming it into my cunt.'

I pull back the bed-covers and slip under the sheets tearing off my knickers and dropping them on the floor. For a second Greg gazes at them looking as if he wants to say something but doesn't. He takes off his shorts and comes in beside me but I have to fondle his cock for a full minute before he becomes hard.

Then I lie nursing it just between my legs and we hold each other tightly as if on the point of a farewell or some disaster. When I look into his solemn eyes, there is a glint of something that I don't at first recognise. Then I do. It's fear. I'm suddenly reminded of the stories he has told me about Celine. How the two of them would cling to each other in the dark when their parents were fighting in some other part of the house. How he'd pray his smaller sisters wouldn't wake up and start to cry. 'We'd just hold on together like orphans in a storm.' Now I press his cock to my cunt. It's my storm now, I think, and it's not fair if I make it yours too.

When he penetrates me he whispers, 'Oh, but you're wet for me, my darling.'

And I am, wet and aching for a man to fill me up, any man.

And so it goes on. For over two weeks I sleep fitfully, eat little, drink too much and need, quite desperately, to have someone in my bed at night. Most of the time it's Steve, but on the couple of occasions he has to go and stay over in town I become panic-stricken and frantically seek Greg out.

'I'll sit up all night then – on the balcony,' I tell him when he says that maybe he won't be around on one particular evening. He laughs at this initially. 'Let's not be a drama queen, Lara.' But then he sees my fear. He takes me in his arms. 'Of course, I'll stay with you, darling.'

Perversely, as my spirits fluctuate from wild throat-closing anxiety to sunshiny optimism and near euphoria, the heart of Old Beach House becomes pale, pure, serene as a temple. With no screening yet delivered to mask or filter the natural light, the interior glows in varying degrees from snow palace softness in the morning to gleaming almost silver white opulence, in early evening. It feels strange walking through iridescent rooms, chatting to the workmen, as if we are all in some vast cloud. I spend a lot of time with Steve, leafing through papers for new projects, doing correspondence. We often sit in the safe, russet, yesteryear gloom of the seventies room or the natural wood and homeliness feel of the large, now untidy kitchen. We eat and talk and frequently make love as if there is no past or future, just an eternal, unstoppable, fervent, twenty-year-old present.

Since Steve discovered the problem with the lighting, I am much more conscientious regarding detail and more aloof and direct with the workmen. Big Spence and Kenny have moved on to be replaced by painters in white overalls. I give instructions cordially but matter-of-factly – matt Ice White on that ceiling, Diamond Frost – at least three coats – on that floor. I feel like an actress. I listen to myself speak, watch myself walk towards people with my authoritarian high heels slapping the exquisitely sanded and wan-tinted floors. I feel myself smile through my shimmering eyes as if I'm someone else. The men in their white clothes look like doctors to me, or moving, climbing, restless breakaway pieces of the white cloud. I lose track of which and how many of Greg's pills I am taking. I forget which are the stimulants and which are sedative. Some days I believe I take none at all, other days I consume about a handful. I give up staring at the phone, willing it to ring and be Jake. Steve takes nearly all the calls including those from my office. Sometimes I don't ring back. When Stacey phones I let her talk mainly to Steve. I don't want her to detect my forgetfulness, the fuzziness in my thinking. I like to watch Steve's face as he talks to the daughter he hasn't seen since she was fourteen, the eagerness, the pride, the small frown when she jokes about the frugality of the student existence. 'But I could help you, Stace. I'm very well placed financially these days . . . no, I know I have no obligation but I want . . . OK, my love, you too . . . yes, another couple of weeks I guess.' The small smile of regret as he hangs up. 'She wants to see me, Lara. But she won't let me help out with money. I don't understand . . .' The noon sun on his face makes him look tired, older. 'She wants your company, Stevie. I understand that.'

It is August and the light is changing. Frailer in the morning, mellower later in the day. Older. One afternoon, I'm sitting on the boxy sofa trying to absorb a contract. Steve is standing by the open window smoking a cigar. He touches the now yellow-green leaves of the tree. 'I wonder if Jake'd like this cut back?' My eyes feel too heavy to reply. The papers slide from my knees to the floor. My head bobs down in the warm air.

'You should go to bed for an hour.' Steve sits beside me. I loll over onto his shoulder.

'I'll stretch out here. Stay with you.'

I sink thankfully down on the sofa. Steve takes my feet on his lap. For several woolly minutes images like half dreams float in my head. A winter's day with Steve. Me, heavily pregnant, resting against him. A blazing coal fire in front of us. The flat strewn with student's notes. With one hand he raises a text book into the glow of the fire. With the other he massages my stomach. Stacey kicks against us. Somewhere else – a party. Steve and Jake arguing over the merits of contemporary architecture. Me applying plum lipstick in a corner, hoping one of them will pay me some attention. Jake storming out, taking his whisky bottle with him. My toes nestle against Steve's hardening cock. I smile as I drift into sleep. When I wake up, I think, he will fuck me.

I jolt upright, a ringing noise reverberating through my head.

Steve is standing, laughing.

'It's the phone, Lara. Take it easy.'

He picks up the receiver, sits by me, idly running a hand up my thigh.

'Hello, Steve Fitzgerald . . . oh, right . . . how are you?'

His voice becomes oddly formal, his hand abruptly withdraws from my body.

'She's . . . she's put a hell of a lot of effort into this place.'

He looks at me when I mouth Jake's name, nods, then suddenly, inexplicably, rises and walks towards the door.

'So where exactly are you?' he asks as the door opens then closes behind him.

I gaze at it for long seconds, stunned, then furious.

I rise and begin distractedly to study myself in a small, oval, wrought-iron-framed mirror above the music system, almost hidden by long candles. I think how when I last looked into it, I probably had maroon eye shadow and clear smooth skin. Now I examine the small lines around my eyes and mouth, my now more prominent cheekbones hollowing daily under my golden tan. I can't decide whether I have become an attractive woman or a stupid tart.

The door opens again.

'Jake wants us to organise an exhibition,' Steve says, calmly, off-hand, as if the proposition was something we'd all being considering for weeks.

'What? *Jake* actually suggested . . .'

'No, I did. But he agreed. He feels a bit bad, leaving the students, Greg . . . everyone. I mentioned that the downstairs renovations would make a great display area and proposed the idea of showing off the students' work. An informal thing, friends, maybe some colleagues. People can buy if they want . . .'

'But not his own stuff – he won't be showing that?'

'Oh, that too. He realises it's stupid to have everything stored in the summer-house and up in the attic.'

'I've been saying that all summer,' I say weakly.

We sit on the boxy sofa. Steve puts his arm around my shoulders.

'Jake sounds much more positive, Lara, looking towards the future.'

'Good.'

I picture Amber's flat stomach beginning to swell, her wonderful body concealed in long chaste dresses. She'll need someone to lean on, now. I think about the value my work has put on the house, how much easier it will be to sell. I take a deep breath.

'He didn't say . . . when . . . if he'd be back?'

Steve has taken a pad from underneath a pile of papers. He begins to enumerate bullet points on it, flicking his wrist to look at his watch.

'Saturday . . . that gives us five days.' Then, not looking up, he says in a soft voice, 'I'm afraid, my sweet, that's something I can't tell you.'

It is three o'clock on the afternoon of the exhibition. Greg sits opposite me on the balcony. He glances at the wine I'm drinking, but says nothing. I slide the bottle across the table.

'You'll get a glass on the dresser.'

He hesitates, doesn't move.

'Steve was wondering if you want to do any more about the window screens.'

For two days I have sorted, put up and arranged various drapes and blinds and screens throughout the house. I shrug.

'What more does he want me to do? The downstairs drapes are pulled well up to get the best lighting for the paintings. Later on they can be released.'

'I think he was considering the other rooms,' Greg says carefully.

'What the hell for?' I burst out. 'It's the lousy exhibition people are coming to see, not my fucking curtains.'

Greg rises, draws his chair back.

'Don't go, please, I'm sorry.'

My heart beats rapidly. I have taken no herbal pills. It's going to be a wine-fuelled evening. The evening seems to have started early.

Greg turns, looks back at me.

I light a cigarette from a packet of Jake's left under the bed. My hand shakes. Greg sits again wearily. 'You've transformed this place. You've done so well. You should be proud.' He reaches across the table for my hand, squeezes it, looks sadly into my eyes. 'Can't you salvage any happiness from this summer, Lara?'

Above the trees two large seagulls streak noisily by. I

think vaguely that this is the first time I've noticed gulls near the house. Surprising, considering how near the sea is. How white they look, how powerful and well directioned. For an instant they rule the sky, then they are gone.

'When have you decided to leave, Greg?'

He looks down at the table where interlocking wine rings dry.

'Probably tomorrow,' he says quietly.

'Ah.'

'You think I wasn't going to say goodbye,' he says with an unexpected desperate fury.

'I think you were afraid to, my angel.'

'Lara . . .'

I put my finger to his lips, then take his hand.

'Come.'

We walk through to the shower-room. I'm unbuttoning my dress as we go.

He doesn't hesitate at all before coming under the teeming cold torrent with me. I hold him as the water blasts me into sobriety and I can smile at him again. This is the way I want you to remember me, I think. Not like your poor depressive mother or your unpredictable stepsister, but smiling with gratitude into your wonderful boy's face. Your lover. As he fucks me I think, Every time I'm in a rainstorm now I'll think of you.

At four thirty, Steve, Greg and I open the first bottle of champagne. Ludicrously, in such a vast pale space, we are all dressed in black, like escapees from a funeral. Steve leans back against a white-damask-covered table, wearing what looks like a dinner suit without the tie. As usual he looks expensive and elegant. Greg, also in dark trousers and white crisp shirt, stands next to him. Behind them on the table is a vase of red fleshy blooms.

'It would be nice to paint the two of you like that, as some sort of keepsake,' I tell them, in a voice which sounds even to me very cheerful. Greg, gladdened by my lifted spirits, gives me a wide smile. Steve's smile is smaller. I walk up the room looking at the paintings, aware that I'm being watched by both of them. I'm pleased at my choice of dress, sensual and black, without being overt. It falls nearly to my ankles, but is split up both sides to mid thigh.

From the middle room beyond the first arch, light, rippling jazz music filters out. Joyful music, but without a singer, I supply my own words in my head.

'No more the virgin, no more the whore.'

Jaunty, bouncy lyrics to suit my champagne mood. I feel as if I'm part of a painting myself – woman in black in late-afternoon gallery. The light is perfect. Neither bright nor weak, just the end of the day retreating somewhere back to the sun. It falls with a hint of late-summer green on the white walls, not sad, but subtly expectant. In order to expose an expanse of leg to Steve and Greg I squat to examine a low hanging sketch which looks vaguely familiar.

'Stevie.'

He comes over briskly, bottle in hand.

'Refill, my sweet?'

He crouches to replenish my glass. I stretch out my hand without looking at him.

'This one. Where did you get it?'

'Can't remember. It's one of the students', isn't it? It's very good anyway, if a bit rough. In fact,' his eyes sparkle suddenly and I realise I'm not the only one affected by the champagne, 'I think it might have been in your room.' He glances backwards at Greg who is otherwise occupied speaking to the first guests to arrive, the student with the large bust and her timorous fidgety friend. Steve slides his hand up my thigh. His fingers rest just against my crotch.

'The sketch is Jake's,' I tell him.

I feel the pressure of his hand a little more, then he withdraws slightly.

'Oh, I see. I'm sorry if I shouldn't have . . .'

'No, it's OK, but don't you think it's . . . freaky?'

He glances at the sketch.

220

'Freaky . . . what do you mean?

'Well the masculine limbs, all that hair, and it's my face.'

He looks puzzled. 'Steve, she's throwing herself from the balcony. It's like a sort of death wish thing. Remember . . . Victoria.'

Steve laughs.

'I didn't see that at all. Certainly, the face is yours. But I took it to be more a statement of male-female concordance. You know, the rising spirit, if that doesn't seem too arty-farty.'

'It does.'

'You're not falling Lara, you're flying, above the trees, towards the clouds.'

I giggle. 'I'm *flying*, that's how you see it?'

'Yes, of course. It's very positive.'

He helps me to my feet. I snuggle against his shoulder, suddenly quite elated.

'Has anyone ever told you that you're absolutely gorgeous – for an older man?'

'Yes, and they're usually as drunk as you.'

He holds me around the waist, letting his hand slide towards my hip. I turn towards him, wanting to embrace him. But he looks at me solemnly.

'I hope tonight is not a disappointment for you, Lara,' he says.

I look at him in astonishment. 'Why should I be disappointed?'

As late afternoon turns to early evening, people arrive in groups and pairs. Some of the younger students are self-conscious at first among Steve's cocktail waitresses and long glasses. As more alcohol is consumed and the music from the middle room rises they begin to thaw, become more gregarious. Steve is the most considerate of hosts, trying to ease the mixing of our own friends – many of the people who were at Jake's party – with some of the more introverted students. I watch him bolster egos with a wonderful sense of schoolteacher fair-play. Angela

221

Lloyd, resplendent in crimson couture is anxious to impress, purely, I suspect, because of the tailoring of Steve's suit. He persuades her to part with a sizable amount of cash for one of the nervous fidgety girl's sketches, 'very now, very New York attic'. I watch the latter glow inside the scintillating effect on her impoverished ego. Steve smiles in my direction, his unforgettable 'told you so' grin. For a moment I love him for it.

In those first couple of hours I talk mostly to Nadia and Richard Gorman – tonight, in my more elegant mood and dress I can't bring myself to call him Dick. After a few exotic cocktails she says hesitantly. 'You and Steve look more of a couple now than you ever did.'

I smile. 'We're wiser now. Hopefully wise enough to know that the last thing we should do to spoil things is become a couple.'

But as we wander the length of the three arch-partitioned rooms, picking like birds at trays of circulating glistening food, changing groups, reaching for yet another glass, I'm aware that Steve is never far away from me. He mingles expertly and confidently but always keeps me in view. Through the floating faces and high garrulous voices, Steve's presence is sharper and more physical. The hour slips from seven to eight and the lights in the ceilings and on the walls pick out revellers and artworks in their dying sunset rays. The buzz of noise and the flush on tanned faces intensifies, but something is starting to fade within me, as surely as if I'm being depleted by some mysterious external source. Voices, other than those up close, are beginning to echo. Close to, people's words seem to physically hurt my hearing as if I'm on the brink of a migraine, although I never get them. At a distance, and then I notice, frighteningly, nearer and nearer, my vision starts to blur. My heart races, but when I breathe deeply it's fine again. My skin feels tight when I move. I become more and more comforted by Steve's proximity.

We are sitting by one of the long windows, looking out at the empty drive and the trees greying towards night. Steve is fondling the back of my neck absently. I continue to sip champagne. It keeps me alert, refreshing my senses. But, like a malfunctioning engine, I am only ticking over. The power is seeping away.

Then, unexpectedly he does that swift, wrist-flicking action to look at his watch. My pulse quickens.

'Who are you expecting?

He doesn't seem to hear, simply moves distractedly to kiss my cheek.

'Stevie?'

After a couple of irrational seconds I'm convinced he's waiting for a woman, a wife even. I start to speculate, wildly. I have never asked. I'm on the point of some bizarre, shrill utterance when a large, gleaming, white car rolls into the drive and four middle-aged men get out. Their faces mist when I look at them.

'Ah, good.'

Steve plants a firm 'must get on with things' kiss on my brow and rises.

'Where are you going?'

Barely glancing back as he walks briskly away, he gestures with his hand behind him. 'One minute, my sweet. Don't move.'

I swallow some more champagne, look at the clusters and pairs of people on the floor as if through a window. The blood is rushing through my veins. I can hear it. I imagine I see Kenny and Big Spence at the far side of the room. The golden-haired youth in his best clothes, the big man waiting to be bumptious and dismissive, but starting to enjoy himself, secretly delighted when people admire the different colours and intensities of light that rainbow the walls. I wave at them, smile for them. He liked me, Big Spence, used to call me 'petal', and Kenny liked me too, otherwise he wouldn't have . . .'

Steve is coming back into the room with the men. They are advancing. I fix my smile. Steve takes my hand, has me on my feet. My smile doesn't falter.

'Guys, this is Lara . . . my . . . we go back a long way.'
'I recall.'

223

A broad man, balding in front, but with straight ginger hair flicking over his shoulders and a red beard grins audaciously. From the murk of my memory is an image of some half-dark hallway, me pinned against a wall, an asthmatic ginger-stubbled chest imprisoning me and a large, repugnant hand clawing at my backside, Steve in another room, laughing, showing off.

'What are you doing here?'

I look straight at red-beard, forgetting to change my voice into actress mode.

Steve grips my hand.

'These are colleagues of mine. They were interested in your work,' he says pleasantly, if a little apprehensively.

I recover myself, grab a glass of champagne from a tray, put my smile back in place.

'Oh, I see . . . Good.'

It is decided that we will view the top floor first. Red-beard, like some school bully, boisterously leads the way up the stairs for his more subdued companions.

I follow behind with Steve. The large hallway, now in vast-seeming incandescence, is peopled on every corner by statues rescued from the garden which careful restoration and bleaching have rendered ghostly. I feel everywhere is watching and listening.

'Just what the hell is going on here?'

I stop Steve at the bottom of the stairs.

He looks at me with genuine bemusement.

'Connections, Lara. These people will be great for your career.'

'But why didn't you let me know they were coming?'

'Because I wasn't absolutely sure that they were.'

He glances strangely towards one of the statues in the corner.

'People let you down,' he says quietly.

I look at him imploringly. 'I don't know if I'm up to this, Steve.'

'Your trouble, Lara Macintyre, is lack of self-belief.' He allows himself a small smile of reprive then reaches for my hand. 'Come on, we've a bit of selling to do.'

Upstairs red-beard is already peering into rooms.

'They're not all renovated,' I say pointedly, dashing up to him on my high heels. A wave of dizziness rushes through my head.

'What I've glimpsed so far is very impressive,' says one of the smaller men in a conciliatory manner. He has glasses and a fatherly smile. Morris or Boris.

'Indeed,' interjects red-beard. 'There's a length of material, gauzy stuff on one of the windows that looks just like a woman's underwear.'

'Yes, I have knickers like that.' I look at him boldly.

Morris sniggers. His other friend, Col or Mal, moustached and twitchy, flushes. Steve hurries to my side.

'Lara has a uniquely eclectic taste in soft furnishing,' he says seriously.

And so we progress – Steve and I like some kind of unrehearsed double act, each one vying for the audience's acclaim. The audience, I realise, is probably in no need of our repertoire. Their lingering glances at the fixtures and the window dressings, their murmurs of approval when I switch on lights that sprinkle, glow or splash, their enthusiasm as they take in the luminosity of the rooms is very encouraging and does not need extraneous embellishment.

But at the first sign of stage-fright on my part, which comes as soon as red-beard asks me a deliberately overly technical question about the light fittings, Steve steps in, hand on the small of my back, reassuring sidelong smile. I am incensed. My dry mouth, my paralysed memory, my feeling of disappearing into myself are all blasted away by a surge of adrenaline. All the lines are in your head, Lara. Suddenly I'm on. References to stately homes I have studied, exhibitions I have visited, new decorating techniques I have mastered, all tumble from my lips with authority and verve. It's as if I'm standing outside myself watching, as if Greg is around coaching me, egging me on. Go for it, Lara – sexy mature woman who knows her stuff, who might later choose to be fucked by any or all of them. What are you saying to them? – a small voice in my head, listening too. Each time I pause or stretch up to release a blind Steve is there aiding and abetting with details of cabling and voltage and the desirability of clean lines.

'Steve, the wall screens. I must show them,' I enthuse, dashing over to a switch near the window. Buoyed by my performance and their attentive faces – even red-beard seems awed into non-quibbling contemplation – I am about to show them my unique selling point, as Steve calls it.

'No, Lara,' he says sharply. 'It's better that they see the large one in the exhibition rooms downstairs.'

I swiftly cover my astonishment with a nervous smile.

'Of course.'

But I feel it all start to fall apart, disintegrate at those sharp words. The curtain's coming down. I gaze at him in shock as red-beard leads his friends out of the room. Steve Fitzgerald, schoolteacher. Suddenly I think of those years he taught me when I was fifteen, sixteen, really skinny, flat-chested, agonisingly shy. He couldn't have liked me in the slightest. Not even be attracted to, but like. My heart is thudding again, louder than before. It hurts. Then I hear a roar, a mechanical noise, then the harsh crunching up of something heavy being dragged. It takes me several terrifying seconds to realise that this sound is not some manifestation of my senses, it is coming from outside. I walk towards the window but Steve stops me.

'Are you alright, my sweet?' His voice is soft, but his eyes are strange, evasive. 'I didn't mean to steal your thunder just now,' he says quickly, glancing over my shoulder to the outside world where the roaring sound has abruptly ceased. 'But the downstairs screen will make a much better impact.'

Suddenly, frighteningly, I don't trust him. What if there's something else wrong with the house, like the problems with the light fittings, would he tell me?

I break away from his gentle hold on my wrist, go once more to the window.

'What was that noise outside?' I peer down. 'It sounded like a bike.'

Steve doesn't answer. When I scan the gravel and the shadows beneath the trees, the same cars are there but no motorbike.

I sit downstairs on a window seat with Nadia and Richard. I tremble and perspire and I can't hide it. I mumble something about the heat, although the air conditioning I have installed ensures that it is, in fact, quite cool.

'Would you like a brandy, Lara?' Richard enquires kindly. 'Just the thing for the jitters.'

He hurries through the now fairly crowded space, through the archway, headed to the far room which has been turned into a well-stocked and waitressed bar for the evening.

I smoke a cigarette which steadies me a little. I feel I have to explain to Nadia.

'I'm bloody knackered, that's all. To hell with Steve and his screens. One more drink and I'm headed for bed – alone.'

Nadia looks down at her manicured nails, hesitates. 'Richard and I were saying you looked a little . . . strained . . . around the eyes.'

Her too, I think, furiously, *and* Dick, the guy who, not so long ago, was slobbering to get into my pants.

I fight to control my runaway emotions. 'I can't believe Steve.' I take a long, furious drag of my cigarette. 'Hauling me upstairs to go through that pantomime with those guys.'

'I think that it was well-intentioned,' Nadia says carefully.

'Maybe,' I concede grudgingly. 'But then he just buggers off leaving me . . .'

Richard returns with the brandy, a large one.

I gulp down half of it at once. Instantly it warms me, steadies me a little.

'Thank you, for being my friends,' I hear myself gush.

What are you saying to them? – the little voice in my head again.

Richard and Nadia look at me in surprise and vague embarrassment. I take another mouthful of brandy and when I look up Steve is back in the room talking to Greg. They chat earnestly, close together. Then both of them, quite pointedly, glance across at me, then look away again.

'Did you see that?' I hiss. 'Steve and Greg talking about me, deciding things. They're . . .'

'Lara, really, honey, I think you're getting a little paranoid.' Nadia laughs rather shakily.

'I am *not* . . . look, he's coming over . . .'

Steve crosses the pale floor. I think how in his dark suit he looks sinister like some sort of executioner. 'Man in black' – who said that?

Ludicrously, now, from the middle room can be heard the strains of the first chords of a Scottish country dance tune.

Steve, with his best schoolteacher bellow, turns towards the sound.

'Someone cut that music, now . . . for a moment,' he finishes quietly.

In the new silence that follows everyone looks at him expectantly. I feel sweat break out under my hair, trickle down my breasts. I close my eyes and tell myself firmly, in a minute you will walk from this room, go upstairs and sleep – a long, long sleep. Then tomorrow you'll go home to your daughter and then a holiday, maybe . . .

'OK everyone, just a couple of words and then you can all get on with the jigging or whatever.'

I listen dimly as he expounds predictably, but very kindly, on the contributions of the students, of Jake's ideas for starting the school, of Greg's effort and imagination. Steve, please stop talking and let me leave. I need to sleep. Then through a haze I hear the words which chill my blood.

'And of course the setting for our exhibition and party

this evening would not be quite so magnificent without the talent of my . . . special friend, Lara Macintyre.'

From the centre of the floor he now walks towards me.

'Oh fucking hell.'

I look desperately at Richard and Nadia, and see the trepidation on their faces.

Steve towers over me in his black suit. I stare at him, frozen.

'Right, my sweet,' he continues in his showman's voice. 'Time for the *fait accompli.*'

I don't move. I hear people giggle. They all look at me. Steve holds out his hand, smiles encouragingly as if I was a timid child. Richard's palm gives me a rather half-hearted push and I am on my feet.

Steve has his arm around my waist as we walk crazily towards the wall.

'Where are we going?' I protest lamely.

'The switch for the screen. Your big moment, Lara.'

'I keep telling you. I'm not up to big moments. I don't feel too good.'

'You're four parts pissed, that's all. You can do it,'

'Steve . . .'

I all but collapse onto the button on the wall near the window.

The loud swish as the huge screen descends to the floor three feet from the glass makes me start.

'Tremendous,' murmurs Steve, kissing me on the cheek.

I turn to look.

The wall-wide, semi-opaque framework hangs like a second sky. There is silence in the room apart from a general rumble of approval. One or two people glance at me respectfully, but most just stare at the pale mountains and valleys and islands of softly painted cloud formation on the screen.

Even red-beard seems genuinely in awe. 'I've got to hand it to you, doll. That *is* fuckin' amazing.'

Then I notice something that strikes me as hilarious.

'But look though,' I splutter, appalled yet delighted, 'There are people in the sky!'

Nadia and Richard behind the screen, by the window, appear to be sitting in a cloud.

People standing beside me – Steve, Greg, red-beard, all seem to think this adds to the overall effect. Steve explains earnestly to a nearby guest that the intensity of the silhouettes is all to do with the fall of the artificial lighting. 'Captivating,' she murmurs.

'Oh Christ, stop it,' I gasp, 'I screwed up again, didn't I Steve. It looks surreal.'

'That's exactly why it's so good, because it *is* surreal, Larissa.' A voice comes from behind me, several feet away.

I turn to see Jake, leather-jacketed, with tousled hair standing about ten feet away from me.

I flinch, unable to trust my vision. He takes a step towards me and I glance behind him, expecting to see Amber or a ghost of someone else. Jake holds up his arms. I wonder if he wants to embrace me, but he just gestures.

'The whole house . . . the whole house is magnificent. Thank you,' he says softly.

But I can't respond, can't even move. Meanwhile more people are walking through my sky. Their silhouettes fascinate me. Although a low level of general conversation and hilarity has resumed, one or two people are now regarding me with curiosity. Everyone seems so humourless.

'Look at all the people in my sky,' I giggle to the phantom that is Jake. 'God, doesn't that sound like an old psychedelic pop song. Steve will be sooo mad, I've screwed up again.'

'Lara.'

Behind me I hear Steve's rather irritated tone, then no-one has a chance to do or say anything further. From the middle room Scottish dance music bursts out with ear-splitting intensity and an arm comes around my waist. Big Spence – it really is him – very drunk and exuberant.

'Mine, I think, petal.'

He literally whisks me off my feet and I'm carried along in the swirls and countercurrents of dozens of jubilant bodies. The momentum of the dance ploughs me through arm after arm: young Kenny, his thin shoulder hard against my back, his excited breath on my face; Stuart McNab, his fingers scouring my outer thigh through the slit in my dress; Greg, wrists crossed, hard and powerful twirling me until the room is a kaleidoscope of faces, relaxed and flying limbs, and sky. For several of the choruses where we stand marking time and clapping while other revellers whirl through our six-body-deep furrow, I can't keep my balance unless supported by Big Spence.

'You and me did all this, Lara.' The arm not holding me up sweeps through the air to indicate the whole universe. I can't stop laughing. I keep thinking of my sky full of people. At one of these respites I am dimly aware of a conversation near me. Steve and Jake.

'How long has she been like this?'

'Oh, since about four thirty.'

'No, I mean days, weeks . . .'

'Lighten up Jake, she's been at the champagne. You know Lara at parties.'

'That's not booze. Have you seen her eyes?'

'Her eyes?' A short blast of mirth. Then, 'What do you mean?' Steve's normal confidence faltering.

'Look into my eyes.' I giggle when Big Spence and I once again take centre stage, launching ourselves inside the jaunty vying accordion and violin music.

'I'm looking, petal.'

'What do you see?'

'A lovely warm woman. Too good for any of them.'

He cocks his head at all other mankind.

'I want to fly, Big Spence, that's all I want now.'

I see his eyes gleam with the excitement of a challenge, a vein in his bull-hard neck begin to throb.

'If you want to fly, Petal, then you shall.'

He hoists me high into the air and begins to twirl me round about six feet off the floor. All the other dancers stop, begin to cheer and clap. Someone turns the music up louder. I hold on to his strong triumphant arms and feel my legs in a straight line slice the air. Round and round, I go, my skirt flying.

I look at no-one, just savour the sensation of being so high so fast, never coming down.

But I do come down, abruptly. On a long jarring note the music stops. Big Spence lowers me carefully to my feet, then supports me while the room spins. People are talking among themselves now, laughing, greeting others, moving on. Poor old Big Spence – I'm holding him back. He deserves better than this grotesque shell of false purity.

'I'm fine now, I can stand,' I say and kiss his large proud forehead. He gives me a wink and turns away.

I stand alone in the middle of the white floor, swaying a little, looking for my people in the sky. But it's no longer there. The sky has gone and a blackness is rushing towards me as suddenly as a storm. My knees give way and I wait for it to take me down, for my face to slap the hard unforgiving white. This time there will be no-one there to catch me.

Chapter Eight

I'm in a swamp. It's sucking me down. I can't breathe.
  'I can't breathe. Help me please.'
The stranger pulls me up, frees my face from the stifling damp, lifts me into the air where it is dryer, cooler. Then, it's too cool. I shiver and he gives me warmth with his body.
  'You're alright, Lara. I'm here.'
I can't see his face, but I feel him in the dark. I feel his arms hold me back from the edge of the abyss. Then I'm back in the hot and wet again, but he keeps me on the surface, lets me lie against his body. When I cry out he shelters me.
There are strips of light over my sea. I look at them and my eyes ache. Is the stranger still on the surface with me?
  'Where are you?'
  'Right here.'
A strip of light shows up his eyes. I gasp.
  'It's OK now.' Hiding my face to his shoulder.
I tumble again to the darkness but his eyes are watching me. Kind eyes. Greg has made me into an angel whore. I am painted, proud, powerful. Greg watches me. Steve is leading me up the long stairs. He won't take no for an answer. Everything must be white and pure again.

I have a sky to paint. Steve watches me. The stranger watches me always. But he expects nothing.

But it's too hot now. There's a fire. Near. I can't see the flames. But the orchard is burning and the heat is coming for me. All the apples are cooking in agony, sweet fragrant death, dropping from the trees. Everything burning out. Blackening. No whiteness any more. So hot. The blackness holds me. I can't get away. Struggle in its grip. It holds me tighter. I claw, push, cry out. Something slams between my legs. Tree trunk, pillar, pinning me down. The force between my legs increases.

'No, Lara, no.' The stranger's voice. Help me. Oh help me.

Then something odd happens. The pressure between my legs is taking over, consuming me, drawing me from the fire. The rest of me calms, then disappears. All is centered on my lower body. I go towards the barrier, want to meet with it, wrap my thighs around it. Feels good. Push more.

'Lara, what are you doing?'

The stranger's voice, tired and frightened. Where is he? The barrier is being removed and I want it back.

'No, no, no,' I scream in frustration.

My eyes open. It's dark, three-quarters dark. There are shadows. I don't know where I am. There is . . . there is the outline of a man looking down. I scream again.

'Lara, it's me. It's Jake.'

I gaze up at the figure. He is breathless, dishevelled. I turn my head to look at how he has pinned down my wrists. My eyes hurt.

'My eyes hurt,' I whisper.

He lies down beside me in the dampness and the twisted sheets.

I'm wearing my white nightdress. It's soaked through. My hair sticks to my head. I peer over Jake's shoulder at the slats of light. I try to remember. Why are those shutters closed? It's summer. Why does it feel like winter? So black.

'I'm thirsty.' My voice cracks. Everything feels brittle, sore, my bones, my muscles.

'Lean on me.' He moves me up on his shoulders, feeds me small sips of water. I have never tasted anything so good. I feel it slide down to my stomach. I want to look at him, say thank you. But I can't move my head or my mouth. I feel myself start to fall away again. I clutch him, want to know he's real. His arm comes around me.

'Lara, I want to get this nightdress off you. Do you think you can help me?'

I feel his hands move me gently, work the damp cotton over my head. I am naked then, more soft, light dryness encases my skin. I feel his fingers, adjusting, pulling something near my neck, over my breasts. I want then to be held. I want to feel his touch on my poor raw skin, I want him inside me, healing me.

'Make me feel good.'

'I'll do my best, sweetheart.'

My body is encased in a sheath of smooth cool material. He rolls me gently over the bed. I remember tumbling down sand dunes, years ago, some other beach, some other life, no Jake. The last few languid rolls before you stop, laugh at the sky.

But now I'm no longer in my satin shell, no longer rolling. I wait for Jake to make himself into my shell but he isn't there. I call out his name to the darkness.

'I'm right here, Lara. Sleep now. You need to sleep.'

There is a rustling noise and a small pink mountain on the floor in the dark. I hear his breath beside it.

'I need you beside me.'

He slides into my darkness, wraps himself around me.

'I don't think the doctor would approve.'

'Doctor?' I murmur.

I fall through clouds, layers and layers. I am letting it all go, the make-up, the pounding heart, the being on show. Gradually the heat inside me ebbs, then is fierce only for seconds at a time, too short a time for terror. And Jake is with me. I will not burn. The wetness is easier now. It's like the wetness on the ledge of the sea pool receding to a glaze at noon, caressing your sex lips, making you want to open your legs. Greg above me, his cock hard. His hand on my cunt. The water, lapping and lapping. My thighs spreading, my knees bending up with need. Writhing harder and harder on the palm of his hand. On fire between my legs. The clouds have given way to blue sky and the sun on fire behind his head. I want his cock, try to pull him down towards me. Want our fires together, need to burn it out. But he holds me like he wants to stifle my passion. His arms hard round my back, his thighs rigid against mine. I try to struggle. My cunt is aflame. But he wants to thwart me.

'Easy, Lara. Just lie back.'

'Fuck me . . . Fuck me, please.'

I try to free my hand, trapped against my chest. I must find his cock, take it down. I know he is hard for me. I shudder with the effort but still I can't move.

'Please,' I implore him. 'Please.'

A gush of sea water, small but frenzied, warms my cunt, makes me need him more. I feel it wash his thigh. I begin to sob with frustration.

'It's alright, sweetheart. It's just the fever. You can't help it. It's alright, just lie back.'

I stop struggling, go limp. Now the sun has gone. I'm back in the dark. Greg doesn't want me but the stranger is here, lying on his side, stroking my brow, unaware of how I ache to be filled.

'I only wanted you inside, to fill me up. That's all,' I say softly to the darkness. I cry quietly, letting it all ebb away.

'Oh, Jesus.'

The stranger sounds as if he is saying a prayer.

Then slowly, with quivering tenderness, I feel his fingers trace a path down my face, my eyelids my mouth, my neck.

He opens some loose fastening on the garment over my breasts, slips his hand inside. One nipple, the other. Uncertainly he lays his hand down. Someone moans, the sobbing stops. An awesome grateful sound, a woman's aching sound, not just from her voice, but from her soul.

He slides a hand under my back, gently tugging the covering from my body. As he bunches it up and hurls it away, a wet edge of it flicks over my thighs like a tongue. His eyes shine a different blackness from the surrounding black, a wondrous dark vibrance as he comes down to me. He drinks the residue of salt water still warming my lips, runs his tongue over the flame between my legs. In the joyous ache inside me, tiny silver fish of desire surge and retreat, surge again.

'Now, now.'

He hesitates, closes his eyes as if in pain but then lies over me. The tip of his penis comes carefully inside me.

My hips heave towards it wanting more, but he stills me with a strong movement in the small of my back.

'Let me come to you. You're not strong enough. That's it. Let it happen.'

Slowly I feel him fill me up, holding me very tight as if I'm going to fall. He moves very gently, cautiously, but I feel his hardness deep inside me, the pressure intense then slightly less, intense again. I lift back his head, tangle my fingers inside his soft curls.

'I can't wait long,' I tell him. My voice shakes.

He misunderstands. I feel him pull back a little.

'I'm hurting you.'

'No. No.'

I wriggle against him, needing to get the feeling back.

I feel him tremble. 'My God you're beautiful.'

Then his face comes over mine, kissing me softly, moving himself slowly back and forth inside me. I feel hot then cold. There is a faint ringing in my ears. I mustn't pass out, I mustn't.

He begins to move more urgently inside me.

'So good, so good,' he whispers. 'You know it's me don't you, Lara?'

I can't answer. I clutch his shoulders as he bears down on me.

I start to cry out, feel him open me right up. We cry

out together. His face is wet. Don't. Don't think you're causing me pain. But at the point of orgasm, when we both clutch each other, wracked in unbearable ecstasy, tears course down my cheeks, too. As soon as he recovers himself, steadies his breathing, the stranger lies on his back and lifts me onto his chest.

'Poor, little Lara,' he whispers over and over. 'Poor broken thing.'

But I'm not broken. I feel quite whole with you. I drift off to sleep still lying on his chest.

When I wake again there is a special freshness about the light filtering into the room. One of the shutters is slightly ajar. I can hear birds singing. A new dawn. I move my body on Jake's chest, look down on him, watch him sleep. I think how exhausted I must have made him. I look at the soft pile of sheets and clothes on the floor. I decide I should get up and take them downstairs. The fever has subsided but when I try to move myself out of bed my limbs are leaden, weak. Jake opens his eyes.

'Lara, what are you doing? Lie down. You need to rest.'

'The sheets have to be washed.'

He sits up, takes me gently back against him.

'You're doing nothing till you're well again.'

I laugh a little shakily. 'I'm not ill.' I see my black dress slung over a chair. Then I remember Big Spence hoisting me up, my legs flying through the air, the people in the sky.

'How long have I been here, Jake?'

'It's Monday morning. You collapsed on Saturday night.'

'Some hangover.'

He doesn't smile.

'Nervous exhaustion, Lara. According to the doctor.'

'I haven't seen a doctor . . . Have I?'

'Yesterday morning. You were pouring sweat, shaking, delirious. All those herbal things in your cabinet, we've thrown them out. Not that there was much left. Greg couldn't get over how much you'd taken.'

238

'Greg too. And Steve was here, I bet. Why didn't you just sell tickets.'

My eyes fill with tears of humiliation.

'We were worried. Christ knows, no-one felt more guilty than me. Steve knew you were overdoing it but he thought as soon as the work was over ... anyway, I should never have left. If I'd been here I would have noticed ...'

'I can take care of myself,' I say quietly, but I'm trembling again, unsure.

Monday. Suddenly I remember where I should be. I push myself away from Jake, look frantically over the floor for something to cover my nakedness.

'It's Stacey. I have to go, get dressed. She'll be expecting me home.'

He puts his arms around me, tries to calm me.

'Stace's alright. Steve's with her. The official line is that you have flu.'

The thought of Steve rediscovering my daughter, our daughter, the child that always looked so much like him, brings fresh tears of pride but also rejection to my eyes.

I blink them away, lie back against Jake's shoulder.

'Do you want to sleep again?' he whispers.

It feels as if my nerve endings, having been in some sort of shock or stasis, are suddenly reawakening. I become abruptly aware of a dull full sensation far down in my abdomen.

'No, I want to pee,' I say hurriedly.

He puts his arm around my waist, helps me to my feet.

In this upright position the pull of gravity makes my predicament more urgent.

'God, hurry, before I lose it.'

'It wouldn't be the first time.'

'What?'

I gaze at him in astonishment as I hobble, leaning against him, round to the shower room.

'During the night. You were struggling, a bit hysterical. Anyway, next thing I know there's this flood against my thigh.'

'Oh Jesus, tell me you're kidding.'

Then I suddenly remember my dream of lying on the ledge of the sea pool, the ocean surging between my legs.

I sink down on the toilet, scarlet with embarrassment.

'You won't want me to wait outside in light of our newly found intimacy.' He squats in front of me, his eyes twinkling.

'Oh fuck off, Fitzgerald.' For the first time in what seems like weeks I feel my face break into real laughter.

When I wake again, half of the room is filled with sun, the other half already in shade. The shutters are wide open and it's early afternoon. The room smells fresh, slightly scented. The tangled sheets and clothes are gone from the floor. There is a large vase of tall feathery-looking flowers with blue and white heads on the dressing table. I smile at this, stretch my arm across the bed. He's not there. I look wildly around, call his name, pull back the bedclothes.

'Out here, Lara,' he calls from the balcony.

I grab his shirt from the chair as I rush outside. The daylight seems achingly bright. Jake sits gazing out over the trees, preoccupied. Then he glances up.

'You're supposed to be in bed.'

'I missed you.' I drop weakly onto his lap. 'What were you thinking of just now, sitting here alone?'

'Oh, just the house and how it's changed. And the future I suppose.'

I feel myself stiffen.

'I was so sure you were going to sell up and not come back.'

He sighs, tilts my face back to look at his.

'Well, I did consider it, after I dropped Amber off with her parents.'

'I thought you might have stayed with her.'

'She has things to work out, needs someone to look after her.'

'I thought you . . .'

'Not me, Larissa.'

A breeze lifts the trees, rushes through their leaves. The mass of green has lost colour, looks frailer. The holes through to the sky are larger.

'So, what brought you back then?'

I think, as long as his chest is warm and he can hold me like this, I won't mind the answer.

'Well, Steve I suppose, in the end.'

He lights a cigarette, blows smoke into the air. It smells toasted, foreign. I close my eyes and imagine we're abroad, with a whole summer and a golden autumn in front of us.

'What do you mean, in the end?'

'I had an instinct something was wrong, that's why I phoned. I always trust my instincts.'

I laugh at this, feel a bond.

'I do, too. It gets me into loads of trouble.'

'Steve told me how much effort you were putting into the house and also . . . that you were pining for me.'

'Pining . . . there's a real Steve word.'

'Then I began to think of all the years that have gone by. I realised Steve only wanted to help, that there was no real feud between us. I travelled around a bit, thought things through. I decided I was needed back here.'

'I'm glad.'

He looks at me seriously, searching my eyes. I feel apprehensive.

'Are you, Larissa?'

'Damn right I am. I really have to take a bath and I need you to help me.

I sit on one of the huge, round, gravestone chairs. It's covered in thick white towels. It feels good, comforting.

I watch Jake drowsily through clouds of scented mist as he prepares the sunken bath. The windows are wide open, the trees seem silent and small.

'Are you up to this?' Jake looks down at me through veils of steam. I blink, vaguely remember silhouettes of people in the sky. For several seconds I can't remember where I am.

I nod, reach up to him.

He lifts me into the fragrant water. For a while he sits on the edge, carefully, shyly almost, skimming water over my shoulders, around my neck, smoothing back the soaking ends of my hair. I gaze at his gentle hands, his strong bare chest, his battered jeans already splashed with water.

'Why don't you come in beside me and do the job properly?'

He stands and undresses, wordlessly, but his eyes never leave mine. He is semi-erect when he climbs into the bath. He supports me with one arm then gently soaps my shoulders, down my arms, over my abdomen, up and down my legs. I start to move myself towards him. My nipples, hard and pink, peep through the foam; I am breathless when I look at him. His hand rests on my inner thigh. He looks at me questioningly, touchingly unsure. I move his hand between my legs.

His fingers sneak inside the folds of my skin, tentatively. A little more water laps inside me. I move round sideways against his arm, push my hips towards him. I reach for his penis. He is now completely erect.

'You take it easy, Ms Macintyre. Remember, you're recuperating.'

'And you do as you're told. I'll decide the best medicine for me.'

I kiss him and his skin tastes faintly of soap. There is a light stubble on his chin, a tiredness around his eyes.

I rub his cock against my clit in the foamy wetness. But he is right. I soon feel weak. Weak, but wanting him too.

'I think I'll need a bit of help.'

He moves further up the slope of the bath, lifts me on top of him.

'Maybe we should leave this till later.'

But suddenly I can't wait.

'Sit on the ledge,' I tell him.

There's a small ridge on one side of the bath. Just wide enough, I think.

'Lara . . .'

'Please.'

He holds me on top of him with my legs spread. His cock is hard against my abdomen. For a long while we hold each other like this. I feel as if I am coming closer to him, feel his hardness increase, but there is no pressure, no hurry. He rocks me against him. When my shoulders cool, he lifts a towel from the floor and wraps it around me. In a kind of half-sleep I feel soothed but subtly aroused too. And something comes to me, some echo of my fever.

'The stranger.'

'What?'

Jake smooths my damp fringe from my brow.

'When I was in bed, burning up, I had this dream. This man, the stranger. He fucked me. I made him. It was wonderful. The best orgasm I've ever had. It was you Jake, wasn't it?'

He stares at me, tries to say something, doesn't. He looks down at his erection between us.

'Did you hear what I said? The best I've ever had.'

He gazes at me solemnly, then smiles slowly.

'Do you think we can better it?'

He holds me onto his cock. I feel the water enter me with his hardness. He is so slow, gentle, afraid even.

'All those years,' he whispers. He looks at me, his dark eyes dull with a sort of misery, confusion. I don't know what he means but my heart goes to him.

'We both have to heal, that's all,' I say simply.

He comes forwards to run his lips over my face, wrap his hands inside my hair, rock me, kiss me more.

We move together. He thrusts himself towards me just enough to enhance the impact of my downwards squeezing, surrendering motion. I feel my face flush, my nails grip onto his shoulders.

'You'll tell me if it hurts,' he says anxiously, 'I don't want to hurt you.'

The insecurity in his eyes makes him look young again. It occurs to me that Steve is right – he always was insecure. It's just that I couldn't see it.

243

I clasp his head to my chest. 'I don't think you could ever hurt me, Jake.'

Something in my soul has gained, feels stronger, but physically I am growing weak.

'I want to come now,' I whisper. My body stills abruptly, exhausted. My open thighs begin to shudder against him. But my clit is alive, pulsating towards him for release.

He lifts back my head, one arm strong around my lower back.

'But you're so pale, sweetheart. I shouldn't . . .'

'Please, Jake.'

He leans back, holds me rigid against him and, with a series of tiny barely perceptible movements, pushes against my clit until I cry out with joy and open and open against and around him. Only my lower body is still alive. The rest of me fades thankfully into him as I feel the spasm of his own release.

A week of mornings where a subtle chill creeps into the air. Out on the balcony early one day, I can't see a single summer bloom although I know, in this huge garden, if I look for them they will still be there.

Jake comes up behind and, without seeing my face, senses the sorrow in my mood.

'What is it, Lara?'

'It'll be autumn soon.'

He turns me around and takes me in his arms. 'Come to bed.'

And I know as he leads me back into the shadowed warmth of the room that I will leave soon. He knows it too.

He gives me his body hurriedly, desperately, rolling me over on top of him, clasping me to him, making me come again and again as if we are both tossed by some sea, slamming us together, making us ride the waves until washed out and utterly sated we can travel no more.

I feel so overwhelmed afterwards I tell him I must sleep, but I don't. I lie at his side with closed eyes but looking out from time to time as Jake stares at the ceiling, around the room, out towards the balcony, out towards his memories. Eventually he gets out of bed and stands on the balcony smoking while the sun warms the day. I want to go to him, say there'll be more summers, autumns, memories, but I don't know if I can.

August deepens, a strange and wonderful time with an odd leaf yellowing overnight, but the noons are still warm and fragrant. One day, walking in the garden we come across a group of dark-coloured, blousy wild roses deep inside the trees, that have sprung up from nowhere. 'Stubborn aging jezebels', I tell Jake and laugh, but he doesn't get the connection.

The pale luminosity of the house astounds me. On my first day out of bed I insist on seeing it all again, all the rooms with their windows dressed in gauze and silk and frail elegant slatted wood, the wall screens that are the sea or the sky or pale heavenly fields, the pure abounding light when all the veils are pulled back into the ceiling or off the windows. I see it all as if for the first time. Too weak to walk, Jake lifts me into his arms and carries me through the house. His eyes shine too with our shared delight.

Downstairs in the exhibition rooms we sit on the window seat in the poignant green light of late afternoon and look at the paintings on the wall. A few have been sold. The spaces that remain lend the empty room a sudden forlornness. I feel my throat tighten.

'Your sketch has gone – the one of me flying through the sky.'

'Steve took it down. It's on one of the tables.'

He rises, crosses the floor to bring it to me. His footsteps echo on the pale-wood floor. I think of his solitary steps around the house in the coming weeks. By the time he hands me the sketch in its thin elegant frame I can barely speak.

'It's beautiful,' I finally manage to whisper.

'It was grotesque, Larissa, remember?'

His old derisive tone is supposed to lighten my mood but when I laugh a tear runs down my face. He rubs it away with his thumb, like a smudge from a painting.

'I'll tell you this once,' he says in a mock stern way.

I take a deep breath.

'I'm listening, Fitzgerald.'

'If . . . no, *when* you leave here, there will be no tears. Right?'

'Right.'

'And you know why?'

I swallow hard.

'Why, Fitzgerald?'

'Because sooner or later I know you'll be back.'

'Confident bastard, aren't you?'

I reach across and playfully grab his balls.

'Horny one you mean.' He grins, and I can't help but smile too.

I look at the bulge in his jeans.

'Take me into the sun, Fitzgerald, and fuck me.'

Jake carries me through the sighing trees to where the ponds and fountains are. He lays me on a patch of sun-warmed grass between two statues of praying women.

'I feel like a sacrifice or something.'

He unbuttons my thin dress, caresses my nipples. I watch the sun light up his dark curls.

'One day I'll paint you like this,' he says softly.

'Not without my lipstick on you won't. Honestly, all those make-up tricks Greg taught me just to get you to put your hand in my pants and I've been going about the past few days without a scrap on.'

'You look like you did when you were seventeen and I always wanted to put my hand in your pants then.'

He lifts my dress above my waist and slides his fingers inside the crotch of my knickers, coming down to lie at my side.

'A bit like this, perhaps,' he whispers, circling my clit so lightly and enticingly that I lower my own hand and press it hard on top of his.

'Mmm, greedy girls need to be punished.'

He removes his hand completely and presses his thigh between my legs.

I rub myself on his leg, quivering with the pleasure, while I unzip him and take his rigid cock in my hand.

My breasts hard against his chest, I writhe against him, frantic for orgasm. I forget how enthusiastically I am working his cock.

'Slow down a bit, sweetheart or I'll drench your dress before I can be any use to you.' His excited breath warms the side of my face.

'Fair deal,' I murmur. 'I'm leaking on your jeans.'

'I'm serious, Lara. I don't want to disappoint you.'

'Inside me now then, Fitzgerald.'

His arousal is so great he doesn't have time to remove my knickers, but simply hauls the gusset aside and gives me his cock.

He penetrates me slowly, hugely, up to the hilt. I close my eyes and breathe deeply to stop myself coming at the first long lingering thrust.

I smell the grass beneath me, feel the leaf-dappled sun on my face.

'My God, Jake.'

'What is it?'

Now he is completely still inside me. His breath comes erratically.

'I'm going to come, very quickly. I can't help it.

'Thank Christ,' he whispers and wraps his arm around my buttocks to prevent excessive friction from the ground as he pounds into me.

'Oh, Jesus,' I begin to sob as my legs open wide, wider, clawing around his back as the final thrust comes and convulses me into shuddering orgasm.

We lie afterwards, letting our sweat and juices dry in the sun, looking out at the tiny clouds floating above.

'There were people in the sky when I was cracking up,' I whisper.

He kisses my mouth, such a soft tender kiss. 'Now you know there are only angels.'

* * *

We still eat outside in the kitchen courtyard although the mornings grow chiller and the light is more frail. In the evenings the stars come quicker. I look at them sometimes and think of frost in winter. Then I see Jake looking at me as if he knows what's in my mind. I still wear my skimpy dresses at the end of the day, but often I shiver and Jake brings me one of his shirts and sits with me on his lap and we wait in silence till the stars are brighter and colder. 'I wish I still had time to shag you under the moon,' he says and I, already mourning and desperate, kiss him hard on the mouth and say, 'There's time.'

Even though it's cool and there's a hint of rain in the air, I stroke him to erection while I sit astride him on one of the garden chairs. Then, when he becomes so aroused he can't do without me, I make him unfasten the small buttons in the crotch of my knickers and penetrate me. I ride him frantically while the moon runs away from us behind the clouds, the heat of our bodies and the frenzy of our orgasm lending us a brief echo of the heart of raging summer.

But most often when night falls, it forces us indoors to the comfort of the scented bathtub and the depth of the pink satin sheets. Days pass and they are as full of promise as a honeymoon, yet as terrible and memorable as waiting for a death.

Once or twice we leave the house. Too disorientated and muzzy to trust myself to drive, I let Jake do it. He drives fast like Steve, but I trust him, feel safe. As miles and miles of coastline and yellow fields speed past, I sometimes drift into sleep. Once, I open my eyes feeling flushed and excited, although the sky is dull and the day breezy. I'm aware of restlessness in my limbs, a strange agitation between my legs which makes me press my thighs together for further sensation. I glance swiftly at Jake to see if he has noticed my inexplicable state of arousal. He looks straight ahead, concentrating on the road. For several seconds I wriggle a bit more, intense frustration setting in, then I try and calm myself, focusing my attention on the heads of poppies rushing by the car, like splashes of paint.

'If you're terribly wet for me, Larissa, I'll stop the car and fuck you in the back seat, unless you think that's too juvenile at our age,' Jake says suddenly, turning to me with eyes full of roguishness.

'How do you know . . .?'

I don't finish my sentence as, unexpectedly, his hand slips under my red and marigold skirt, steals up my thigh and finds its target of tiny and very damp cotton knickers.

'It was you, wasn't it? Jake, you swine!'

'I just wanted to see if I could make you come in your sleep. You were getting well turned on,' he smiles.

'Well don't leave me in limbo.'

I settle my pussy on his fingertips, squirming furiously. Infuriatingly, he withdraws his hand.

'Sorry, sweetheart, junction. Tell you what, there's a small restaurant along this road.'

'A restaurant? What the hell can we do in a restaurant?'

'You'll see.'

The restaurant is next to the beach. It's small, dark blue-green with lots of wood. Two young girls with dramatic, nighttime make-up drift around half-heartedly serving a half-dozen people: two middle-aged women in town attire and a group of sun-bronzed young girls. Jake walks past them all, to a table in a shadowed corner.

'I should have sprayed some perfume on,' I whisper, 'I must smell a bit . . . musky.'

'I wouldn't bother if I were you,' Jake remarks intriguingly.

We order coffee and croissants and the waitress with silky black hair and over-painted mouth gives Jake a lowered-lash smile as she brings him an ashtray.

'She fancies you,' I hiss, trying to work out if he is watching her tight, round bottom move away from him.

'I could be her father,' he says idly.

'I hope you're not,' I mutter.

He pinches me lightly on the thigh.

'Now, are you going to be jealous or co-operative?'

'Co-operative?'

He gives me a long lingering kiss. The girl with the red mouth stares. I look at him with apprehension and delight. I sip some of the coffee. In the moody shadowed blue corner I begin to feel warm again, expectant. Through the window the wash of silver sea is motionless. Jake lights a cigarette and moves it from his right to his left hand. He holds my hand on his lap, squeezes it. He has the beginnings of an erection.

'Alright, Lara?' he murmurs.

'Alright.'

I drink more of the coffee, luxuriate in the warm buttery taste of the croissants. It's so good to taste food again after weeks of eating so sparsely.

I close my eyes, rest my head on the back of the long soft seat, breathing in the scents of fresh coffee, Jake's fragrance of warmth, cologne and faint cigarettes.

Then I feel his hand on my knee, under my skirt, snaking up and inside my thigh. I glance at him, breathless.

'Let's see if you can carry this off,' he says mischievously.

'What?'

I look at him uncertainly, but I can't help moving in my seat when his fingers come hard inside the crotch of my pants.

'You will never resist, Lara,' he whispers and leans over to kiss me again.

The waitress wiggles her way over to supply Jake, quite unnecessarily with a fresh ashtray.

'Thank you, sweetheart,' he says, smiling at her and inserting a finger inside my lips. The girl blushes and turns away. I jerk slightly under his hand. I feel myself grow wet. I'm not going to be able to do this.

'You're flirting with her.'

'Yes, but I have my hand in *your* knickers, Larissa.'

I glance around, wondering whether anyone else is aware of what's happening under our dark tablecloth.

'Oh, Jake.'

'Oh Jake, what? "Stop it, behave yourself" ...?'

He rubs me so swiftly and intensely I let out a small squeal.

'... "Do it more, Jake." ... What?'

'Infuriating pig.'

Abruptly he takes his hand away, lights another cigarette. Warm-faced and frustrated, I feel my clit pulsate against the seat.

He takes a few drags on his cigarette, drinks some coffee and doesn't immediately put his hand back, though I know he will.

I bear down on the seat, squirm a bit. I pick up my cup to feign normality and my hand shakes.

'I almost came on my handbag strap once,' I say in a light shaky voice.

'How decadent, Larissa.'

He kisses me again very softly, touching my face. I smell my musk from his fingers.

'You were sitting behind me in the back seat of the car. Steve was driving. I was thinking of you and trying to bring myself off.'

Abruptly the gleam in his eyes softens. 'I wish I'd known.'

Then his hand steals back again, traces a path up the juices wet on my thigh, immediately seeking out my throbbing clit. The red-mouthed waitress puts some rock music on the jukebox, and keeps glancing over. Now, I no longer care if she suspects what's going on. The harsh rousing beat of the music provides a perfect foil for the small cries of pleasure I can no longer suppress.

Jake's teasing attitude has changed. His fingers move more slowly but unknown to him, this is arousing me more.

'Will I stop, Lara? We can go out to the car, or down to the beach if you want.'

'Too late, Fitzgerald,' I gasp.

I bite my lip and press down hard on his hand. Hot waves of colour surge through my body as I come explosively, my abdomen shuddering in ecstasy.

This time my cry of 'Oh, Christ' is more audible. The two well-dressed ladies glance over. My knee jerks up against the table and my empty cup flips over with a tinkling sound onto the saucer.

The waitress is over in a second.

Now I can't stop the smile on my face. Jake grins also, rubbing my arm.

'She has muscular problems,' he explains solemnly, 'I'm her physiotherapist.'

The girl nods wisely and begins to clear the table. Jake gives her a huge tip.

As we make our way from the restaurant, barely able to control our mirth, I overhear the red-mouthed girl.

'See, Justine, I told you he fancied me. Did you see his erection when he passed by?'

We drive down to the beach, still laughing, and Jake fucks me in the sand dunes until I'm raw.

One morning I see the first leaf drift from the trees. Pale yellow, soft as tissue, it floats and twirls and disappears somewhere into the morning shadow of the woods. I go back into my room and stand for several minutes gazing around at the high curved walls, the dark wood, the long oval mirror. Then I look at Jake sleeping, bare-chested and peaceful. He opens his eyes and looks at me in a solemn way.

He reaches his arms to me wordlessly and I go to sit by him on the bed. He touches my hair, traces my eyelids, my nose, my mouth, with his fingers as if wanting to commit them to memory.

'It's today, isn't it?' he says quietly and smiles. I love him for that smile. I think, I never told you, I love you. You never told me.

I nod, dry mouthed, numb.

'Remember, no sadness, Lara.'

I lie in my robe beside him for a while. I don't go

under the sheets again. I can't bear the proximity of his body. We lie in silence holding each other while the sun lightens the room.

Then I go alone to the marble bathroom and take a long bath. I comb out my wet hair, put on make-up, my high-heeled strappy sandals.

I go out to my balcony one last time, smoke a cigarette. I laugh at this. OK, you're stressed, Lara.

My holdall at the door, I take one last look around the room. Ten o'clock in the morning. The room is full of sun; young, optimistic. I go back, close the shutters. Now it is outlines, shadows, mystery – the way I remember it best. Jake and I have breakfast in the sun. Ironically, it is one of the hottest mornings for a week. I feel slightly foolish and self-conscious in my make-up and heels. Jake sits opposite me, not too near, watching.

'You look beautiful, Lara.'

'Thanks,' I whisper.

He leans forward, reaches for my hand.

'You can talk to me you know,' he says softly.

'It's difficult.'

He sighs, stands up. 'Come on, it'll be easier if we walk. This is like being in a film set.'

We go through the tall trees to the orchard. The young apples are much more profuse than I would have expected. The scene of the fire, not so harrowing now, more like a fading stain on a carpet.

We sit on the grass under the slender boughs of growing fruit. I put my head on his shoulder. 'What will you do now, Jake?'

He laughs. 'For God's sake, Lara, don't sound so melodramatic. I've paintings to finish, to sell, classes to organise, autumn, winter. I need to buy a car. I plan to get to the city much more often.'

'Jake Fitzgerald, young blade about town.' I manage to laugh. It feels good.

'Rusty knife, more like. I'd like to come and see you, Lara. And Stacey . . . if it's OK.'

'It's OK.'

Sure now I can smell the first hints of fruit in the air, smell life, glimpse the future, I stand up suddenly stronger.

'Right, Fitzgerald, it's time.'

I kiss him briefly and smile.

Walking towards the house, I glance up a last time. The sun glistens on the ivy, brightens the odd dead leaf. Then something strange, unexpected arrests my gaze.

'Jake, that tree – it's been cut back. Isn't that the one outside the seventies room?'

'Yes, I had someone round to trim it the other day when we were out.'

'Could we go up, look at the room? I'm curious.'

The room is very different, softer, more wide open. The dimensions of the window also seem enlarged. Now it's silent, no incessant grazing of the branches on the glass, Looking out over the trees, I can see the orchard now and the rocks by the sea pool.

'You approve?' Jake puts his arm around my waist.

'Absolutely. But what possessed you to have it trimmed after all this time?'

'Your idea of letting in light to the rest of the house. New beginnings and all that.'

'God, that's ironic. I closed the shutters in the upstairs bedroom.' I give him a half-smile, avoid meeting his eyes.

He puts his arms round me.

'That's because I'm an optimist and you're such a doom and gloom merchant ... and why I ... care for you so much.'

We look into each other's eyes a little too long. I feel him become hard against me. My pulse quickens. I grip his shoulders and don't want to let go. From the corner of my eye, I see the remains of the candles we have burned, the tapes we have listened to, the table that has supported our wine and hidden our restless limbs. I close my eyes and hold him tighter.

'You do know I'd be stupid enough to ask you to marry me if that's what you wanted.'

He says this in a perfectly calm, even way.

I take a step back, stare at him.

'If that's a proposal, it's the most feeble one I have ever heard.'

He looks at me with shining eyes. 'How many have you heard, Larissa?'

'OK, it's the *only* and most feeble proposal I've ever heard.'

'And . . .?'

I feel a tremendous wildness surge through my blood. The tawniness on the walls, now an autumn-flower-rose swims before my eyes. I cling to him and say the only thing possible.

'Fuck me, Fitzgerald.'

'What?'

'Here, now, immediately.'

He lies over me on the corded sofa, unfastens my dress very slowly. I open my thighs and raise my knees for him.

'I'll smudge your make-up,' he whispers.

'Please.'

I take his cock in my mouth. I caress it, lick it, hold it to my throat. I suck it as if my life depended on it. My head comes forward to him only two or three times before he asks me to stop, trembling and with a glaze of perspiration on his chest.

He puts his mouth to my cunt and covers it with soft fragile kisses, puts his hands solidly beneath my thighs when they quiver.

He lies on his side to penetrate me. I look into his eyes as his cock slides in. I feel every small movement, every swelling. My eyes never leave his face. I love you, I think, I love you, as I press myself further into him and feel the small ripples of my desire blend together and surge. I tighten my muscles around him and he closes his eyes and shudders.

'Oh, Lara.'

I run my hands down his back, clutch at his hips as I feel the imminence of his climax. I feel myself begin to melt, push my clit towards his slow powerful thrust. Then I hear myself cry out his name as the wave rises that will take me with it, as if, on the other side of it, I won't see him again. I feel him convulse against me, quite silently, then he turns his face from me, the first time he's ever done this, to quiet his breathing, steady himself. I gaze at the warm ceiling and rosy walls, imagine the lamplight on them in winter, the first spattering leaf shadow of spring. All those years, I think, just as Jake had said. I can think of no other resonance, just the words themselves.

Some vague kaleidoscope of seasons to come and past, memories of the summer, hopes for the future, gets me from the sofa to the bathroom, to the front door with my holdall and Jake standing beside me warm, calmer almost respectful.

He opens the car door for me, hands me a cassette.

'I would say to remind you of me, but then I hope you won't need too much reminding.'

I kiss him briefly, numbly. He squeezes my hand and I am gone, down the drive with the potholes still as fierce and unexpected, past the trees that, driving this way, mask the secret place of fountains and ponds, down to the long empty road back.

I take a deep breath, insert the cassette, put my foot hard on the accelerator.

> *Reach for my hand and take me*
> *we'll go higher than the sky*
> *warming tears as they come down*
> *Swallow them inside our ground*
> *And we'll stay close forever.*

I drive about five miles or so to where the sea, vast and crystalline blue, is in sight. Then I pull over to the side of the road, put my head on the steering wheel and sob.

After a few minutes, calmer, I switch off the cassette, wind down the window, smoke a cigarette.

Three young girls with streaming hair are dragging two boys between them towards the pure white crashing waves.

I redo my eye make-up, switch on the music again. This time the beat is vigorous, the lyrics energising. The song bounces round the car and through my head. I start up the engine.

> I can take your funny moods
> the feelings that you lack
> I can watch you play around
> Lay me out on the rack

I start to hum along, unable to recall having heard it at all over the summer. But it cheers me, makes me smile at my slim, golden, expertly made-up face in the mirror. You're definitely improving Lara Macintyre – a successful career woman, an amazing lover, with one iffy marriage proposal behind her and a very positive future. I turn the music up, throw back my hair. Maybe I'll phone him first, I think. As soon as I get home. The words of the song come back to me. Suddenly I remember every one. All those years. I laugh, start to sing, loudly raucously – through the open window to the wind, the sea, the vast eternal sky.

> I can show you to my door
> Though the night will be so black
> Because sooner or later
> I know you'll be back.

Visit the *Black Lace* website at

www.blacklace-books.co.uk

Find out the latest information and take advantage of our fantastic **free** book offer! Also visit the site for . . .

- All *Black Lace* titles currently available and how to order online
- Great new offers
- Writers' guidelines
- Author interviews
- An erotica newsletter
- Features
- Cool links

Black Lace – the leading imprint of women's sexy fiction.

Taking your erotic reading pleasure to new horizons

BLACK LACE NEW BOOKS

Published in May

PLAYING HARD
Tina Troy
£6.99

Lili wrestles men for money. And they pay well. She's the best in the business and her powerful body and stunning looks have her gentlemen visitors begging for more rough treatment. Her golden rule is never to date a client, but when James Travers starts using her services she relents and accepts a date.

An unusual and powerfully sexy story of male/female wrestling.

ISBN 0 352 33617 X

HIGHLAND FLING
Jane Justine
£6.99

Writer Charlotte Harvey is researching the mysterious legend of the Highland Ruby pendant for an antiques magazine – a ruby that is said to sexually enslave any woman to the man who places the pendant round her neck. Charlotte's quest leads her to a remote Scottish island where the pendant's owner – the dark and charismatic Andrew Alexander – is keen to test its powers on his guest.

A cracking tale of wild sex in the Highlands of Scotland.

ISBN 0 352 33616 1

CIRCO EROTICA
Mercedes Kelley
£6.99

Flora is a lion-tamer in a Mexican circus. She inhabits a curious and colourful world of trapeze artists, snake charmers and hypnotists. When her father dies owing a lot of money to the circus owner, the dastardly Lorenzo, Flora's life is set to change. Lorenzo and his accomplice – the perverse Salome – share a powerful sexual hunger, a taste for bizarre adult fun and an interest in Flora.

This is a Black Lace special reprint of one of our most unusual and perverse titles!

IBSN 0 352 33257 3

Published in June

SUMMER FEVER
Anna Ricci
£6.99

Lara Mcintyre has lusted after artist Jake Fitzgerald for almost two decades. As a warm, dazzling summer unfolds, she makes the journey back to her student summer-house where they first met, determined to satisfy her physical craving somehow. And then, ensconced in Old Beach House once more, she discovers her true sexual self – but not without complications.

Beautifully written story of extreme passion.

ISBN 0 352 33625 0

STRICTLY CONFIDENTIAL
Alison Tyler
£6.99

Carolyn Winters is a smooth-talking disc jockey at a hip LA radio station. Although known for her sexy banter over the airwaves, she leads a reclusive life, despite the urging of her flirtatious roommate, Dahlia. Carolyn grows dependent on living vicariously through Dahlia, eavesdropping and then covertly watching as her roommate's sexual behaviour becomes more and more bizarre. But then Dahlia is murdered, and Carolyn must overcome her fears in order to bring the killer to justice.

A tense dark thriller for those who like their erotica on the forbidden side.

ISBN 0 352 33624 2

CONTINUUM
Portia Da Costa
£6.99

Joanna Darrell is something in the city. When she takes a break from her high-powered job she is drawn into a continuum of strange experiences and bizarre coincidences. Like Alice in a decadent Wonderland, she enters a parallel world of perversity and unusual pleasure. She's attracted to fetishism and discipline and her new friends make sure she gets more than a taste of erotic punishment.

This is a reprint of one of our best-selling and kinkiest titles ever!

ISBN 0 352 33120 8

To be published in July

SYMPHONY X
Jasmine Stone
£6.99

Katie is a viola player running away from her cheating husband. The tour of Symphony Xevertes not only takes her to Europe but also to the realm of deep sexual satisfaction. She is joined by a dominatrix diva and a bass singer whose voice is so low he's known as the Human Vibrator. After distractions like these, how will Katie be able to maintain her serious music career *and* allow herself to fall in love again?

Immensely funny journal of a sassy woman's sexual adventures.

ISBN 0 352 33629 3

OPENING ACTS
Suki Cunningham
£6.99

When London actress Holly Parker arrives in a remote Cornish village to begin rehearsing a new play, everyone there – from her landlord to her theatre director – seems to have an earthier attitude towards sex. Brought to a state of constant sexual arousal and confusion, Holly seeks guidance in the form of local therapist, Joshua Delaney. He is the one man who can't touch her – but he is the only one she truly desires. Will she be able to use her new-found sense of adventure to seduce him?

Wonderfully horny action in the Cornish countryside. Oooh arrgh!

ISBN 0 352 33630 7

THE SEVEN-YEAR LIST
Zoe le Verdier
£6.99

Julia is an ambitious young photographer who's about to marry her trustworthy but dull fiancé. Then an invitation to a college reunion arrives. Old rivalries, jealousies and flirtations are picked up where they were left off and sexual tensions run high. Soon Julia finds herself caught between two men but neither of them are her fiancé.

How will she explain herself to her friends? And what decisions will she make?

This is a Black Lace special reprint of a very popular title.

ISBN 0 352 33254 9

If you would like a complete list of plot summaries of Black Lace titles, or would like to receive information on other publications available, please send a stamped addressed envelope to:

Black Lace, Thames Wharf Studios,
Rainville Road, London W6 9HA

BLACK LACE BOOKLIST

Information is correct at time of printing. To check availability go to www.blacklace-books.co.uk

All books are priced £5.99 unless another price is given.

Black Lace books with a contemporary setting

THE TOP OF HER GAME	Emma Holly ISBN 0 352 33337 5	☐
LIKE MOTHER, LIKE DAUGHTER	Georgina Brown ISBN 0 352 33422 3	☐
IN THE FLESH	Emma Holly ISBN 0 352 33498 3	☐
SHAMELESS	Stella Black ISBN 0 352 33485 1	☐
TONGUE IN CHEEK	Tabitha Flyte ISBN 0 352 33484 3	☐
FIRE AND ICE	Laura Hamilton ISBN 0 352 33486 X	☐
SAUCE FOR THE GOOSE	Mary Rose Maxwell ISBN 0 352 33492 4	☐
INTENSE BLUE	Lyn Wood ISBN 0 352 33496 7	☐
THE NAKED TRUTH	Natasha Rostova ISBN 0 352 33497 5	☐
A SPORTING CHANCE	Susie Raymond ISBN 0 352 33501 7	☐
TAKING LIBERTIES	Susie Raymond ISBN 0 352 33357 X	☐
A SCANDALOUS AFFAIR	Holly Graham ISBN 0 352 33523 8	☐
THE NAKED FLAME	Crystalle Valentino ISBN 0 352 33528 9	☐
CRASH COURSE	Juliet Hastings ISBN 0 352 33018 X	☐
ON THE EDGE	Laura Hamilton ISBN 0 352 33534 3	☐

---------✂----------------------

Please send me the books I have ticked above.

Name   ....

Address   ....

                                   ....

                                   ....

                        .... Post Code ....

Send to: **Cash Sales, Black Lace Books, Thames Wharf Studios, Rainville Road, London W6 9HA.**

US customers: for prices and details of how to order books for delivery by mail, call 1-800-805-1083.

Please enclose a cheque or postal order, made payable to **Virgin Publishing Ltd**, to the value of the books you have ordered plus postage and packing costs as follows:

UK and BFPO – £1.00 for the first book, 50p for each subsequent book.

Overseas (including Republic of Ireland) – £2.00 for the first book, £1.00 for each subsequent book.

If you would prefer to pay by VISA, ACCESS/MASTER-CARD, DINERS CLUB, AMEX or SWITCH, please write your card number and expiry date here:

....

Please allow up to 28 days for delivery.

Signature ....

---------✂----------------------